BAD COMPANY

JOCELYN DEXTER

BLOODHOUND
— BOOKS —

Also by Jocelyn Dexter

Shh

Uninvited

ONE

Penny

NOW

P enny Crisp closed her eyes and stood still in the garden. Remembered way back to when she was fourteen and her father had said, 'It's called "hoarfrost".' She recalled smirking and had settled her weight on one hip, crossed her arms and made an exaggerated visual scan of the trees, the grass, the shrubs and the bushes. '*Whore* frost? Really? Seriously? Where are they then? The prostitutes?'

In her mind she'd pictured sparkling, frozen women dangling from branches, swinging by their leg garters and suspender belts: stiletto heels, fishnet stockings and red-slashed lip-sticked mouths. She'd laughed.

Her father hadn't tried to hide his smile. He was good like that.

Two years ago, she'd lost that sense of humour, lost that joyous sense of the ridiculous that she'd had as a young girl and adult. As she now crouched to touch the needle-like ice crystals on the ground with her mittened hands, instead of envisaging glistening ladies of the night, glittering with alluring promises of the flesh, she could now only enjoy a disturbed and relatively new fantasy as she rocked on the hoarfrost, back and

1

forth on her wellington booted heels, thinking dark, black thoughts. Listened as the frost creaked under her feet and hands.

She heard only the sound of death.

The icy shards clinging to every blade of grass crackled and yielded to her bodyweight. In her mind, a corpse made that same sound as it rotted – the bones decomposing as she shattered them.

So, she hoped, a skeleton would give up that strange little snapping noise in a last attempt to be noticed and heard.

That's what she hoped the brittle, dried bones of the man she'd killed would sound like.

And those of all the bastards she would kill in the future.

But this early morning cold was a transient thing and already the winter sunshine was destroying the haunting sound of the newly dead.

Breathing in the cold, huffing out her warm breath in a shivering puff, she trudged back towards the house. Cold and flushed with the icy temperature, both external and internal. Trudged back towards her house and her parents.

Her mother who knew absolutely nothing about her.

Her father who knew absolutely nothing about her.

Not anymore.

Not since *then*.

TWO

Penny

2 YEARS AGO

Penny, although twenty-eight years old, still slept like a baby. She'd wake in the morning, in precisely the same position as she'd gone to sleep; her fists semi-curled in relaxation on either side of her head, her arms bent at the elbow. In sleep, not one muscle twitched. Impervious to the sounds of the night, she might as well have been dead.

However, as she was jolted awake from a deep sleep, she knew she was very much alive. Right at this moment, possibly *too* alive. Something had awoken her. Some*one* had awoken her. There'd been a sound – wrong and out of place.

Her parents were in bed, and once there, it was rare that either of them ventured out of their room until the morning. Her father's declining health meant he spent most of his time propped up in bed, as if in-waiting for death, whilst her mother quietly and sadly struggled to cope.

So it definitely wasn't either of them moving around.

Penny's eyes bulged into the black, grey light. Blinking wildly.

There it was again. A noise. A noise that didn't belong.

Lying still, lying *very* still, she realised that she'd stopped breathing. Her ears strained, attuned to anything audible that shouldn't be. There it was again. *Damn it.* At first, she failed to identify it, but then she placed it. A muffled footstep. And then the very distinct and instantly recognisable sound of her bedroom door being opened.

Shit.

Her eyes felt like they were bleeding as she stretched her lids as far apart as was possible, trying to penetrate the darkness and recognise the figure who'd stepped into her room and stood stationary at the door. The *male* figure who'd stepped into her room: she knew that much from the form of his outline. He turned slightly but quickly to close the door behind him.

Sudden light split the blackness, blinding her. Automatically, she closed her eyes. And then the white bright torch beam was gone, leaving a smudge of orange burnt onto her retinas.

Having apparently got his bearings, the man walked softly, softly towards her: his steps barely making any sound at all. But she could smell him. Aniseed. He smelt of aniseed.

And she continued to lie there. Involuntarily, her arms moved swiftly but silently into a defensive but useless gesture. There she remained, paralysed; her hands tucked under her chin, bunching the duvet tight up to her neck. The terror inside her, sounded like the deafening clash of cymbals – so loud that surely he would hear it and she waited for his anger at the clamour that shrieked from her.

She knew with certainty that her pupils would be huge black circles, diminishing the colour of her eyes, as they desperately tried to *see*. The man stopped. 'Are you awake?' his voice whispered out.

She didn't answer. Didn't know what the best answer was.

Oddly, flat on her back, eyes wide open but blind to anything more than the shadowed silhouette of the man next to her bed, she felt him smile. It was if the air had shifted, and she imagined the corners of his mouth tilting up. She smelt a stronger smell of aniseed as he opened his mouth again and whispered. 'I *know* you're awake.'

Unable to speak, she listened to him smiling loudly. Her heart beat so strongly that it matched the pulsing throb in her temple. Penny waited.

He waited with her.

Then he stopped waiting and grabbed her by the throat.

She couldn't move. Couldn't scream. Couldn't fight. Couldn't do anything. Knowing what was coming, she gritted her teeth together and vainly and pathetically attempted to keep the duvet to her. Of course, she couldn't compete with his strength. He ripped it off her and she felt ludicrously naked, although dressed in a pair of cotton pyjamas.

Instead of raping her straight away, thrusting himself on to her and into her, he slipped into bed beside her. Turned her gently but firmly on to her side and tucked himself tightly up against her spine, bottom and legs, keeping her physically restrained, forcing her into a position where they were cupped together like two spoons in a drawer. Snuggled up behind her, as if they were lovers. He stroked her hair. Her shiny black beautiful hair.

She couldn't tell if he were young or old, only that he was around about the same height as she. Because, horribly, their bodies fit. Obscenely, *they fit*. A physical match.

Wanting to wail, to scream and shout and swear, she remained utterly quiet. Acquiescent. Accepting of her fate before it had begun. Before it had started, before it had stopped, she already felt raped.

He had no knife, he had no gun, he didn't threaten physical violence. It was merely his presence that terrified her so. Kept her obedient and obliging.

And she just carried on, silently letting him frighten her.

Why am I letting him do this to me? I'm giving my permission. By doing nothing, I'm saying, you may go ahead.

Because I am frozen.

The man ran his fingers through her hair, flattening it to her scalp, with long sweeps of his hand against her head. Her marvellous, thick hair. It fell naturally like the crest of a wave, dark and sleek on the pillow. Stunning. Magnificent. *Hers.*

He carried on flattening and smoothing it with his hand. Dampening it with the sweat from the flesh of his hand.

The more he stroked her hair, the less magnificent it felt. Now it was more like a burden, weighing Penny down, making her head feel heavy and useless. How could something so beautiful be made suddenly so repulsively ugly.

'Lovely hair,' he whispered.

When it inevitably came, the actual rape, the very physical penetration of her, the visceral violation of her body, she felt detached from it. Remote. He grabbed her hair tightly, holding on to it as he did whatever he pleased to her. She didn't want to engage with it, or him, and so she did nothing. His thrusting barely registered on her body, so far away had her mind taken her. It was happening to someone else. Some other poor bitch.

At last, with an agonising but muted wail of release from him, he patted her on the head as if she'd been a very good girl. Tousled her hair, as if she were a child. He handed her something in the dark. Automatically, her fingers traced its outline, felt the stick and the round hard circle shape at the top. She heard the crinkle of cellophane. Instinctively, she knew what it was.

Emotionally freezing, but not actually physically cold, she continued to lie there in her bed. Not shaking, nor trembling. But deep-down *bone* cold. Dead. She might as well have been sculpted in ice.

'Bye-bye. And don't tell, will you? I know you won't.' He still whispered and he stroked her hair one final time. 'See you later. And thanks.' She felt his smile again in his words. Smelt his smell again. Died just a little bit more. Again.

It took a while, still curled foetus style, stiff and immobile, before she could move. Turning on her lamp, she winced at the sudden glare of artificial light. Looked down and examined what she was holding.

Realised that he *had* given her a lollipop.

Alone. Dry-eyed. Fists clenched.

Holding a fucking lollipop.

THREE

Penny

1 YEAR AGO

P enny no longer slept like a baby. Instead, she rarely slept at all; more the dozing of a person mimicking slumber. She was too full of rage. Constant rage.

And hatred.

That's who I am now. Angry and hateful.

She'd also never told anyone. Not a soul. Certainly not the police. She didn't like authority, *especially* the police.

As a teenager, walking home from school, she'd been cautioned by an over-zealous policeman for smoking a spliff, and consequently been expelled from school because of his unnecessary intervention. The powers that be had been over the top then. She assumed they'd be equally useless this time. The justice system was too often underwhelming in rape cases. *Every*one knew that.

She was better using her own authority.

That night, after the Aniseed Man had left, she'd felt as if he'd cored and peeled her – leaving her stripped: emotionally naked. That first year, it had been like walking on thin ice. One misstep and she'd have sunk: never to re-surface again. She'd

8

have drowned, without bothering to come up for air – too destroyed to even kick for the surface.

So, she focused. Better, she thought, to march on. Alone and silent, keeping her secret to herself as if its release would further wound. Would further damage. She told herself she was better on her own and in charge of herself. Reliant on no one. No one *at all*.

All that remained inside her was rage. A rage with no outlet. Penny hated everyone, except her parents, whom she loved. But she hadn't told them and so they didn't know. They had no idea. It would have been beyond their comprehension, but as angry as she was, Penny had no desire to stain them with her own filth. She protected them. From herself and her hatred of the world.

Instead, she moved out. Couldn't bear being in her old room: the rape room – now impossible to think of it as her bedroom. It had become simply a dwelling. Bricks and mortar filled with filth.

She lived in a small bungalow in town and busied herself despising everyone. She fumed and ranted at the universe, despising all the stupid fools that surrounded her; wanting to destroy everyone's pedestrian lives, their petty existences. Men, women, children – anyone who breathed, she loathed. She could almost taste her anger.

She particularly hated men.

She specifically hated the Aniseed Man.

But most of all, she hated herself.

Her beautiful, glorious hair had been cut. She'd had it cut like a man's soon after the rape: a brutal short back and sides. Gender-anonymous. Her clothes were now always black and most importantly, they were baggy, floating, formless, making it impossible for people behind her to identify her as female. Even from the front, her sex was questionable. Others would have to really look to make sure that she was indeed a woman. Make-up was a thing of the past.

Hiding in her bungalow, surrounded by a clan of geriatrics who'd gathered in these houses that differed only by their front gardens, furious with anyone and everyone, she thought of revenge. It obsessed her, filling her mind with violent thoughts.

Revenge against the Aniseed Man.

Against *all* the aniseed men out there.

She was going to get as many of the bastards as she could.

Let the vendetta begin.

FOUR

Penny

Vengeance was a cosy bedfellow for rage. The two emotions had become best friends within her mind, and Penny nurtured both as if they were her babies. One drove the other.

Initially, she'd experimented with a hammer on a watermelon. It was a frustratingly difficult tool to wield with the correct amount of heft. Too small a tap and all it produced was crescent-shaped cuts in the flesh. Too big and powerful the hit, using a full arcing backswing, simply obliterated the fruit. The impact and carnage of a hammer had completely thrown her. She hadn't expected such utter devastation: she'd been covered in red flesh and black pips and pink juice. Splattered from head to foot.

It wasn't a difficult decision for Penny to make: no hammer. It was far too messy and more to the point, it was too sudden and final. And far too unpredictable. She had no control with it.

Something more subtle and in keeping with her nature was in order. Although subtlety wasn't a thing that had ever come naturally. She was more of a doer, a think-later type of woman.

But Penny wasn't a maniac, nor a homicidal lunatic, so wasn't prepared to beat the brains out of anyone.

Homicidal, yes. Lunatic, no.

What she was looking for was something that wasn't so abrupt. Something that would make it a bit less obviously final. She didn't want anything quite as unceremoniously and immediately fatal for the man. But certainly it had to have the risk of *potential* fatality. Therein lay the fun. The danger.

For her and for him. Whichever *him* she found herself with. It wouldn't matter which man, just that it *was* a man.

The time had eventually come. She was ready, and Penny knew it was time to *do*. Since her attack, this had been her reason for living. Had spurred her on.

And the drunks that staggered from the bars and clubs were a pool of prey into which she could dip. She the bait and they the catch.

Because it was her first time, she allowed herself to accept the nervous apprehension that filled her. Although deep down, was disappointed to see her own hands shake as she prepared to go out searching for her first victim. The tremor of her fingers felt like a failure, a weakness.

Bad-temperedly, she made an effort to forgive herself. *It's understandable*, she consoled herself, *and not worth giving myself a hard time over.*

Adjusting her short black hair around her ears, she looked for one last time in the mirror. Smiled at herself. Didn't believe it for a moment. Undoing two more buttons on her top, and squeezing her breasts together, she felt sleazy and wondered why she was bothering with this part of the charade.

Her old and once-favourite perfume now smelt cheap, her lipstick seemed too red, her mascara too phony. She'd always enjoyed wearing make-up. *Before.*

All it made her feel now was that beneath the powder and

paint there lay a large red bullseye. Right in the middle of her forehead. *Here I am. Come and get me.*

The irony was that it didn't matter *at all* what she looked like. She knew that now. That was the whole sad point of it. Any woman would do; irrespective of how they looked. She had a heartbeat – good enough. *I am an available sex machine. Nothing more. That's all I am,* she reminded herself. Everything and *any*thing extra will be a shock. For *him* the evening would be shocking. But not for her: she knew exactly how the evening would play out.

Angrily, she wiped the lipstick from her lips. Completely redundant. He wouldn't even notice. She was female – that was the only criteria which she had to satisfy, and she had that covered. Shaking her head, she changed her mind again. Dithered and felt stupid for doing so. Cleaning her lips with some tissue, she reapplied her lipstick and grinned again at her reflection. Tried to give it a bit more oomph. Looked at her white teeth shining back at her and thought, *Here we go then. In for a penny…*

The last thing she did was to check her pocket for pepper spray. Tick. Easy to get at quickly and to use if things went wrong. Feeling her toolbelt under her loose-fitting top, where normally secateurs and a small knife and twine would sit, she caressed instead a satisfyingly *large* knife and a Stanley knife – if things went *really* wrong. But she was relatively confident. She'd been over and over this scenario a million times and was as prepared as she possibly could be. Opening her front door, she slipped out into the night.

Knowing she was armed made her feel as if everyone else knew she was armed, and she giggled nervously at the stupidity and enormity of it all. Gardener by day, killer by night.

Getting herself under control, she walked slowly, got into sauntering easily and effortlessly. Her road had no CCTV so she didn't have to worry about being picked up on film. There were no lights showing in any of the bungalows anyway – everyone was in bed. The real bonus of living in this road for the aged was that no one spoke to her and she had no reason to speak to them. They were all tucked up safe and sound with their cocoa and their partners. Or alone and probably lonely. Being surrounded by the elderly, made her feel safe: certainly she didn't feel at risk from a mass octogenarian attack. Nothing to worry about here.

She reached the end of the road and glanced at her watch. Five to midnight and the male dregs, with some females mixed in with them, were stumbling alone and in groups, back home from the pub. Ignoring the groups, she waited for the solitary drunks. Knowing that at least one of them would use her road as a cut-through. They always did. But this time she'd pick one of them.

Now it was her turn.

It was freezing but she patiently bided her time, giving each of the men the once-over whilst keeping herself off the main road under the branches of a tree.

One man approached, zigzagging his way down the pavement, obviously drunk. He stumbled, tripping on the kerb. Regaining his balance, he suddenly veered off from his course and approached her road. She stood back and waited again, making sure that none of his friends caught him up.

But he carried on alone.

He staggered past her and she fell into step behind him. Noted his bare arms beneath his T-shirt. *Mr Cool*, he thought. *Mr Fool*, she knew.

As her house approached, she quickened her pace until the two of them walked abreast. Her mouth suddenly dry, she made a silly, girlish giggle to get his attention. He turned. She pretended to stumble and took hold of his arm. 'Excuse me. Hope you don't think I'm being rude, but could you do me a favour, please?'

He closed one eye to focus better and then beamed, like a child being offered an array of treats as he saw her for the first time. 'Course I can, love. What's your problem?'

Nodding at her house, she said, 'I'm a bit drunk. I only live there, and when I'm drunk, I always get just a bit freaked out. You know, in case there's someone in the house. Hiding under the sofa or something.' She laughed. Ruffled her hair. Coquettish. 'Stupid I know. But would you mind…?'

Furrowing his brow, as if this were a really, seriously difficult question, he said, 'Would I mind what?'

'Coming in with me. To check.' Again with both hands through her hair, jiggling her chest just a little. 'There's a drink in it for you.'

'How could I possibly resist an offer like that?' He laughed drunkenly, not believing his luck. 'It's just you in the house, you said, right? No boyfriend or anything?'

'If I had a boyfriend I wouldn't need you, now would I? You silly.'

Puffing out his chest, he placed his hand over hers, which was still linked through his arm. He bowed in a theatrical way, staggered and said, 'Lead on.'

'What's your name?' She took out her key and slipped it into the lock. Waited for his answer before she turned it.

'Keith.'

'Okay, Keith. Come in, please.'

She went in first and stood back to allow him access. 'Just carry on walking in a straight line. The sitting room's right in front of you. Well, this *is* the sitting room actually. Handy, eh?'

'Yeah, great. Nice place,' he lied, not bothering to lace his words with any real belief. He looked down, as she knew he would, and said, 'What's all this on the carpet. Plastic sheeting? What's that for then? You haven't got the decorators in have you?' He tittered and burped.

'Course not. Well not today at any rate. I'm painting this room. I was thinking red. What do you think, Keith?'

He didn't think anything apparently and angled his head back in front of himself, chin jutting forward. Concentrating on reaching the sofa without falling. 'Do you want me to check *under* the sofa, for real? Or shall we have that drink first?'

'You just go and sit down, Keith. You're a real love. Thanks so much. I feel safer already. I'm pretty sure there's nobody under the sofa, so I'll go and pour us both a drink. Make yourself comfortable.'

She gave him a gentle nudge in the back to steer him forward and closed the curtain across the front door. To shut out the cold. As he paced two, then three paces from her, she bent slightly at the waist and grabbed the baseball bat from its hiding place in the corner, where the closed curtain usually hid it.

The sound of it hitting his head surprised her. It was really loud. Noisy, even. She'd decided to go with her nature and ignore subtle. She didn't want subtle. She wanted harsh and bold and cold. And the strike was all of those things. Pleased that the blood landed mostly on the plastic and minimally on her, showed that finesse wasn't a must. Her face had been instantly freckled by his blood. Breathing hard, she wiped her sleeve across her cheeks.

Penny wasn't surprised that he didn't get up again. Perhaps she'd hit him *too* hard. But what *was* too hard? This evening only had one ending. And it wasn't going to be hers. Not this time.

As Keith lay face down, she tipped his jaw to the side with her shoe. Squatted and felt the pulse in his neck. Still alive. Moving quickly now, she trotted around the sofa and pushed her until-now hidden wheelbarrow up to his still-breathing body. Being a gardener, she was well versed in the art of manoeuvring heavy deadweight and with the added bonus of the expected adrenaline rush, she manhandled Keith into the barrow relatively easily. Tying his hands quickly with rope, she then bound them to his feet, bending his knees, behind his back. His head lolled back, hanging over the end with the handles.

Perfect.

Dragging a chair up behind his head, Penny sat down, avoided the blood trickling from his scalp, and whispered into Keith's ear. Whispering was *key*. She was following the script that she had been a part of. But this time, she was the director. *This* time, she was the one in control and not an unwilling participant.

'Right then. I rather think it's time we got started. I'm Penny, by the way.' She bent in closer and enunciated clearly, hoping that he could actually hear her, and said, 'It's nice to meet you. I've been waiting a long time for this.'

She allowed her lips to brush his ear and she spoke again, her voice as whispery as the Aniseed Man's had been.

'Welcome to my nest. Just to let you know, before you decide to up and leave, you'll be staying for most of the evening. Here. With me.'

Leaning over his head, Penny held his hand, as if in comfort. 'If I'm being completely honest, I don't actually think you'll be leaving here in a very compos mentis state at all. You won't be leaving *alive*, that's for sure.' She shrugged. 'Sorry. But what can a girl do?'

Stroking his hair, over and over again, she felt her heartbeat slow.

FIVE

Penny

S he leant in close to his face and inhaled his breath. Nope. No aniseed. She hadn't really expected to smell it, but you never knew your luck.

'You've got lovely hair, Keith,' she whispered. And he truly had. For that she was pleased. It fit. 'I wonder how old you are. I don't imagine that it matters – not really. You're here and you're available. That's good enough for me. Perhaps you should be grateful that I picked you. And do you want to know *why* you are the chosen one? Because you're vulnerable. Simple as that. Does that make you feel very special? You with your beautiful hair. You *should* feel special.'

Penny continued to run her hands through his blond hair, now peppered with blood-red highlights.

'How young you are. What, mid-twenties maybe? Such youthful innocence. But are you? Innocent, I mean. I don't think so, somehow. You're a man. So, let's make it fairer. Make it so that we're on a similar level: no misplaced hierarchy, no gender bias, no male physical domination. I'm going to girly you up. You'll love it. Promise.'

Laughing, she went and got her make-up bag from the kitchen worktop, next to the hair clippers. She picked up the essential items needed for the evening's entertainment, keeping an eye on Keith through the arched doorway which separated the two rooms.

Sitting again, she softly took his hair in her hand as it flopped from his neck over the back of the wheelbarrow: it was thick. *Probably his pride and joy. My heart is fucking bleeding right now.*

The clippers razored a neat trough of baldness through his locks, revealing his pink scalp, as she pushed it from his brow, backwards. Very satisfying. Carrying on without stopping, she winced and sucked in air through her teeth as she shaved around the bloodied gash in his head. *Bet that smarts.* Almost without breathing, she was finally able to sit back and admire her completed handiwork. *Nice*, she thought. She'd created an android. A robot-like male face looked up at the ceiling, his eyes glazed and still. Watching closely, Penny saw him blink and close his eyes.

But still his chest moved up and down.

Slowly.

'That's right. You just lie there and pretend it's not happening. But you won't want to miss out on the fun part, Keith. You are going to just *love* being a girl. Don't worry, I'll make you a pretty one. We'll start your make-over with some powder. Give you some foundation. We all need a solid foundation from which to operate. Now, don't move. This may take some time.' She bent into her task. 'What colour do you fancy for those lips of yours? Pink? Dusky pink or full-on, unapologetic tarty red? Okay, then. Dusky pink it is. I agree. I'm going for the vulnerable, don't-mind-me-I'm-not-really-here look, not the femme fatale. You couldn't carry it off anyway. Now, hold still.'

Bending, she gently pressed the lipstick against his mouth,

making sure that it didn't smudge. She patted the excess off with a tissue. Arching her back away from him to get a better overview, she was pleased with the effect. 'Now for the eyes: eyeliner, some mascara, but I think eye shadow would be overkill, don't you think? Keep it classy is my motto. And I'll pluck those pesky eyebrows of yours, tidy them up just a smidge.'

The wet sound from him when it came, the sort of gargle from deep down in his throat, startled her and her hand slipped. 'Jesus Christ, look what you've made me do. Now you've got a wonky eyebrow. Well, it doesn't really matter, does it?' She reined in her anger. She'd wanted everything to be perfect. 'At least I know that somewhere in there...' She tapped his head in the middle of his forehead with her index finger. 'Somewhere in that shitty little head of yours, is an awareness, sucking all this up. Are you enjoying it? I don't think so. In fact, I sincerely hope that you are excruciatingly and painfully *too* aware of what's happening. I want you to *feel* everything. The humiliation, the shame, the degradation of your situation.

'Are you feeling it, Keith? Blink once for no.'

There was no blink forthcoming, so Penny happily convinced herself, lied to herself, that he was suffering. Suffering like she had.

Shifting in her chair, she realised her back ached from her skilful facial administrations on the young man. A small price to pay. And there, look, he was as pretty as a picture.

Following her own internal script, keeping it as similar to the real thing as she could, she said, 'I don't know whether I want you to struggle, put up a fight, or at the very least scream and shout, or... I don't know, maybe, *tell me to stop.*'

She took a deep and calming breath, not wanting to lose her temper with him. She gave him the benefit of the doubt: 'I appreciate you're not at your physical peak at the moment, but could you not feign even just a little annoyance? Could you not have the decency to show *some* fear?'

Delving into her bag, she brought out a little something. 'Would you like a lollipop? For being such a good boy. I suppose it's like a prize. For not making a fuss, for not making a noise. For allowing me to do whatever I want with you. I imagine I should be experiencing relief and maybe a feeling of immense power and superiority right now, at your pathetic acquiescence. Well done for not struggling. *At all.* I take it from your meek and accepting demeanour that you are ultimately giving me your permission to do with you as I see fit. Thank you, kind sir.'

Looking at his stupid painted face, a wave of complete and all-consuming hatred filled Penny. Hatred for him.

Or for herself, she wasn't sure.

'You should have put up a fight, you idiot. You should have stopped me. Why didn't you stop me? You're pathetic. You should consider this a life lesson. I'm showing you how easy it is to take advantage of you, how simple it is to steal your very self from you. And I will leave you with nothing. I will leave you utterly *broken*.'

She patted his bald head and thought what a silly sound it made. A sort of hollow slap. Holding the lollipop under his nose, she told him to breathe. 'If you deeply inhale and keep it close to your nostrils, you can still smell the aniseed. See? Are you getting it? Weird, right? Even through the cellophane. Still, after all this time. Think of it as an award for what I've done to you. For what you've told me was fine to do to you, by your silence.'

Her lips touched his earlobe as she whispered, 'How's it feel to have your soul ripped out of you? To be left irreparably damaged? To own nothing except shame and hate and anger. How's it *feel*, Keith? Are you glad you accepted my invitation tonight? No. Probably not so glad now. Funny, isn't it, how one's life can change…' She clicked her fingers. 'Just like that. One minute you're happily living your life, and then someone comes and takes it all away. And there's nothing you can do about it.

'And you've accepted everything I've done to you so politely. With no complaining. No fuss. You just took it. Sucked it up. Just like I did. Perhaps we're more alike than I care to think.'

His breathing suddenly seemed to stall. For a moment, his chest stopped rising. She put the back of her hand to his mouth. And there it was: a breath. Just one. Big gap. Another breath.

Lifting both of his eyelids, she couldn't help but notice that one of his pupils was dilated. Very little iris was visible. Like a big black hole.

Sitting there with her hand on his chest, she felt him exhale.

Minutes passed. He didn't inhale again.

'Typical,' she said. No longer whispering. Not having to. The selfish bastard had gone one step further than giving his agreement and acceptance to her. He'd actually given up. Totally.

She punched him suddenly in the face. '*I* didn't give up. *I* had to carry on. Live with what was done to me. You've got off lightly. How dare you. How fucking *dare* you.'

Sitting in silence, Penny stared at him. Studied him. *What a fool he looks*. And to top it all off, he'd done the final job for her. Instead of her actually having to kill him outright, he'd manufactured his own demise. By being too weak to see it through to the end.

Before leaving the room, she put on a pair of latex gloves. Penny closed her eyes and inhaled deeply. Preparing herself. She didn't like mouths and dental work. It was almost a phobia with her. She particularly hated the disgustingly shiny-smooth little enamel gnashers. But she had to do this. She placed her fingers in his mouth and counted his teeth. Twice. To be absolutely sure. Satisfied, she stood. 'Don't go anywhere, Keith. I'll be back in a jiffy. We're going for a little drive. With my tools. And they're sharp. I always keep them sharp.'

SIX

Butty

You didn't even know that I stood, at twelve years of age, peeping around the doorframe, just looking at you; one year older than me. Admiring you. Taking you in. Drinking you up.

I watched as you inspected the windowpane, your body bent forward, your nose pressed up against the glass. You put your hands on your hips and tilted your head to the side. Thinking. Choosing.

And then you turned. You saw me and smiled, and everything was perfect. 'Hey, what're you doing there, lurking in the doorway?'

'I'm not lurking. I'm *loitering*. With intent. Very different.' I came over to you and punched you on the arm.

You smiled and said, 'God, you're a weirdo. You do know that, don't you?'

I did know that. Knew that I was definitely a bit weird.

'I've got one,' you said, tapping on the glass.

I saw the raindrop that you'd claimed as your own. You pointed it out at the top of the windowpane. Dead centre.

Heavy looking. After much thought, I selected mine, pressing my stubby index finger with a bitten fingernail to the glass.

'Ready?' you said.

'Ready.'

We both leant forward, with faces to the window, steaming it up with our breaths. You tapped the glass, impatient. Then you pulled back so that we could both watch.

Immediately, your drop fell suddenly and swiftly. Mine was left at the top, sluggish and seemingly unwilling to drip down. 'Come on, come *on*,' I shouted.

And then it did drop. Slowly at first, but then it gathered speed, picking up another raindrop as it went, making it doubly speedy. Faster and faster it fell. It passed yours. My stomach churned with the unexpectedness of it all. Was it possible? Was I actually going to win? I laughed with unexpected anticipation.

Your gaze was intent on your raindrop. Smiling, not bothered by its slow progress, you watched its now rather hampered journey as it slid ever slower and finally it came to a complete standstill.

Watching both my now racing raindrop and your face, I felt pure joy at this simple game. At the pleasure we both got from it.

You raised your voice and shouted, 'Come on, my raindrop, come on.'

You jumped up and down as if that would help your selected drop.

And then your face changed, lighting up your whole expression: laughing, laughing. Hollering and whooping with joy.

Your raindrop had copied mine and picked up another, fatter drop. It fell like a bullet, screaming down the glass until it splashed to victory, leaving mine in its wake. It burst into tiny victorious droplets as it crashed and broke. I could almost hear the explosion as your drop burst into a thousand teeny tiny water bubbles.

You pumped your arm in the air and said, 'Boom.' Then you rubbed my hair and beamed. 'Never mind, Butty. Next time.'

I took out five boiled sweets and handed them over. Your winnings. You laughed and unwrapped a sweet before popping it into your mouth. Ruffled my hair and said, 'Don't worry, your day will come.'

My parents had started calling me Button when I was very little, probably in reference to my button nose. I mean, even I knew that all babies have button noses. It certainly didn't make me special. But as my life went on, as I grew up, it became patently obvious that I was growing into an ugly, gawky child. Especially when compared to you, Jack. So the once-endearment, 'Button,' had quickly become Butty to my family, and Butt to school friends. Then the inevitable school jokers had added the Bot to the Butt and I was officially known thereafter as Buttbot. Or Butt for short.

Butthole for long.

But it didn't matter. The only thing that mattered was you. You made everything okay. Normal. Happy.

Bearable.

We were all falling in love with you that hot summer, all watching you grow as if from afar, your hair so beautiful and your skin so golden, kissed by the sun. The golden boy. You were like a summer's day. You really were.

I felt like a cloud by comparison.

But I was safe and happy at home. Inside. With my family.

It was only the Outside world that I hated. *Inside* the home, happy. Outside, that's where I didn't like life. The people. The cruelty. You, Jack, could only do so much, after all. But Outside, with you – bearable.

After your victory raindrop dance, our mother strode into

the room, breaking the perfect bubble that was us, and clapping her hands briskly, said, 'Come on now, hands and faces washed, hair combed. Supper's in ten minutes.'

She looked at you and cocked her head to one side, taking in the deliciousness of her first-born. Luxuriating in your beauty. My parents' love, especially our mother's, was a loud one – like you could actually hear it. It bounced off the walls, echoed around the house, around the room. Around you. I surreptitiously side-stepped into the glow. Basked in it: second-hand.

Second child. Second best.

I was the unfavourite.

No one had ever said that, nor treated me as if I were unfavoured, but that's just how I felt. Rightly or wrongly.

Our mother's eyes flitted down to me. Frowning, as if only just seeing me, she said, 'What exactly are you wearing and what is that on your knee?'

'Shorts. Old ones. I'm wearing shorts and it's blood on my knee. I was playing football earlier and fell over. It's nothing. Don't worry.'

'Yes, well, that is one thing you're very good at, Butty. Ball games. Good hand-eye coordination.'

'Good *foot*-eye coordination,' I corrected her, smiling.

Mother smiled back quizzically, as if she didn't really understand. Not unkindly, just in her normal sort of way as if I was a mystery to her. Then she surprised me by cupping her hand under my chin and kissing me on the nose. My button nose: although less button now – more a sort of shapeless blob in the middle of my face.

She finally turned to leave, saying over her shoulder, 'Come on, both of you. Chop-chop.' Surreptitiously she smiled at you. As if you both shared an unspoken secret. She clapped her hands again and left the room, waving the fingers of one hand behind her in farewell.

I knew my mother loved me. And my father. They just did it in a quiet, gentle way. But I knew they absolutely did love me. No doubt about it. Just not so loudly. But that was my lot and I accepted it. It was weird because really it felt more like that was my little.

While I understood that we all adored and loved you, I was equally aware – on some level that I didn't really, truly understand – that my love for you, was maybe a little bit *too* much.

Perhaps a little unhealthy.

But I was only twelve.

And twelve's too young to recognise danger.

Too young to realise how horribly wrong life could go.

But really, your perfectness overwhelmed me. I didn't just want to be like you, I wanted to *be* you.

I loved you so much, that I would die for you.

I really would.

SEVEN

Butty

Two years had passed, and you and I had moved on from raindrop racing. Moved on to being more involved in Outside life. And to be honest, I still wasn't a lover of school. You were obviously a year above me and had your own friends. Because you were popular. With both students and the teachers. A rare accomplishment.

But as always, you still looked out for me. In a discreet way: nothing over the top. You never did anything that would cause me embarrassment. It wasn't that I *needed* you. Just that I felt less… less open to abuse from the bold and the strong when you were there.

There was a mixed assortment of boys and girls, brains and idiots, the beautiful and the ugly.

It was a blast being fourteen.

'Still sucking on your mummy's titties, Buttbot?' Tommy said with his unique flair for language. Tommy Green – the school bully. There's always one.

'Yup, still sucking away,' I said, feigning brazen. I gave Tommy a withering look that you and I had practised in the mirror. I didn't think I'd mastered it yet: it was less withering and more squinty-eyed. Tommy laughed and casting his eyes quickly around him, pivoting on his toes, he checked oh-so-casually that you weren't around. Yup. Just me. He spat at me and laughed. 'Stick that up your butthole and swivel.'

Behind me, I felt my best friend, Willy, tucking himself away from trouble, putting me between him and Tommy. He was frightened, always frightened – frightened of everything. He shouldn't show it so much, but ironically, I didn't enjoy my role of protector of the weak. I was playing *your* role, although I doubt I carried it off with as much style. But I bumbled through. And it was good enough for Willy. Ergo, it worked.

I really didn't like the role. It didn't suit my nature. I had enough difficulty ducking and diving and avoiding Outside-the-home life, without having to take on such a screamingly-obvious sitting target as Willy. He might as well have *victim* indelibly inked on his forehead. I'd told him, warned him. But it wasn't in *his* nature to stand up for himself at all. He was a dependant. Mine, apparently.

Clearly, what with his name and mine, we were a match made in heaven for the literary elite of this world. Willy and Buttbot. The jokes were endless: 'Where's Willy? Up your Buttbot?' 'Oh, look, here comes Prick and Bum,' or 'Watch your backs, here's Dick and Hole.' Ad-bloody infinitum. Truly thigh-slapping stuff. I could hardly contain my mirth. Willy could hardly contain his tears.

I turned away from Tommy, the school's biggest shithead and said, 'Come on, let's go, Willy.'

And then I smiled. I could see you, over Tommy's shoulder, with your arm around Cindy's waist. Both of you wrapped up in big winter coats, scarves and hats. I didn't know what you saw in her. Admittedly, she had the biggest tits this side of the Watford Gap, as my father would say (the Watford Gap bit, not the big tits bit). *I* thought she was as cheap as chips, if anyone cared about my opinion.

My face must have relaxed at seeing you, as Tommy glanced around and realising that you were headed this way, he quickly adopted a cool but stupid mock saunter, and slithered off. His leg buckled on an unexpected lumpy piece of rogue tarmac. He tripped and I made a big show of laughing. Too loudly. Willy punched me softly in my back. 'Don't,' he said, keeping his voice low. 'He'll hit us.'

'Nah. He won't. Trust me, Willy. He's a total knobhead.' I liked swearing: had recently taken it up. Thought it gave me a hint of sophistication and adultness that I wouldn't otherwise have been able to attain. 'Look, here comes Jack,' I reassured Willy.

Knowing you were coming to save me, I should have been mortified, but what the hell. I didn't care, because I didn't really care what anyone thought about me. Maybe I lacked something. Maybe they did. That was just the way it was. This world that made me feel like a bit of an Outsider, a little bit odd and a lot different, frustrated me. I didn't conform. I was a misfit, and I didn't really quite know why.

Perhaps because I wasn't you. Maybe that was it.

I didn't know who I was, but whoever I was, I thought I was a bit pathetic. And that made me angry. Angry at the world and with anyone who wasn't our family. Who wasn't you.

Willy and me dawdled home, not following you, but just going the same way. I watched you hug Cindy goodbye, squeeze her, kiss her. With tongues.

A wet, sloppy visual display that I could have done without seeing, to be honest.

Willy peeled off at the end of the road to go home, and shuffled slowly away, his thighs chafing as he walked, the tips of his earlobes pink and pulsating with the cold.

You and me joined up. 'All right, Butty?'

'What do you see in her? She's like a Barbie doll. Except

she's a Cindy doll.' I shuddered in an exaggerated way to show my distaste.

You just laughed. 'You'll get it one day. She's great. She's more than just tits, you know. She's really nice. Clever. Funny.'

I grunted. Looked up at the sky. It was already getting dark and looked like it might snow. Shivering, I told you to get a move on. We hurried our way home, noses dripping from the bite of the wind. Five o'clock and already the sun was long gone.

Christmas decorations glowed in the early evening from the windows of houses and made the world look like a stupid Disney film. All happy families and gaiety. All unreal. Not like real life. With real *stuff* going on In *and* Out of the home. Sometimes, not nice stuff. So I thought they could stick their big Christmas trees with their outlandishly oversized baubles, straight up their jacksies. I wasn't impressed and didn't believe in their fakery. No one was happy all the time, *were they*? No. Definitely not. That would be impossible.

I was pretty sure that Tommy Green was adored and doted on by his parents, who no doubt saw him as kind and strong: *Inside* their home.

Cindy, I was equally certain, pretended a prim and proper façade Inside, but *Outside*, she was a different girl entirely.

And poor old Willy. Perhaps his Inside was as bad as his Outside world. His parents could hardly fail to see his suffering and mental anguish, his beaten-down fat body with his sloping shoulders forever in defeat, his embarrassed and eternally pink face shamed by others.

That's why I hated these houses. They mocked and they lied. Fuck them all.

I stopped looking at them and joined in joking about with you. Falling into the house together, we wrestled and fell into the hallway. De-booted, de-coated, defrosted. Piled in tandem into the kitchen to get a hot post-school snack. Our father suddenly loomed large from the other side of the open fridge door. 'Hello, you two. Cold enough for you?'

We both nodded, laughing at something I couldn't even remember. Dad said, 'If you're after hot chocolate, you're out of luck.'

You moaned and asked the obvious question. He replied with his very over-used and even more obvious answer. 'Why? You want to know why?'

We both looked him in the eye, avoiding each other's, waiting for his seriously boring and very sad answer to everything. It would be a joke. What he thought was a joke anyway. 'I was playing with my trains and got thirsty. Came down to the kitchen and before I knew what I was doing, I'd drunk all the milk. Bloody trains. I just lost all track of time. Get it? Lost *track*?'

He stopped for us to smile at his latest but oft-repeated hilarity. We both did, out of politeness – or pity: I was never sure which, but he came out with thousands of sad puns that weren't funny at all, *all the time*.

Before our father could finish, Mum came in. She eyerolled as she heard the train track joke and said, 'For God's sake, Gordon. We've all heard it a million times. Change the tune.'

'I was just saying,' he said, unfazed. 'I was about to make a hot drink to take back up to the attic, only to discover that we've run out of milk. Well, we ran out of it because I drank it. Sorry.' He shook the empty carton as if we needed proof of the no-milk crisis. He wiped his sleeve over his face, trying to clean his white milk moustache around his mouth. Like a five-year-old.

I looked away, embarrassed for him.

Mum, obviously irritated, said, turning to you and me, 'Would you mind? Here…' She rummaged in her purse and took out a ten-pound note. 'Nip down to the shops, would you? Get some milk and whatever you want for yourselves. A treat.

On me. Off you go and don't dawdle. It's cold and dark.' She clapped her hands. Our mother was a great hand-clapper. A professional.

Groaning, we re-wrapped in winter woollies and left the house. Not really bothered. Because it was nearly Christmas and nothing really mattered. It was nearly the school holidays and together, life was fun. On my own, *meh*, life wasn't so much fun. I just pretended. Because it was easier than admitting that I couldn't really do life single-handedly. I just went through the motions and hoped no one noticed that I was just a performance. A person with no substance. Empty.

It was easy to accept that I would never be like you. You were beyond me. Your perfection was out of reach.

I was just watching, happy to be along for the ride.

EIGHT

Butty

We walked in a friendly, easy silence. But then you said, 'Dad's a moron, isn't he? Embarrassing. Like a bloody child, sometimes. With his stupid bloody trainset. His tracks and his platforms and his stupid little plastic commuters. He actually moves them about like they're real. What a saddo. We live with the fat controller himself. *God.* He's turned into one of those embarrassing dads that you wished didn't belong to you. What a bloody dickhead. He's getting worse. More old and more past it every single bloody day. Don't think Mum finds it amusing.'

I was shocked at your assessment; even though it was an accurate one. You weren't normally wound up by such trivia, and let's face it, Dad was seriously trivial. I secretly blamed Cindy. I'd noticed that you'd become a little more distant from the family since you'd started going out with her. A little more distant from me. You were leaving me behind. I said, 'Dad's all right. Just a bit stupid. He's old. What do you expect?'

'He's weak. I expect him *not to be weak.* I don't want a weak freak father. That's not much to ask, is it?'

I laughed, trying to get the nice you back, not the Cindy-influenced version. '*I'm* the weak freak. Dad's just an idiot.'

You stopped walking and so I stopped. You stood so that you were opposite me and put your mittened hands on my shoulders. 'You are *not* weak. You can do or be whatever or whoever you want. Unlike Dad, who's a complete tosser. He doesn't like Cindy. He doesn't even know her. He should stick to playing with his stupid trains and keep his nose out of my business.'

So that was it. I should have known. The reason for your anger at Dad. He didn't like Cindy. Big boohoo. But I didn't say that of course. Mostly because I *am* weak. But I didn't know *what* to say either. This wasn't you talking. It was Cindy talking through you, with her silly treacly voice; all fluttering eyelashes and big blue eyes. I laughed instead and told you to ignore Dad.

'What have you got Cindy for Christmas? Jewellery? Chocolates? Roses? Romantic shit of any description?'

You smiled. 'Actually, you're not far off. I've got her a chain with a heart on it. Bit soppy I grant you, but it's real gold. She'll love it. It'll go with her toe-ring: it's got her initials inscribed on it. I got the necklace engraved as well so they'll sort of match. I'm going to give it to her before she goes away for Christmas with her family. By the tree. And I don't mean the kissing tree in the forest, where all the kids go and carve their names into the bark. That's just so sad and pathetic. I mean *our* tree: in the copse – the biggest one there. Out of the three of them, it's the tallest. The one on the bank, on the edge. But we always walk through the thicket to reach it. It's a real battle in the winter; like a personal challenge with thorns like knives.' He smiled. 'It's like a quest, getting through it unscathed, to reach our tree. Mine and Cindy's tree. You know where it is, right?'

You didn't even see my nod of recognition. Too caught up with the telling. Too *in love*.

'When I pick her up after her karate class in town on Thursdays, I walk her back through the alley and into the little patch of trees. A cut-through to her house. She'll only walk through there when it's dark if I'm with her.'

Your chest puffed out a little and I smiled, not really understanding your feelings for such a stupid girl. You ran your hands through your hair: 'That's *our* place.' You beamed with pride.

Fair enough, I supposed: because you'd made it sound like an almost heroic tale of romance. But I didn't know about love. Hadn't experienced it. Not yet anyway.

And I did know the tree. 'Sounds dead romantic,' I said and laughed. Taking the piss. But you didn't mind. Because nothing mattered. We were happy and that's what life's like when it's normal.

Even though the little local shop was in sight, I suddenly didn't want to talk about Cindy anymore, so I slowed down and changed the subject. 'Got a fag?'

You delved into an inner pocket. 'Coming right up.' You took two cigarettes out and giving one to me, I watched as you cupped the flame of the lighter in your hand, the glow lighting up your face. Then you threw back your head and inhaled deeply. 'Luvverly,' you said, laughing and teetering on the kerb as you threw the lighter at me. I caught it one-handedly and bent my head to my fag, seeing you out of the corner of my eye. A second passed, maybe two, three, and the next thing I knew, your arms were cartwheeling frantically as you tried to recover your balance, one leg cycled in mid-air in a vain attempt to keep you upright.

I saw the car coming but didn't register it properly. Not the speed it was travelling.

But I heard it hit you.

It was like a hard but soft sound all at the same time. Metal hitting skin and bone. A loud, squishy thump.

And then you weren't there anymore. I turned to look up the road and saw you. Just before the road vanished around a corner. In a heap. Not moving.

Everything fell quiet. Like a great big pause. I felt my world tilt. I remained standing, but the ground beneath me seemed to shift. It was as if all the sound had been sucked right out of the entire universe.

Utter silence.

I couldn't move. Couldn't speak. Couldn't shout and scream.

I couldn't breathe.

I couldn't even cry.

You lay there, all crumpled and wrong-looking. Dead-looking with awkward limbs splayed at impossible angles.

The globe had slipped on its axis and you were gone. I knew that. I knew it with an awful finality.

Transfixed, I could only stupidly stand there and do nothing. In the silence.

Eventually, I don't know when, sounds, one by one, started to come back, as if someone were turning the knob on a radio, turning up the volume slowly – one random noise at a time. Until everything was suddenly *too* loud. The wind, a dog barking, the sound of Mrs Evans, the shopkeeper, running down the road. Her shoes hit the tarmac and I could hear every stride she took. Her footsteps thundered and boomed and echoed and her screams shattered the stillness of the night. Even the silence was loud in its quietness, at odds with the shrieking woman. A neighbour's house opposite the shop suddenly lit up and I imagined I could hear each and every light switch as they were flicked on, one by one; the family rushing and crashing down the stairs. Out into the street to see you.

And I just carried on standing there. Alone. Watching Mrs Evans as she crouched over you, and the neighbours huddled around you, and I realised that the car that had hit you hadn't stopped. It was gone. You were gone.

Then I could hear the worst sound of all. Someone was wailing. Louder and louder. *No, no, no.* I cupped my hands over my ears to block it out: *no, no, no.* It wouldn't go away, just got more insistent. Like a mad chant, never-ending and so *loud.* Why wouldn't they shut up? *No, no, no.* I wanted them to stop. Just stop now. *No, no, no, no, no.*

Then I recognised the voice.

It was mine.

I don't know how long I stood there. I can't remember. It didn't matter.

Nothing mattered now and it would never matter in the future.

You were dead.

And I wasn't.

NINE

Butty

NOW

Today was the first time that I felt like me.
Me without you.

And now I didn't feel like a cloud, as I once described myself in comparison to the sunshine of you. Now I was a storm waiting in the wings. A furious tempest, gathering strength. The winds whipped up inside me, fuelled by such an intense anger I felt paralysed by it. Pure fury. I couldn't move past it. So, I continued to lie on my bed, summoning up the energy, the courage to move; trying to remember the fucking point of getting up at all.

I didn't even know how long I'd been here. Days? Weeks? Forever? Mum had been in with food, looking bleached white with grief, but I hadn't seen her since yesterday, I think. Or maybe the day before. Dad hadn't bothered putting in an appearance at all. Probably lost himself in his train world. As you said, what a tosser.

Getting up, I looked out of the window. Cold, harsh, empty. Missing something. Some*one*. Changed forever. Had Christmas been and gone? Did it matter? I clenched my fists and checked my mobile. A million texts from Willy:

> Are you all right?
>
> I'm so sorry.
>
> I'm sorry about Jack.
>
> Please text me.
>
> Hello? Are you okay?

On and on they went, getting more and more needy, as if he expected *me* to comfort *him*.

I clocked the date: the twelfth of December. I knew you'd been killed on the second. So ten lost days. I was so angry I didn't even feel sad. Didn't have time. Wasn't brave enough to stop and feel your loss. I got dressed. I got ready.

Ready for what, though?

It was like I was on a mission. Mission-Reclaim. To reclaim me. To *be* me. To remember your last words to me: You can be whoever or whatever you want.

I wasn't sure who or what I wanted to be, but I was pretty sure it wasn't good.

I was an accident waiting to happen. A walking trauma case. Steer clear. Chaos coming through.

TEN

Butty

I t didn't take me long to find Dad. He was slumped in the big armchair in the sitting room in front of an empty, cold hearth. At first I thought he was sleeping. It didn't take long to discover that he was totally off his face. His lips vibrated noisily as he inhaled and exhaled, breathing out the toxic fumes of whisky. I kicked him in the leg, not too hard, for signs of life other than breathing. Like maybe he was actually alive and sad that you were dead. Could perhaps voice those feelings and have a conversation. Not that I wanted one with him. Or anyone.

But no, decent parenting was obviously too much to expect from the station master at this time. His ability to communicate had been delayed by a leaf on the line. A dead son in the road. Stop. Halt. Sorry for your inconvenience. Normal service will be resumed shortly.

I didn't think that likely.

Back upstairs I found Mum. In bed. I shook her shoulder. It took an age for her eyes to open and then for them to register the presence of her now only child. 'Hello, Mum.'

She drew herself up, sloppily, on her pillows, on shaking

arms, wearing only her nightie with one of your jumpers tied around her neck by its sleeves.

'Why are you in bed?' I asked.

Her breath caught and she held out a sweaty hand to me. Obligingly, I walked into it, letting her touch my face. 'Butty. Dear Butty. I'm so sorry.'

I almost laughed, having to stop myself from saying *Sorry? What for? Were you driving the car?* But of course I didn't say that.

With an unexpected strength, she pulled me to her and cradled my head against her shoulder. I could feel her sobbing into my hair. Wanting to shout at her to stop blubbering, to get up, to do something, *any*thing, I instead just stood there quietly seething and curling and uncurling my fingers: fist, no fist, fist. Unable to contain nor control this terrible urge to hurt. Anyone or anything would do. My anger controlled me, not the other way round. Intellectually, I could see the dangers in that, but right at that moment, I didn't care. Not one tiny bit.

Managing to pull myself away from her desperate clutch, I stood back and said, 'I'm going out for a walk. Want anything?'

'Don't go, Butty. Stay a minute.'

'No. Sorry. Can't. Got to keep moving.' I smiled to take away the harshness of my words. She had a record for 'taking to her bed' in times of extremis; rare occurrences admittedly, but I asked anyway, hoping that she'd done at least this: 'When's Jack's funeral?'

'I was going to tell you. They're still looking for the driver who, you know…'

'Killed Jack.'

She blanched and nodded. 'Yes. I talked to the police earlier this morning. They wanted me to ask you if you'd remembered anything from, you know, when it happened. The night of the accident. If you'd perhaps remembered the colour of the car or seen the driver. Since they talked to you straight after the… the accident. You know. Anything, really.'

I kept still, having no recall of talking to the police. Ever.

'*Have* you remembered anything, Butty?'

'No. Nothing.' And I hadn't. The car hadn't had any lights on, I knew that, but I hadn't seen anything else. Only heard that dull thump as it hit you. I said again that I didn't remember seeing the car. Couldn't, wouldn't recognise it. Because it was true. Thankfully. My mother stopped herself from sighing and said, 'I'll let the police know not to bother you then. If you *do* remember–'

'Yeah, Mum, I'll let you know. Leave it now.'

She did a weird sort of wet smile thing and said, trying to be brisk and efficient and strong, 'The funeral will be this week. Saturday. I've organised most of it already.'

Bully for you, I thought. I was suddenly pissed off with her but knew I was being unfair. I closed my eyes and stood there. Soaking it up. Trying to be kind.

'If there's anything you'd like to say at the service, or a hymn you'd like, let me know, won't you? I want you to be included in everything, Butty. All of it. I know how you adored Jack. We all loved him very much.'

I just wanted this conversation over. Now. Making an effort, I said, 'Yeah, fine. I'll let you know. I'll give it some thought. I've got to go, Mum. Can't stop. Later, okay? We'll speak later. Promise.'

I heard her calling weakly from her bed of grief, entangled as she was in her sweaty sheets of anguish, and I ignored her, running out into the street where the wind screeched and the wind blew.

Turning to the left, I walked as fast as I could. Rounding the corner, I careered straight into the arms of the trumpet man's daughter. I couldn't remember her name. And she looked different. Penny Crisp, that was it. Except she was hardly recognisable.

You and me, Jack, remember how we'd often see her, in the

background in their front garden, pushing a wheelbarrow, or digging busily in the soil with her trowel? Rolling her eyes and laughing at her father behind his back, as he played his trumpet? Do you remember? She'd hold a spade to her mouth and pretend to blow, moving her fingers up and down the handle. And she'd wave at us with her huge smile, beaming right across her face.

Penny with the beautiful hair. Even I had appreciated that. But now it was gone. Cut off – short. I still recognised her though, but she looked so different. Much thinner. Sad. And changed in some way. She'd always been fun. Now she looked very… *un*-fun. More angry than anything and her face was twisted and bitter as if she were sucking on something sour.

Surprised, I realised she looked like I felt.

And what was she *wearing*? She had been a bit of a looker, as Dad would say, but now she just looked plain, dressed in nothing-type clothes. All black, and with nothing-type hair. What had happened to her? Looked like she was off to a funeral for someone she didn't love.

She held out her arms to steady me, 'Whoa, stop. Watch where you're going. You'll knock me or yourself over, and I don't do nursing. Just so you know.'

I manged a polite smile and murmured 'sorry'. Went to move on. Forever running. That's how it felt. If I stopped, the tears might catch me and I would never stop crying. I'd drown in my own salty tears and choke on them. They'd fill my lungs and I wouldn't be able to breathe. I'd cry forever and ever. So I had to carry on. Sprinting.

But Penny stopped me, holding me in place with her hands gripping hard on my shoulders. 'Why the hurry? Got a bloody train to catch?'

Clenching my jaws together tightly, I had a sudden vision of stupid Dad and his stupid trains and me wanting more than anything to catch one now.

Tilting her head back, she peered down at me, screwing her face up. 'I know you, don't I? You're the Hawthorne boy, aren't you? Charlie, isn't it?'

'Yeah, but you can call me Butty. And no. I haven't got a train to catch. I'm just in a hurry, so see you later, Penny. Can't stop.'

Her hands still prevented me from moving. 'I'm so sorry about your brother. Jack. Your older brother, Jack – that's his name, isn't it? An awful, terrible thing.' Her head moved towards the shop and Mrs Evans. She didn't actually roll her eyes but her face made it clear. Mrs Evans was a gossip. 'She told me. How are you holding up or is that a stupid question?'

'It's a stupid question.'

'Yeah, thought so. Sorry. Thoughtless of me. But what else can one say to someone who has suffered a real trauma like that? Really, what can I say. But I *am* sorry. Truly. And of course, sorry for Jack.'

'There's no need, thanks. Don't be sorry. He wouldn't want you to be sorry for him.'

She sort of smiled, and leant in nearer for a closer look at the freak boy with no brother. The way she looked at me, made me feel like I'd just shat in the front pew in church. A major curiosity. 'Don't be sorry? Shouldn't I be? I *am* sorry. Life's shite, right?'

Life's shite. That was unexpected. And a bit bonkers. Definitely weird vibes coming off her.

'And why do you call yourself Butty?'

'Because everyone else does.'

You called me Butty, Jack. You always did.

Shrugging her shoulders, she accepted my explanation. 'Right, fair enough. Butty it is, then.' She paused, peering at me. 'Isn't it annoying having a stupid nickname like that?'

'Yeah, it's a real pain in the buttbot.'

Penny laughed. 'Fancy a fag around the back of the bike shed?'

I gaped. I mean really couldn't stop my jaw from falling slack from its moorings. 'What did you say?'

She smiled, her face crinkling up like she hadn't smiled in a long time. Like she wasn't used to her lips moving like that. It seemed to surprise her. That's what she looked like. Surprised and sad and with a really stupid haircut – like a weird sort of grown-out man's short back and sides. But thicker. At least she had that going for it.

Her face was white and sort of empty. Blank holes for eyes. And what the fuck? *Fag behind the bike shed?* I thought she must be about forty? Was she a forty-year-old perv? Who talked like that to a child? She was a grown-up, after all. And even I knew that you didn't have to be a man to be a nutjob. Women could be mad as well. *A fag around the back of the bike shed?* I couldn't get over it. *What the fuck?* I reckoned she was off her rocker.

But the danger, the potential risk of her – or the hint of it, excited me. Her oddness was a good and possibly a bad distraction. What was the worst that could happen? The worst had al*ready* happened, and I was still here. I could fight off this woman, if she tried anything funny, so I said, 'Yeah, why not,' and laughed. The noise of my laughter sounded mad, but I was embracing my madness now, my differentness, so why not enjoy and take a chance. *I might die, she could kill me*, my internal voice warned me. *So what? Bring it on.* This was the Outside. Without you. A possible battle with a whack-job woman: that's exactly what I felt like. A war. I wanted a fight. A battle. If she wanted one, I'd give her one.

Or we'd just have a fag together around the back of the bike shed.

She laughed back at me and said, 'Surely your mother wouldn't approve? I haven't even ever met your parents properly. Not been introduced formally, anyway.'

'They know who you are. The trumpeter's daughter. Anyway, Mum's resting and is busy grieving,' I said, discovering that I actually meant it. Could understand it. Was jealous of her ability to do it.

'And you want to grieve on your own, right? You look like a chap who'd appreciate a quiet smoke. A smoke sounds like a good plan to me. But better to smoke in company I always find. We can smoke in the comfort of my parent's house just down the road, or we can hang out on the corner like a couple of old bums and just chew the fat and smoke in the cold. What's your fancy, Butty?'

No contest, the new Outside me thought. 'Your place, Miss Crisp. Penny. Let's go. Now. Come on. Get a move on.' And I grinned and clapped my hands in the style of my mother, feeling truly demented.

ELEVEN

Penny

P enny was surprised that Butty had come so willingly with her. But then again, she was hardly a threat to the boy.

She was the first to admit that she'd never really had a lot of interaction with children before. Couldn't seem to get on their wavelength – odd little things, kids. They always managed to make her say ridiculous and outlandish statements that wouldn't normally leave her mouth. Especially now. Now that she had stopped speaking to people, *any* people, except when she truly couldn't get out of it. *Do you fancy a fag behind the bike shed?* Where did *that* come from, for God's sake? Speaking to a child at all, was completely out of character for her and she wondered why she'd done it. But of course she knew. Deep down, she knew.

It was simple. Looking at Butty was like looking in the mirror. He was a little mini version of herself. Raw. Feral. Wild.

Very damaged and definitely not coping.

Different reasons, but same result.

As soon as he'd ran into her, she'd looked into his eyes and she'd *known*. He couldn't control that scary, skittish chaotic look. Something terrible had happened to him, and he was trying to cruise through it, sailing on anger and hate. She couldn't resist him.

This was simply an altruistic act. Nothing more. It was a long time since she'd been kind. Too long, she realised. This was the first time that she'd initiated conversation with anyone in so long. The art of natural and easy communication seemed an effort, as if her tongue were coated in verdigris. Her social skills had rusted. It was all such an effort, but she persevered. Because she'd instantly felt a connection with this strange, unhappy child. A deep familiarity.

She was astonished to find that she genuinely wanted to help the boy.

'One marshmallow lump, or two, Butty?'

'Five, please.'

Butty's tone was still blunt, verging on belligerent, but she knew she had the boy's interest. She smiled gently and threw a handful of marshmallow balls into a mug of hot chocolate. Presenting the steaming mug to her young guest she said, 'Now, how about that ciggie? We could partake in a puff either here or in my dad's Trumpet Room. Your choice.'

She watched with interest as Butty's eyes swivelled in thought, clearly wanting to pick the more exciting option of the Trumpet Room but weighing up the potential risks that might come with that particular choice. It was clear that Butty was on self-destruct, careering head-long, all caution thrown to the wind, into whatever calamity welcomed him the soonest, and the more possible danger involved, the better. He wasn't risk-averse. He was risk-*seeking*. And she knew *that* feeling.

Grief chased the boy, and the boy was running for his life in a frantic mania, hardly able to contain his anger. Penny could see and feel his fury. It was right there. Steaming off the child. Merging with her own.

She was aware it wasn't a healthy combination.

'If you're not careful, Butty, you'll get eaten up by this world.'

He smiled but looked confused at her comment. She realised that she wanted to save him. Maybe by doing so, she could save herself.

Lucky for Butty, he'd only bumped into her, and not some lunatic with evil in his heart. It came as no surprise when the boy opted for the riskier – in *his* head – of the two options, having not as yet seen anything other than the normal warm and welcoming walls of the Crisp kitchen. She wondered what the Trumpet Room looked like in his mind. Probably full of trolls and ogres. He pretended to give the question some thought, but she knew he'd already made his decision. 'Let's smoke in the Trumpet Room. Lead on.'

Penny smiled at the imperiousness and cavalier tone of Butty's voice, the sweep of his spindly arm towards, what was for him, an unknown destination, and it was with an effort that she kept her face straight.

She knew the child was lying. Was pretending to be something that he quite patently wasn't – untouched by trauma. And for that she liked Butty. Hugely. In the face of adversity, amidst his own sudden grief, the child was rising to the occasion. And that demanded admiration. The boy was ready to meet head-on any danger that may be coming his way, albeit prematurely and unadvisedly, which made him a rare breed in Penny's experience.

Of course it meant he was a fool, but she understood and forgave him that. He was only a child. And Butty's end would certainly not come from *her* hand. She had nothing against children. Just people. Men in particular.

They walked in silence, holding their mugs in their hands, as their feet walked across the huge expanse of lawn. The building they were headed for was at the bottom of the garden. A considerable distance from the house. A one-storey breeze-blocked rectangle, not dissimilar to a shipment container, perhaps a little smaller. Penny fumbled around in her pocket and came out with three small keys. She systematically unlocked the impressive triple-lock padlock, drew back the deadbolts and opened the door. 'After you.'

'Thanks,' the boy said automatically, his voice flat – all bluff and disinterest. But nevertheless, he retained a level of alertness that was admirable.

Despite Butty's bravado, both his voice and his step faltered, and he tripped up one of the two stairs that led into the Trumpet Room, nearly spilling his drink. Stepping over the threshold, he pulled up suddenly and stopped. Turned back to her. 'But it's empty. Just a single bed and a chair.'

'What were you expecting. A prison? A torture chamber? Dead bodies piled high?'

He shrugged, clearly embarrassed. He conceded, 'And a trumpet. There's a trumpet.'

They both turned to look at the brass instrument on the chair.

'Yeah, there is a trumpet. It's my father's. The Trumpet Room is exactly that. *Was* that. Except now it's my guest room. And what else would I need in here? It's an empty, calm space. Just for me and my bed and my chair. For when I stay here. My dad's not well, so when I come to the house, I sometimes sleep here when it's too late to go home.'

She watched the child as he scanned the admittedly spartan room. She'd de-cluttered before making it her own. By making it empty. 'The bed used to be just a slab with a cushioned top. For Dad. When he played his trumpet. He loved to sit and play in this room. Just him and his music.'

'Sorry. I didn't know he was ill.'

'Yeah, well, you wouldn't know, would you? I moved out a couple of years ago, but I come back here every day. Have to muck out the pigs, feed them, do general piggy duties. I help around the place, you know? More to the point, I look after my parents. Dad's dying. He doesn't come in here anymore – he's too sick. But he used to be in here all the time playing his bloody trumpet.' She eyerolled in what she thought was a youthful, conspiratorial way.

'Look, there's even a small en-suite bathroom, so I don't have to go into the house in the middle of the night. Everything that I could possibly need is right here.'

'So, that would be nothing but a bed and a bog and a trumpet, then,' and Butty turned to her and raised his eyebrows in question. 'Bit weird, isn't it? Where's all your stuff? Your possessions? What makes you, you. Books and photos and shit. Where's that?'

'I like it simple. What's wrong with that? It *was* a Trumpet Room; now it's just a Guest Room. For me. Sorry if that's not exciting or dangerous enough for you. I love this room. It was Dad's. Now it's mine. We both love it.'

'I'm very happy for you.'

'Why are you being such a rude little shit? I didn't have to bring you here. Go on. Tell me something fascinating about yourself. What are your interests? Got any?'

Butty hopped from foot to foot, blushing.

'Astronomy. I like the galaxy. And sorry. I didn't mean to be rude. Sorry.'

'Accepted.'

He looked angrily at Penny and the room. Not knowing why she bothered, it suddenly seemed important that he understood the simplicity of the space. 'It's my favourite room in the house, even though it's not strictly *in* the house. It reminds me of Dad when he was well. Normal. Playing his trumpet. There's nothing wrong with keeping nice memories.'

'Your father's not dead yet.'

'Yeah, but he doesn't play the trumpet anymore. But he *did* and that's what I choose to remember.'

Psychology for Dummies: Get in touch with your innermost positive and happy memories. What a crock.

Butty tapped his foot with exaggerated boredom. Didn't look at her. She wanted to ignore him right back but refused to let him go. She wanted him to connect with what she was saying, realise that it applied to him. Whatever had happened, had happened, and you had to get on with it. Positivity and all that. *God, believe that and you'll believe anything.*

She couldn't be more negative about life if she tried. Thought positivity was over-rated. But in theory... well, in theory, a lot of things.

Butty would come to accept the death of his brother, but not now. Now was too soon. He wasn't ready. Maybe she could help him.

Maybe *he* could help *her.*

But she was happy to wait. It was evident that the child *needed* a friend. Someone to confide in when he felt ready. It was evident that *she* needed a friend. Even a child would do.

How bloody pathetic was that?

Picking up the trumpet which perched on the chair, Penny fondled the brass in her hands, running her fingers over the golden instrument. 'When my father played outside, people heard him. I'm sure that sometimes it must have seriously annoyed them. But no one can hear him playing his trumpet in here. That's why he built it. The room is completely soundproofed. No one can hear you scream in there. Go on. Give it a go. Scream. See what happens.'

Without thinking, she shut the door and shouted. As loud as she could. Before she could tell him to go outside and see if he could hear her, she saw the terror in his eyes and his body stiffened. Too late, she realised her mistake. *Too* bloody late, but she got it. Felt ridiculously stupid and heavy-handed and unthinking.

'Sorry, Butty, of course you don't have to scream – only

joking. I only meant that be*cause* it's soundproofed, of course no one would hear you, would they? You don't have to scream to prove that point. We'll go now. Leave your mug on the side and we'll go and see the pigs. And then, we can do what we came outside to do in the first place – *smoke*.'

Leading the boy away, she gave him a cigarette and they both lit up. The wind stole the smoke away as soon as it left their mouths. Butty drew on his cigarette so hard that the tip turned big and red and hot-looking. Penny pointed, waving her hand over to the left. 'The pigs are this way. See? Over there.'

Butty shrugged. Penny sighed. Why am I even doing this? Persevering with a boy. Trying to make friends. *What the fuck am I doing?* She really wasn't sure she even liked children. They were so unformed, so not ready to have a decent conversation with. Not one that really counted. But there was something about Butty that she found intriguing.

He was an odd-looking child: it was as if he didn't quite fit his own body yet. His voice hadn't broken but sounded like it might at any minute. Everything was slightly off-kilter, his limbs not in sync with the rest of him. He was painfully thin; his hands were too big for his arms and he was uncoordinated. Like a toddler who hadn't yet got to grips with how its own body moved. Every step was a new discovery.

He spoke, having to shout against the wind. 'How old are you, Penny?'

'How old do you think?'

His eyes squinted and he tipped his chin up and to the side, assessing her. 'Forty?'

Penny laughed. 'God, no. Not that old. Not by a long shot. Do I look *that* crap? I'm thirty. How about you?'

'Fourteen. And you should grow your hair again. I liked it better before.'

'Yeah, me too.' Conversation stopped for a while as they both puffed away, trudging against the wind. Penny leant forward into it, feeling its sting, her face angled down to the child. 'I don't suppose you're looking forward much to Christmas this year, are you? A really crap time for you. I can't imagine.'

She could imagine.

Butty shrugged, his little face suddenly set in rigid lines, refusing to let any emotion reveal itself, keeping everything under wraps; all tied up and safely tucked away with a slash of red-ribbon rage.

'I don't suppose there's anything I could do that would help you through it?'

The boy's face wrinkled and furrowed in sudden visible anger. He shouted, trying to stop his words being torn from him by the wind, stopped them being muffled and snatched away. His voice rose to a scream. 'No, there isn't anything you can do. And why would you want to help me anyway? *You don't even know me.*'

'I don't have to know you. Anyway, we've met now, so now I do know you.'

'I want my brother back. That's what I want. Try doing that. I want Jack back. Can you do that, Penny, can you? Nobody can give me Jack back and that's all I want.'

He threw his half-smoked cigarette in the grass and said, 'And fuck your pigs. I'm not interested.'

'Suit yourself. You can walk yourself out. See you around.' She spoke to the boy's back, as he stomped angrily off and away. 'And hold on to your socks in this wind.'

She expected no reply and got none.

Penny knew, with a satisfying confidence, that by inadvertently frightening the child, she had inextricably bound him to her. She had unwittingly played to the child's chaotic need to experience risk. The boy thought he wanted to die. He'd get over that idiotic notion but Penny had stumbled upon the boy's Achilles heel and now Butty was hers.

That was why Penny thought about what the boy had just said. About wanting his brother back.

She wanted her *life* back.

As odd as the situation was, perhaps they would be each other's salvation.

A hopeful and bright future.

Perhaps.

Or the coming together of two broken people, both in the wrong place at the wrong time. Penny wondered if she was in fact creating an unholy union between the two of them.

If that was the case, she'd stand back and wait for the explosion.

And hope it wasn't too bad if and when it came.

TWELVE

Butty

W*ell*, she *was weird*, I thought, as I ran down the road. Making my escape. Turns out the nice daughter of Mr Trumpeter was way off the normal chart – raving; stark staring mad. *The room is completely soundproofed. No one can hear you scream in there. Go on. Give it a go.* Who says that? To a child?

If she was an abductor, then she was pretty useless at it. She lacked the social skills for it. If you wanted to kidnap a child, you'd want them to like you and ultimately *trust* you. Her efforts at coercing me had been laughably woeful and had fallen well short of any self-respecting weirdo. Her whole demeanour had been sort of… off. Almost inappropriate. Not sexually, just in general. As if she wasn't used to dealing with children. So, not in my opinion, a child molester. But there was *some*thing weird about her.

Meanwhile, me and anger had things to do in the Outside world.

And anger kept me safe. That's how it felt, anyway. And that's why I decided there and then to visit batshit crazy Penny again. I was taking the brakes off my life and seeing where I'd hurtle. I knew that I wouldn't tell Willy about her. Penny was my secret. For the time being.

Rage would look after me, be my shield, and I liked the spice of risk that she offered. It was like rolling a dice and playing the odds. I was always going to lose, but I liked those odds. I wanted to lose. I just wanted to lose by someone else's hand, because I was a coward. I didn't know how or what to do myself, so would happily rely on Penny, or whoever, to do it for me. Make a game of it. Maybe my ability and possibly very-deeply-buried desire to carry on breathing would surprise me, and I'd come out fighting for life. Without you. I'd never know if I didn't try. Maybe I'd simply surrender to whatever Penny wanted.

And despite her oddness, I'd kind of liked being with her. She said it as it was. Didn't speak to me like I was a child. She just spoke like she would to anyone. And there was something else. She had an 'other' quality about her. People would call it that, but I thought she had a 'same' quality about her. Same as me. We matched.

And at least she had the front to actually say, 'Sorry about Jack.' Most people, I just knew, would skirt around the issue, tiptoe around it as if I might crumble at hearing the news. Like they'd be breaking the news *to* me. *As if I didn't already know you were dead.*

Penny could definitely be my new friend. A titter or a snort or something derisive and loud exploded from my mouth and nose at the thought. I managed to tone it down to a more normal smile and then felt immediately guilty. It was a bit soon for laughing. And anyway, what was there really to laugh about? My stupidly smug smile about Miss loony-tunes Penny Crisp being my mate, felt disrespectful to you. My lips fell quickly back into a straight, frozen line.

I slowed to a saunter, unaware of the cold. As if in some sort of stupor, I ambled along. Inside, inside my *head*, I was completely cut off as I walked. I thought I might be slowly but quietly unravelling. Working on the premise that speed of mind and fleet of foot could outpace my own disintegration, I made a conscious effort to quicken my stride. Hurried to find Willy.

I had to keep my mind blank so that sadness wouldn't seep in and settle. A refusal to give grief houseroom, I broke into a run. It was all about mind over matter and I had a lot of mind. I focused it on excluding and banishing sadness and grief.

Wanting to gallop, I instead did a polite sort of trotting thing.

Instead of getting on the bus to school, I walked.

The twenty-minute walk seemed to take five minutes and at the same time forever, but finally, there they were: the school gates. Looking at my mobile, I realised school wouldn't finish for another thirty minutes. Time to do some more avoiding. So, I sat down on a bench, not bothering that it was cold, and did nothing. Just killed time. I was sure I was thinking nothing, had made my mind a blank, but then I noticed that as I sat, my fists, as if of their own volition, were pummelling my thighs. I'd become my very own punch-bag. Making myself stop, I abruptly stood and went to seek out Willy. Anger in check.

For the moment.

Looking up, I realised that I'd let time slip. School had closed and most students had already gone. I almost missed my friend. Relieved, I finally saw him, instantly recognisable by his eternally slumped shoulders weighing him down as he walked. Alone, without me. 'Hey, Willy,' I shouted.

His pink, round face looked up and a smile split his face. And then instantly, he sobered his expression. I saw his hesitation as he thought: *Don't smile in front of the grieving. It's not allowed.*

I phony-smiled and raised my hand, releasing him from his torment, showing him that the world, including him, was still allowed to crack their face in my presence. That I wouldn't break and shatter.

'Butty. How are you?' He slapped me on the shoulder and then quickly returned to his default stance: fat and awkward and sweaty: even in this temperature. I knew he wanted to hug me but didn't know how. Embarrassment stopped him.

So I gave him a brief back-slapping semi-embrace and said, 'You know… Not bad. Well, I'm shit, actually. Anyway, let's walk.'

The silence stretched between us. Finally, Willy said, 'I'm so sorry about Jack. Really. So sorry.'

I turned to him in surprise, delighted that he'd actually said it. 'Thanks, mate.' And we smiled sadly at each other. It was more than I could have hoped for and for a moment I considered that I might actually love Willy.

Then Willy stopped unexpectedly. 'Shit,' he said.

'What?'

'Nothing. Let's walk round the other way. Come on.'

I scanned the road ahead of us and saw them. Cindy and Tommy. My gut twisted and my face coloured. 'Leave them, Butty. They're not worth it.'

'Oh, they're worth it. Definitely. Come on. Stick close and don't speak. Leave it to me. I've got this.'

Cindy-Doll and Tommy Green were holding hands and stood, shivering at the bus stop heading for town. There was no one else around. Cindy's face was buried in Tommy's shoulder and he looked like he was smelling her hair. I saw him bend his head to kiss her and she upturned her mouth to his, puckered up her lips, already waiting. I walked straight up to Cindy who didn't see me until the very last minute. She had the grace to blush and dropped Tommy's hand as if it were burning her. 'Hello, Cindy. Missing Jack, I see.'

'Leave her alone, Butthole. Just bugger off, you moron,' Tommy said.

'Don't,' Cindy said to him. 'Stop it.' She turned back to me. 'Hello, Butty. How are you? I'm sorry about Jack. Really, I am.'

Apparently, it wasn't as difficult for people to say as I'd imagined. But that didn't change the fact that she'd been holding hands with Tommy. Had been *kissing* him. I said, not even trying to keep my voice on an even keel, just letting it scream out of me: 'Jack's not even cold in his grave; he's not even *in* his grave – not yet, but here you are, already holding hands with someone else. How dare you?'

She went to speak but I repeated my last words. '*How dare you?*' I felt Willy's hand tugging on my top, trying to pull me back and I realised that I'd advanced on Cindy, my face inches away from hers. 'Well?' I said. 'Jack liked you. God knows why, but he did. And now, what? You're going out with Tommy Shitface? *Really?*'

Tommy did the manly thing and came to her rescue, stepping closer to me, his fists clenched. I confused him by stepping closer to *him*, our noses nearly touching. 'Don't you even think of speaking to me, Tommy. Do not touch me, do not breathe on me, get out of my space before I make you.'

And then I gave him the withering look. The one you and me had practised and I'd never got right. But this time it worked. I watched in fascination as Tommy took a step back, vainly trying to keep his mouth from falling open, desperately thinking of something witty and cruel to say, but coming up with nothing. I pushed his shoulder. Hard. Pushed it again. 'Why don't you just sod off, Tommy. Nobody likes you. You're an idiot. Fuck off before I kill you.'

I heard Willy gasp, saw a flicker of surprised shock cross Cindy's face, heard her sharp intake of breath, I heard the sudden rain fall and the wind blow and the blood in my ears roar. My body was so tense and ready for battle that I wished stupidly and childishly that I had any sort of a stabby thing, a thing with a point, a very sharpened point, a shiny blade. *A knife.* It was such an alien thought I had trouble even naming it. But I swear to God, if I'd had a knife, I would've stabbed Tommy through his heart. In and out and in again. And I'd have enjoyed it.

Instead, I punched him square in the face. A sucker-punch. And it was true: the bigger they are, the harder they fall. When he was down, it took a moment for me to realise that he was lying there because of me. All common reason disappeared and I fell down on his chest, straddling him, and punched him again. And again and again and again. I lost myself in the savagery of it. And I *loved* it. His cheeks and his eyes and his lips were red and puffed and bleeding and I only stopped because the adrenalin finally ran out, and my knuckles ached, and my chest heaved with exertion. I couldn't catch my breath. Panting, I finally allowed Willy to pull me off the now unmoving Tommy.

I'd frightened myself with my own violence.

But I'd also pleased myself.

My Outside world had just got a little smaller. I was a little less marooned in a vast expanse of water: less bobbing hopelessly about, lost at sea. And for that I was grateful.

For the first time in my life, I had surprised myself and really achieved something that I thought was beyond me. I had won my one-and-only-ever fight. And initially, I felt triumph. But deeper down, deeper down where it really mattered, I was a little scared. Because I'd recognised in myself the ability to do harm. Serious harm. And I wasn't sure what to do with that knowledge.

Should I act on it? I didn't mean now. I didn't mean, should I actually kill Tommy now? He was of no consequence. He was just a stupid teenage boy. Not worth the fight. No. I meant, should I really hurt someone? Physically. Anyone would do. I thought it would make me feel better. Give me a reason for carrying on without you. It would give me a reason for being. For breathing. For staying alive.

It would give me something to *do*.

Instead of being a nothing, I would finally become a person of substance. I would become real. A real me. Even without you. And everything that I would do in the future, from here on in, would be for you.

Good or bad.

I imagined you proud.

Now I felt ready for the Outside.

I wondered if the Outside was ready for me.

THIRTEEN

Butty

'See you later, Willy. Sorry if I freaked you out, okay?'

'You really went mental. Totally over the top. You need to keep your temper under control. You *did* freak me out. You nearly killed Tommy.'

'Yeah, well.' I couldn't think of anything else to say. Didn't feel I had to explain myself. Not to my best friend. We carried on walking, me thinking, him worrying, and I left him, with relief, at his house. I walked back past Penny's house and didn't see her, and I didn't stop at Mrs Evans' shop even though I wanted some cigarettes.

I didn't look at where you had lain in the road.

Reaching our house, I was sweating from too much walking, and all that fighting. But I felt very different. In a good way.

As I walked in, I smelt food smells. On the kitchen worktops there were bowls and bowls of Tupperware containing, on inspection, lasagne, stews, soups and pieces of fried chicken. Loads of it. Enough to feed lots of people. For a very long time. Mum must have had one of her mad batch-cooking sessions. Investigating further, I found neatly labelled and dated tubs in the fridge and freezer: plenty of food for weeks.

I couldn't remember when I'd last eaten, so I heaped lasagne on a plate and threw it in the microwave. Gulped it down, burning my mouth in my haste.

After I washed my plate up, I called out to my parents. One or both would do. Checked the sitting room. Dad hadn't moved. There was no answer to my greeting. Nothing. Nada. Diddly-shit. Sighing, I got up and went upstairs, already knowing what I'd find.

Standing in my mother's bedroom, I repeated my question. 'Want anything?'

It took her a while to sit up, and even more time for her eyes to focus on me. 'You're bleeding, Butty. Your hands. What have you done?'

'Why have you gone back to bed, Mum? Get up. Don't you want to get up? Come on. Please, Mum. Get up.'

'Not now, Butty. I can't. I got up earlier and cooked a load of lasagne, and some other stuff. You can reheat it when you're hungry. I'll just stay here for a bit.' She rubbed her face, as if cleaning it with her palms. 'I've taken a little something to help me sleep. Show me your hands. What have you done?'

Knotting my fingers behind my back, I promised her it was nothing. Just a graze. Told her I'd already eaten, thank you. Mum was more than happy with all of that information. 'Go and find your father. Make him eat something.'

'I don't have to find him. I saw him on the way up here. He hasn't moved since this morning. He's in the chair in the sitting room. Off his face. Pissed as a fart. Why should I find him? I can guarantee he's not hungry. I've found him and he's still lost. It's not my fault.'

'Of course it's not your fault, Butty. God, your father's a selfish man. And I do so love you, my little one. And I'm sorry that I'm being so bloody useless at the moment. Forgive me. Tomorrow. Tomorrow I'll get up. Promise.'

'No need to apologise. I'm fine. I can look after myself.' I bent and kissed her on the cheek. Before I could leave she reached out her hand and pointed at her purse on the dressing table. 'Pass me that, would you, please?' She took out a twenty-pound note and held it in her hand. 'Tell me what you're doing with yourself every day, Butty? I'm so sorry.'

'Don't start, Mum. I'm just hanging around. Seeing Willy. You know, the usual.'

'School?'

I shook my head.

'I don't blame you,' Mum said and handed me the money. 'In case you need it, darling. Sorry.'

I took it and kissed her again. Quietly closing her door, I went into your room.

God, how empty it felt without you. Hollow. I remembered us laughing our socks off in this room. Now there weren't even echoes of comedy in here. It was dead – and I do mean *dead* – silent. I imagined I could hear us, I *wanted* to hear us, I even cocked my head and *tried* to hear us, but there was nothing. Nothing at all.

Dust. There was dust. *Already*. Dust to dust. Seemed a bit premature. Seemed so wrong. I hoped Mum wouldn't make your bedroom into a shrine. I'd hate that. This room needed to be lived in because at the moment, it was like a hole, a deep hole with no bottom. It needed filling with life again. You wouldn't mind, would you, Jack, if I moved in? Slept in your bed? Wore your pyjamas? Wore your clothes? The ones that fit, anyway.

Opening the wardrobe door I ran my hands through your hanging shirts – ironed by Mum. Riffled my fingers through the neatly folded tops, again, Mum's work, and I even smelt your socks. Clean. Fresh air fresh. Again, that would be Mum.

Ripping off my jumper, I picked out your favourite stripey top and put it on. Long sleeves, black-and-white hoops and a round neck. I posed in front of the mirror and tried out a smile. A sad, watery grimace reflected back at me. I turned up the cuffs and started my search. You had lots of secret places.

Under the bed. Bit bloody obvious. Behind the wardrobe. Nope. Behind the chest of drawers. Again, no. Where would you hide something precious? Lying on your bed I stared up at the ceiling. Thinking about you. About everything.

And fell asleep.

Later – much later, I realised as I checked my mobile and found two hours had passed – it was dark and I was cold.

Putting on the light I knew immediately and instinctively where you'd put Cindy's necklace. Because I knew you inside out. Instead of under the wardrobe, I felt under the lip of the wardrobe at the bottom: *behind* it. I wondered why you bothered hiding it at all. Who would be looking for it? But it was just your way. Secret squirrel and all that.

I flitted my fingers along the underside and there it was. Feeling a small box, I pulled at the tape which held it in place. The box was blue and about three inches by three inches square. Sitting cross-legged, I gently lifted the lid, and there it was: a delicate gold linked chain with a love heart on it. Bringing it closer, I realised it was actually a locket. When I undid the catch, the two sides of the heart parted, showing me two teeny photographs. One of you. And one of her.

You were smiling directly at the camera. You looked so young and perfect and powerful and alive. So alive.

She still looked cheap.

Standing, I slipped the box into the pocket of my jeans and sat on the bed. Moved the box to my front pocket. I wanted to text Cindy, but I didn't have her number and your mobile was with you. I thought so anyway. Surely the police must have returned whatever you'd been carrying on you, given it back to Mum?

Quickly, I ran into Mum's room. She was sleeping. Shaking her, she rolled onto her back, her mouth open. 'Mum, wake up.' Shook her again. '*Mum.*'

I heard Dad's voice behind me. 'Jack. Hello, son. I couldn't find you anywhere and here you were, all the time.'

I jumped. 'Dad. You nearly gave me a heart attack. And what do you mean, "Jack?" I'm Butty.'

He must have come up the stairs behind me. Bloody lunatic. Why was Dad creeping around like a weirdo?

'What are you wearing?' he asked.

'Nothing.'

Stupid answer. Of course I was wearing *some*thing. And why shouldn't I wear it? It made me feel closer to you. It smelt of you. 'It's Jack's top. He wouldn't mind.'

'What are you talking about, *Jack's* top. It's your top. It's always been yours. Silly boy.'

Folding my arms, I planted my legs into the ground like immovable steel girders, bracing myself against… I wasn't entirely sure what was going on. Dad had lost the plot.

He was standing there with a bottle of whisky in one hand and a glass in the other. I decided to argue for the sake of it. Do anything but talk about your top, and me wearing it, and Dad thinking it important and obviously confused as to who I was. Ignoring the more obvious fact that it was wrong that *you* weren't here anymore.

Except apparently Dad thought you were. 'Are you still drunk, Dad?'

Stupid question. Clearly he was. Even his outline looked blurred to *me*. But I'd never seen him lose his mind before. Mild-mannered Gordon Hawthorne, married to Helen, father to me and you. *Now* he was seriously confused. Could grief do that to a person? Red flushed his cheeks like a red train signal. Sign-posting him going off the fucking rails.

I was frightened by the unexpectedness of it all. He didn't seem like Dad anymore. This was the unfamiliarity of my new life. The Outside had come Inside.

'Do you want to come upstairs, Jack? I've got a great big new engine for my collection. A steam one, obviously. It's beautiful. I've ordered a bus as well. It's one of those oft-needed rail-replacement buses they put on these days with ever-increasing frequency.'

'No, it's all right, thanks, Dad. Got things to do. Maybe later.'

I realised my breathing had gone all funny and I was on the verge of tears. Fuck it. Bloody Dad.

He suddenly changed tack and tried to adopt a nonchalant pose, leaning against the door frame with his ankles crossed. Very casual. Very casual for a drunk man. He was unable to disguise his slight unsteadiness and his words, though clear, ran into each other – joined up with alcohol.

'I'm sorry about your brother, Jack. Sorry about Butty. It was an awful, awful accident. Unthinkable. But we'll pull through. Together, we'll all pull through. Okay? Butty's dead. My son is dead. But you're alive, Jack. Alive and kicking, thank God. You are my perfect son.' His eyes filled with tears. 'Thank God you're still alive, Jack. It would have been intolerable if you'd died. But you didn't.' He beamed at me, eyes misted and glazed.

My face was hot. Boiling hot and wet. I was crying and shocked. 'Do you wish I'd died instead, Dad? Are you left with the wrong son? Is that what you mean? Is that what you're saying? *The wrong boy died?*'

'What are you talking about, Jack? You *are* the right son. You were always the right son. Now off you toddle. Go and play. I want to talk to your mother about Butty's funeral.'

Mum chose that moment to wake up. Saving Dad the difficulty of digging his grave any deeper. Or rather, digging my premature grave deeper. But he didn't need to spell it out any further than he already had. He'd said it without words. His stupid red drunken face had said it. He wished it had been me, Butty, that had died. But here I was, alive and kicking, as confirmed by him, but as Jack.

I am the wrong son.

'What are you two doing in here? Butty, are you okay? Gordon, what have you said to the boy?'

'Nothing, Helen. We were just talking, right, Jack?'

'Right, Dad.'

We just looked at each other, our relationship forever changed. So quickly, it had changed from loving father to bad, mean, cruel bastard father living in a mad delusional world – and me. Me alone with no ally to back me up. No you.

I wanted to kill Dad, right then and there. I really did. I literally wanted to kill him.

Maybe I would.

I didn't need your phone. I'd meet Cindy myself outside her karate class tomorrow night. I knew you picked her up at seven in the evening. Instead *I'd* be there. With the chain. From you to her, via me. That's what you wanted. You wanted her to have the chain. It wasn't what *I* wanted, but I would do it for you.

Running down the stairs, away from pissed shithead hallucinating Dad, I heard Mum shouting at him, her voice shrill but slurred – not Mum-sounding, more stoned-Mum coming awake from a deep sleep. 'Are you drunk, Gordon? What did you say to Butty?' Flattening my hands to my ears, but unable to block out their continuing raised voices, I skidded into the sitting room and then into the kitchen. I had no place to go, no place to run to.

My world was breaking.

Automatically I checked the sweetie jar. I unscrewed the orange top and stuck my hand in. Inspected assorted chocolates and sweets, made my choice and crammed a sweet and sticky slab of spiky home-made peanut brittle into my face. Crunched and crunched, the nuts hurting the roof of my mouth. I wanted it to bleed. I looked for blades of honeycomb and found some at the bottom. Threw them in and crunched on them too: crunched down hard, viciously swallowing big, jagged slivers of hard, crystalised sugar. Had some more. I savaged them. I crushed them until my teeth ached and my mouth bled. Stupidly desperate for I don't know what.

I did know I wanted to hurt Dad.

I wanted to really hurt him.

I wanted to kill him.

I wanted to die.

FOURTEEN

Butty

I didn't sleep in your room after all. I'd been too angry and hadn't wanted to taint your space with Dad's poison, which still clung to me like black sticky oil. *The wrong son.* I'd been right all along. I *was* the unfavourite. Always had been.

So, instead I'd curled up in a ball in my own bed under the duvet. Like a baby hiding under the covers.

And quietly, oh so quietly, I had plotted and I schemed. Not really knowing what it was that I was plotting and scheming, just that I needed to feel alive and by alive I meant I needed to feel bad. I had to feel really *very* bad. Bad made me feel more whole. It was that simple. I'd learnt that lesson from beating up Tommy.

Dad had destroyed and betrayed me. Destroyed me more than I already was. I couldn't get over the betrayal. Maybe, if I was being generous, I could sensibly put it down to him being grief-stricken over the death of you. But I couldn't convince myself that that was true.

What he'd said, he'd meant because he so wanted and needed it to be true. Even if he apologised now, told me he *hadn't* meant it, of course he hadn't, what was I thinking, of course he loved me, *Butty* – still, I'd never forgive him. That was it. Finished. Done. Dad was history.

Today was a new day. It was Thursday. Cindy's karate night. Pink Cindy wearing her black belt.

I left the house early and headed for town. Avoided the possible getting up of either parent. I'd let Dad carry on destroying, hoping he wouldn't destroy Mum as well. I couldn't save her. I'd try, but I didn't think I could save Mum. Wasn't sure she even needed saving. Perhaps it was only me that was crying out for a rubber ring and arm bands.

If someone had asked me what I did all day, I don't think I could have said. I know I considered trying to find Penny, but I didn't. I wanted to be on my own.

It was raining. Cold, hard rain. I was still wearing your stripey top under my blue jumper. And a big insulated black waterproof jacket. Zipped up to the chin. With a hood. And gloves. Once in town I just walked about. Went in and out of different cafés, decided to have a Coke and a sandwich in one egg-smelling workman's place that I'd never been in before. It stank of farts. I didn't think I'd be going back. The food was tasteless but that might have been me. My body didn't seem to be reacting normally: my senses had gone AWOL. I was just a boy: walking, sitting, running, sitting, walking.

Finally, I took refuge in the cinema. I don't know what film I watched. I was killing time. Time that felt endless, relentless, overbearing and heavy. But it was something that I could at least kill. That made me smile.

At twenty to seven, I came out from the dark, nameless unwatched film, not bothering to watch the end: I had a date to keep after all. I stepped into the nameless place that was the Outside. I was instantly surrounded by hordes of Christmas shoppers, pushing, shoving, hurrying – their faces pulverised by the cold. Like a small fish caught in a shoal of bigger fish, I was swept along, hooded and unidentifiable. Not that anyone was looking for me, but I liked the anonymity. People not knowing it was me.

Me not knowing me.

The karate class was held in a boring building, with a lot of windows. It temporarily hid its dreariness behind the sparkle of Christmas lights, trying to cover up the fact that it was seriously dull and faceless. Cupping my gloved hands to the glass I peered in. My breath steamed up the pane and I was suddenly transported back to betting on raindrops.

I couldn't see any karate class going on but presumed it would be carried on behind closed doors: chop, chop, chop with Oriental whoops of intent. Unseen and unheard from the Outside. I wandered away and stood at a bus stop, my back to the gathered straggling queue, and faced the only exit to the building. I didn't want to miss Cindy's departure.

Rigid with cold, I sauntered closer to the 'lover's lane' entrance, stamping my feet to get some feeling back. Still keeping an eye out for Cindy's appearance. I leant casually at the opening to Grope Alley, the cut-through to the copse and the three trees. Glancing up I noticed that the CCTV camera was turned skyward; catching only the dark and the moon. Dirty old men and dirty old women probably, not wanting their touchy-feelies caught on film for eternity.

As it was, I was starting to feel like a dirty young boy, loitering by the entrance. A couple walked past me, already all handsy and quickening their pace so they could do it properly in the relative privacy of the lane. I assumed. I didn't really get it. Why not do it inside where it's warmer and more comfortable and they'd be less likely to be interrupted? Or maybe that was half the fun.

My mobile said ten past seven. *Come on, pink Cindy. I've got something for you*. I stamped my feet to keep the blood flowing. The rain had stopped, and the temperature was icy. Belatedly, it occurred that Tommy might have taken over walking-home duties. Feeling deflated and beaten, I was about to walk home when she appeared.

Thankfully she was alone, all furry-coated and holding a big bag. My heart jumped. Knowing she would go to the bus stop I left my seedy lurking spot and intercepted her. 'Hello, Cindy.'

Her face remained blank, non-recognition plain to see.

I pulled the lip of my hood back. 'It's me. Butty. I've brought something for you. From Jack.'

Her expression matched the weather and frostily she held her hand out. No greeting, no smiling, no nothing. Just her stupid hand thrust out at me.

'Not *here*. That wouldn't be right. Jack was going to give it to you by your tree in the copse. For Christmas. It's *gold*.' I breathed that one out in an excited rush and saw her eyes light up. I swear to God, they literally fucking lit up. 'I'm delivering it instead, though. For obvious reasons. Think of me as your little festive elf.' I did a false ingratiating beam, lips turned up as high as high could be, as befitting the bearer of forthcoming bejewelled delights. I kept my hands firmly in my pocket, feeling the box. Started strolling towards Grope Alley. Heard her behind me. 'Wait. Butty, wait up.'

Turning innocently, I waited. It was no surprise that she was unable to resist offers of a present. She was a grabber of all that glitters, I knew that. Could see it from a mile off.

You never saw that though, did you? But that's because you were nicer than I am. You were blinded by her.

'How do I know that you won't bash me up, like you did Tommy? You don't like me, so how do I know?'

'You don't, but why would I? And for your information, I

have never, and *would* never, hit a girl. That's wrong. Are you coming or what?'

Walking off I heard her stupid little greedy steps hurrying after me. Transparent in her haste to get a promised gift. What a bitch. Without waiting I sped off towards the lane and *then* waited. Offered her my arm like a gentleman and said, 'Don't worry, no lovey-laney stuff with me.'

Snorting with unconcealed derision, she nevertheless slipped her hand through my elbow and off we went. We passed and ignored some saddo old people 'in a clinch' as shitface Dad would say and hurried on – me ignoring them.

Cindy turned her head and stared at them, fascinated. 'God, gross or what. Old people. They look *way* too old to be doing *that*. Get a fucking room.' She giggled but it wasn't a fun sound, more dripping with contempt and arrogance.

Coming out on the other side of Grope Lane, its effect on both of us, *nil*, we crossed arm in arm onto the common. She tightened her grip as I steered her towards the three-treed copse. It was virtually deserted, the weather making it an unlikely time and place for a night-time stroll, whatever your sexual desires were. Cold killed sex, apparently.

'Let's walk round. Get to the tree that way,' she said.

'No, we'll walk through. More exciting. Come on.' I tugged at her hand.

'That's how me and Jack always did it. Through the brambles and shit. I don't want to go that way now. Let's go round.'

'No, we'll do it Jack's way. Yours and Jack's way. He would have wanted that.'

Shrugging her shoulders with irritation, we ducked our way under wet leaves and branches, and forced ourselves deeper through the heavy undergrowth; now all spiky sharp branches, naked without leaves. But still like a jungle – a lot of nature was at work; all big scratchy bushes and low-slung thick boughs for us to fight through. Carrying on, pushing back the heavy and dense shrubbery, we eventually came to the three trees, spaced out – the tallest easy enough to spot. One side of it, facing out onto the common. Standing free.

The trees formed a sort of large canopy, the ground mostly dry beneath so many branches. It didn't look like anyone had been here for ages.

Around the bottom of the tree, a few small rocks lay, as if they'd been discarded in a mini-boulder-throwing frenzy.

Standing at the base of the tree, the side facing into the copse, Cindy put her bag down and stroked the bark and said, 'Look. This is it. Here's our initials. See? Jack carved them using my little pink penknife.'

Using memory and a familiarity I didn't like, I saw her trace out with her fingers something marked on the tree. But it was too dark to *see*. Surprised, unbelieving, I bent in, using my mobile torch. "Jack 4 Cindy 4 ever" and a crude carving of a heart. I smiled.

So you *were* just like the other kids by the other tree in the forest, with your babyish loved-up etched inscriptions on a tree. Not so grown up after all. I thought that made you a teeny bit of a liar.

Turned out you were a bit of a two-faced lying twat, as it happened. No different from the rest of us. And soppy. Especially soppy because of who the recipient of your undying and forever love was directed at. Silly you.

I was surprised that Cindy hadn't said anything about her and Tommy yet, hadn't apologised, hadn't come up with any bullshit excuse, but that was Cindy for you. She couldn't see nor think beyond the gold.

She stood, trying not to look too obviously desperate for something valuable to be placed into her grasping little hands, underneath your tree. Well, yours and Cindy-doll's tree. Seeing such brazen desire and desperation for a golden trinket, my estimation of her dropped even lower.

Again she held out her hand, palm upwards. 'Well, where is it, Butty? Hand it over.'

'Really? Just like that? I might be the messenger boy, but show a little class, Cindy. First of all, I want to know about you and Tommy. How come you're with him now? Did Jack mean nothing to you?'

Putting her hand down by her side and trying to look all chastened and ashamed, she bowed her head, as if in humiliation.

But I wasn't you, Jack. Not so easily taken in by her obvious theatrics.

'Course I loved Jack. You know I did. But he's gone now, Butty. I'm really sorry, I really am. But I can't grieve forever, can I? I've got my own life to think of. I have to move on. Live my own life. I'm young. So, come on, don't be silly. I'll always remember Jack. I'll remember him forever and ever. Cross my heart and hope to die.'

I stared at her. What a speech. She was even more stupid and unpleasant than I'd imagined. 'But it hasn't even been two *weeks* since he died. What the fuck are you talking about, Cindy? *Move on with your life*? What does that even mean? You going to marry Tommy and settle down and have children? God, you're only fifteen. "I have my own life to think of",' I mimicked, in a singsong girly voice. 'What about Jack's life? What about *his* life?'

'Don't shout, Butty, you're frightening me. I don't like shouting.'

'I don't like cheap tarts and you took advantage of my brother. You're only here for the necklace. You make me want to vomit.'

'Look, you've got this all wrong. Tommy's nothing. He's nothing like Jack. Not in the same league. Tommy means nothing. He's a bully. You know that. I'm glad you beat him up. I'm not with him anymore, anyway. So Jack is still the *only one* in my heart. Honest, Butty. Don't be angry. I'll never find someone like Jack again. I loved him and I know how lucky I was to have him, even for such a short time.'

She squeezed her eyes tight shut and managed to push out a tear. One fucking tear which I watched fall down her cheek, showing wet and glistening against her skin by the light of my mobile as it shone in her face.

Cindy seemed impressed with herself, with her show of grief, with her *one* bloody fake tear. 'Come on, Butty. Just give it to me. Jack wanted me to have it, so it is actually rightfully mine anyway. You're just the delivery boy.' She waggled her fingers in a gimme, gimme way. 'Hand it over, Buttbot. And I promise, I *swear*…' She put her right hand to her heart and held her left hand aloft. 'I swear I shall be forever grateful for everything Jack gave me. I'll never forget him. Never. Never, ever, ever.'

Did she really think she'd convinced me with the tear, with her words, with her fucking lies? She smiled at me, keeping her face set in a well-practised sad and insincere wobble of tragedy.

I took the box out of my pocket and opened it. Took out the chain and held it, dangling it from my fingers. If there'd been any lights other than my mobile, I'm pretty sure it would have glittered garishly for Cindy. It would have lit up her whole little world. 'Here it is, Cindy, in all its finery. Just for you. From Jack. With love. With *real* love.'

When I didn't move towards her she got tired with waiting and made a lunge for it. I laughed and whipped my hand backwards, keeping it out of reach.

She snatched at it again. 'Fuck's sake, Butty, give it to me.'

I laughed properly for the first time since you'd died, and danced away from her, around the tree. First one way, and then the other. She, like some mad person, so desperate for a cheap

necklace, dropped her Outside façade and became the real
Cindy. Nasty, greedy, selfish. Your girlfriend, Jack. This is who
you picked. You could have done better. Could have done
shed-loads better. You'd picked a real wrong 'un. Dad's words.
Cheapshit bitch in my words.

Cindy wouldn't give up. Chased me around and around
that tree. Until I suddenly stopped, and she bumped into me.
'Give it to me, Butty. It's mine. Give me my necklace.'

She made a grab for it, touching it, nearly ripping it from
my hand, but I held on tight.

'Fuck off, bitch. I'm not giving it to you. You don't deserve
it. You deserve nothing. You didn't deserve Jack. So you
definitely don't deserve his necklace that he bought for you.
You wouldn't appreciate the love that goes with it. You don't
know what love is. Jack did.'

Our circles around the tree became larger. So we could see
each other better. She was standing on the outer side of the
tree when I pushed her away. She came back at me. I pushed
her again. Harder. Much harder.

Time went all weird then. It all happened very quickly but
in slow motion all at the same time. I saw her fall backwards,
her arms flung aside in the air, in a second, in an hour, in a
forever fall that was over before it began. It conjured up images
of you, pinwheeling in the air, before you had collided with the
car. It was so similar to a mini, but heavily edited, version of
the horror that I'd never forget.

Cindy hit the ground, and her head bounced off a large
rock on the slope. I heard the impact of skull on stone. It was a
very loud crack.

I stopped moving. Our dance of the necklace over. She
stopped moving. Her dance of life over. Quickly, so quickly, a
black puddle spread out from the back of her head. The blood
looked black in the night. Bending down, closer to her, I turned
on my little torch and directed it at her. All it highlighted was

red. Red blood. Blood everywhere around her head. Blood, blood, blood. It's all I could see.

And the fact that she wasn't moving.

At all.

She'd never move again.

Cindy, the Karate Kid, was dead.

FIFTEEN

Butty

It was an accident. Definitely an accident. I hadn't meant it. I really hadn't. I wanted her to wake up. To say everything was all right. No hard feelings. I wanted her to be alive again. I didn't want her dead. It was an accident. I swear to God it was an accident.

But *was* it an accident? Or had I meant it? Had I wished it and made it happen. Fuck, fuck, fuck. I hopped from foot to foot like a dog on hot tarmac, not knowing what to do. Forced myself to breathe. *Calm down, it's all right. I didn't kill her. It was an accident. This is not murder.*

I *had* pushed her, though. If not for the push, she wouldn't have hit her head. That meant it *was* my fault. Even if I didn't mean it. And I *hadn't* meant it.

Suppose someone had seen us come here? I didn't think they had, but just suppose. And what about me beating up Tommy? That wouldn't look good. It would make it seem like I was on some kind of jealous vendetta. Harm those that have harmed my dead brother. Would they think that? They might.

Supposing Cindy had texted Tommy about the fight? She *definitely* would have done that. That would again implicate me.

My involvement with him, and more importantly, with *her*. Even if Cindy had deleted the texts, I knew the police could always find them on her mobile. They never really went away.

They'd think I was on a murderous rampage, angry that my dead brother's girlfriend had already forgotten him. I'd shown I was violent by beating up Tommy. I would be presumed to be traumatised and a little touched with grief and loss.

They'd think I'd murdered Cindy. On purpose.

What to do? What to do?

Mum would know what to do, but she wasn't here. And how could I involve her in this? *Sorry your oldest son is dead, even sorrier your youngest son is now a murderer.* I couldn't do that to her.

I realised I was standing there doing nothing.

But then I had an idea.

A good idea.

An idea that would get me off the hook and save everyone.

Save everyone except Cindy. She was past saving.

I'd make it look like a pervy murder, a sex crime, a killing by a monster. Good, good. That was a good idea. Quickly, panting now with anxiety and nerves and full-on fear, I bent down and grabbed Cindy's pink wellington boots by the heel. Started pulling, tugging her deadweight. Trying to get her back in*side* the copse. Out of view. We were on full display – the wrong side of the tree. What if a car drove past and I was caught, highlighted by headlights, silhouetted, dragging the feet of a dead girl? I heard myself whimpering, little panicky sobs escaping. Why was she so heavy?

I couldn't get her completely back, hidden behind the trees, so had to work quickly. Thankfully, the night was clear but dark. As long as a car from the road below didn't decide to come along, I'd be fine.

It seemed like hours had passed but I didn't stop to check. I had another quick think. What would a perv do? Cut. He'd cut her. And he'd remove some of her clothes. Pull down her trousers at the least. And probably her knickers as well. Her top too. Maybe her bra.

But he'd definitely cut her.

Brainwave.

With my back to the road, I went and picked up her bag left by the tree and popped it open. Praying it was there. And it was. You must have been looking down on me, Jack. Helping me. Though I wasn't sure how you'd feel at the turn of events. But I reckoned you'd understand. You'd see that it was truly a very unfortunate accident.

Cindy's little pink penknife nestled next to a mess of nameless girly stuff deep inside her bag. Grabbing it, I returned to the body. Gingerly, I started unzipping her jeans. I didn't look, I swear. Then I *had* to look to see what I was doing in the gloom. I pulled them down to her knees and then, and I really did not look this time, I tugged at her knickers until I could feel they were off and halfway down her legs.

Pulling her various layers of upper clothing up, I finally exposed her bra. I had to get one breast out – to make it real. But I didn't touch it. Not in *that* way.

Now for the cutting. Opening the stupid pink penknife, I examined by feel, the length of the blade. About two inches but it was quite sharp. Sharp enough, anyway. I made a few half-hearted superficial cuts on her stomach. Felt bad. I pulled off her coat and rolled up her sleeves. Cut again. A bit deeper now. Less personal on the arms compared to her stomach. That had felt way too intimate.

To make it look really good I slashed at her face. Once.

Twice.

A third time.

Easier. Weirdly, *much* easier cutting her face. Savaging her oh so pretty Outside veneer face. Revealing the rotten core beneath the flesh. Literally, showing the Inside. Beautiful on the Outside, filled with maggots on the Inside.

There, that looked maniac enough. Serial killer enough. It had felt... I wasn't sure how it had felt – the cutting. Refused to admit that there had been just a teeny bit of... enjoyment? Was that it? Satisfaction? I tried not to linger on emotions best left hidden and unexplored.

Standing back, I examined by torchlight my desecration of her body. I admitted to myself that that's what it was. But now, no one would suspect me. I was a child after all. Not a murderer of young girls. *I* didn't suspect me. It hadn't *been* me. Just an Outside version of me, fighting to stay one step ahead.

I rolled her along the flat ground and stopped as the slope beckoned. Should I shove her down and *hope* she'd land in the right place. I knew she wouldn't, *couldn't* land in the road as the ground flattened out like a table, before it sloped again sharply to the tarmac. There were bushes to the left and a lay-by at the bottom of the second hill. I could negotiate the final resting place after the first roll.

I pushed. Pointing her more to the left. Hoping the speed she gathered wouldn't make her fly off the levelled six-foot flat ledge, before the second hill, and go crashing into the road.

Holding my breath, I watched her turn over and over again like a thrown-away sausage roll, gaining speed as she went. But her course remained true. She kept on track, thank God.

I'd hide her in the bushes in the lay-by. Didn't want her found too quickly. I had to get home and establish an alibi. Although that bit was easy. I'd just lost my brother in an horrific hit-and-run, I was grieving, I was at home at the time of the murder, and neither of my parents were in a fit state to either confirm nor deny that. I was positive on that score. And Mum would lie for me anyway; swear blind I was physically with her. Even if she was too stoned to notice.

Not so sure about Dad. I rather thought that particular

bridge might have been burnt forever. Irretrievable. Like you, Jack. Like you.

Before I left, I remembered Cindy's pink mobile in her bag. I ran back for it, popped it in my pocket along with her penknife, and carried the bag and her furry coat down the hill as well.

The last part was easier. Cindy had stopped at the edge of the plateau and teetered scarily near the edge. Disaster averted but only by inches. It didn't require much strength to jump down onto the lay-by and pull her body from beneath. Pushing it quickly into the bushes. Throwing her bag in after her and then tossing her furry coat over her, I checked that she was properly concealed. Made invisible to the lights of oncoming traffic. Satisfied that Cindy's body couldn't be seen unless you were actually looking for it, I climbed back onto the common and ran.

And wondered where I'd go. I realised I didn't want to go home. But worse, what kept nagging at me, I wasn't sure I'd left the 'murder scene' properly. Suppose I'd left traces of myself? Evidence that I'd been there? With Cindy? I didn't want to get caught. I needed help. Adult help.

An unpleasant and tricky thought occurred. Leave the knife or take the knife?

Take it or leave it? *I* didn't know. Please help. Someone. You, Jack. Take or leave? Which is right? Would a crazed killer leave the murder weapon, or would he take it?

I took it. Took a risk. Took the plunge.

Decision made, I set off, through the common, finally reached the forest, keeping out of range of people, and kept on running. No one saw me, I was sure.

I hoped Penny was in.

She'd help me.

She had to.

SIXTEEN

Penny

'Dad wanted to go to bed early tonight, Mum, so that's where he is. All tucked up.'

'But's it's only half-past seven. Is he all right?'

'He's fine, don't worry. Just a bit wheezy. Had a coughing fit, but he's better now with the oxygen. I'll go and check him again in thirty minutes or so. He'll probably be asleep.'

'No, I'll do it. And thank you, thank you so much for looking after him for me. I'm a useless coward of a woman. I just can't bear to see him like that. All that gasping for air. It breaks my bloody heart. I couldn't do it without you, Penny, I really couldn't. So, thank you.'

Her mother sighed, a deep and trembling outpouring of breath; long and sad. Penny hated seeing her like this. Unable to cope with a dying husband of thirty-two years. Chronic obstructive pulmonary disease. A mouthful of a condition. A lung condition that killed. The abbreviated term 'COPD' was catchier, rolled off the tongue more smoothly. Sounded somehow less crippling. Less lethal. More a jumble of random letters that spelled out some meaningless acronym. Except of course it wasn't meaningless. It was the fatal disease of smokers.

Her mother passed her a cigarette and they both lit up, both women choosing to ignore the irony of their habit. To make life just that little bit worse, her mother sat with, Penny knew, a now emotionally inaccessible daughter.

Penny couldn't help it. How could she tell either parent about the rape? Bad enough that it had happened to her, but she certainly couldn't violate them with the fall-out of that terrible event. She *couldn't*. Fuck the physical rape; it was the mental rape that had stayed with her. If she told them, she didn't want that particular movie playing on repeat for eternity in her parents' head.

She looked at her mother fondly. Sarah Crisp was like one half of a condiment set: the shape of a pepper grinder – finished off with her hair tied in a top knot in the middle of her head. Her hips made her pear shaped and her mid-section attractively grabbable, according to Penny's father.

The dog at their feet, Baggage, the chocolate brown Labrador, whimpered under the table and rested his snout on his paws. Settled in. Penny leant down and fondled his ears with one hand and was then surprised when her mother took her other hand in hers over the kitchen table.

'Are the pigs done, Penny?'

'Course. They are all in their blankets, warm and toasty.'

'Good.' Her mother nodded. With the handholding, Penny had expected a statement of some gravitas from her mother, instead of chitchat about the state of the pigs. She realised then that her mother was working up to something. Saw her huff and say, 'You are coming for Christmas, aren't you? I know it can't be that exciting with your knackered old parents and Baggy here, but you will come, won't you? It's never the same when you're not here at Christmas.'

'I'll come. Count me in. Anything for free grub. You know me, Mum.'

Her mother rolled her eyes but was clearly relieved that Penny would be coming and staying over the festive period. Her face sobered unexpectedly, and she looked her daughter in the eye. 'Why won't you tell me what's wrong, Penny? It's been two years now, and I've never pushed you on it. I'm pushing now. Tell me what happened to you.'

It's true, Penny thought sadly. She'd always managed to swerve the concern of her parents – I'm absolutely fine, thanks, please stop bothering me; yes, I know I've cut my hair, I love it. Okay, I'm lying, I hate my hair. But I don't want the attention it brings. And yes, I do know it looks like crap. But I am growing it – see, it's almost a bob now. Yes, I do like these black loose clothes, Mum, I promise you. Honest. Leave me alone. Nothing's happened. I swear. I'm fine. The end.

Penny was surprised that she'd avoided this conversation for so long and quickly thought of ways to divert the inevitable barrage of questions. She felt the squeeze of her mother's fingers as they tightened their grip on hers. 'If you're trying to protect me, don't even think it. I'm your mother. I know something awful happened to you and I want to know what it is. Where's my loving, kind, amusing daughter? Where's she gone? I'm left with a horrid version of her: all dark and hostile and angry. Tell me what happened.'

'Really, Mum, it's nothing. Maybe I had a nervous breakdown.'

'Bollocks, Penny, that's a complete fabrication. Don't try and pull a fast one on me. I'm your mother. I know you. And I know when you're lying. And anyway, why on earth would you have had a nervous breakdown. They're not something that suddenly pounce on you, completely unexpected, for no reason at all. You're my daughter: you're not a nervous type. You've never been a nervous type. You're still not. But you're frightened. Of something. You're not quietly and nervously breaking down: you're too busy champing at the bit with hate – so much hate. What are you doing with it all?'

You don't want to know, Mum. Stop asking. 'Wow, Mum. What a speech. That's been building up.'

'Of *course* it's been building up. I love you and I know you're suffering with something. How bad can it be that you can't tell me? Whatever has happened, either to you, or possibly *by* you, I'll still love you and help you through it. You know that. Come on, tell me.'

'Mum…' Penny unentwined their fingers. 'Nothing happened. Just personal shit. You know the kind of thing. Men… you know. It's always a bloody man, right?'

'Again, bollocks, Penny. Don't take me for a fool. And anyway, I'm not aware that you were having an affair with any particular man two years ago. I don't believe you. You're bullshitting me.'

Her mother's love of swearing had been passed down to her daughter. Penny knew how to swear like a scaffolder. Could make a labourer blush without even trying. 'How do you know I wasn't having a secret tryst, though?' Penny tried a smile but knew her mother could see past the pained facsimile of her vaguely uptilted lips. She was an open book. *Go ahead, Mum. Read me. It's written all over me. Just turn the page and see the horror that I went through. But I'm not a book to be read at bedtime, as you snuggle cosily beneath your duvet. I'm a book for reading with all the lights on.*

Penny got up. 'Stop it, Mum. I'll never tell you because nothing happened, okay? Please drop it.'

Her pepper grinder mother sighed and said, 'You are such a big fat liar, Penny Crisp. If you won't tell me, I can't drag it out of you. But when, and I do mean *when* you see fit to reveal all, I'm here.'

Penny kissed her on the cheek and whispered a thank you.

Then said it louder. Didn't like whispering when it wasn't a requirement.

'But I do miss your smile, Penny. Your humongously huge smile that just killed everyone. That smile. Where's that gone? I miss it.'

'I'm resting it, Mum. Saving it for something special.'

'I'm special.'

'I know. You are. Very.' She smiled but both of them knew it wasn't a real one. Didn't even touch the sides.

'I'll change the subject then,' her mother said. 'Drink? Gin and tonic do you?'

'Great idea. Ice and a slice and make it a whopper of a double. I'll just go and check on Dad and be back down in a min.'

'When don't I pour whopper drinks?'

'Never.'

'Exactly. And I said I'd see to James. After a drink. Just a sip. Dutch courage and all that. Then I'll take up my glass, and one for him, and have a gin and tonic *with* my husband.'

Penny watched her mother as she waddled and rolled around, getting bottles and ice and glasses. So desperate for her happy, normal daughter back. Penny was convinced that if she *did* tell her mother about the Aniseed Man, if she *did* tell her what she herself had done, maybe then her mother would rather have wished she didn't know.

She re-joined Penny at the kitchen table and they both sipped their drinks.

Her mother interrupted the familiar easy silence, asking, 'Was that the Hawthorne child I saw here yesterday? You were both looking very earnest, in deep conversation. How is he? Poor little boy.'

Penny stupidly felt guilty that she'd been caught out doing something wrong. As if being with Butty was an arrestable offence, or their odd little relationship certainly not one to be encouraged. She shrugged carelessly. 'He's all right. Considering. He's being very brave, actually. I invited him here because he looked like he needed a friend. He's heartbroken. Obviously.'

'Well, he would be. A dreadful thing. And his poor mother. Such a nice woman. Don't know the husband so well, but a nice family. What a tragedy.'

'I liked him. But he was so desperately sad, Mum. I tried to help but what could I do? He's lost. Lost his brother *and* himself.'

'And *there's* my daughter. Right there. There she is. Putting in an appearance for old time's sake. My kind and sweet daughter who's only briefly visiting at the moment, folks. Blink and you'll miss her. But she's here for more than one night only, I hope. Here because she wants to help Charlie. Because that is her nature: kind, generous and sweet. Hopefully she will return on a more permanent basis when it suits.'

'Don't, Mum. It was awful, seeing him all bereft and alone. I had to help him'

'Of course you did. My deepest sympathies are with the boy, they really are. Unimaginably awful. Little Charlie. And I'm so happy you were there for him. My lovely, *kind* daughter. Poor, *poor* boy.'

'It's Butty. He doesn't like his name, Charlie. Prefers to be called Butty.'

The doorbell rang.

'Are you expecting anyone, Mum?'

'Not at this time, no. Are you?'

'Who would I be expecting? I'll get it.'

Opening the door, she saw Butty.

The porchlight illuminated him. His youth, his face, his obvious cold. And something else. 'What's that on your coat?'

He glanced down at himself. 'Blood. It must be blood,' he said and then burst into tears.

SEVENTEEN

Penny

'Take it off. Your coat. Whose blood is it? Yours?'

Please let it be Butty's blood.

He shook his head. He fumbled with the zip using awkwardly stiff fingers. He was so cold his hands weren't working properly. Penny wanted to rip the coat from him. To rid him of the bloodied coat.

She guessed it was bad: her gut told her so. Judging by his expression, she was frightened to ask exactly whose blood it was, if not his. She watched him wrestle out of his coat and let it drop to the ground behind him. He was seemingly past caring.

'Your gloves. Is that blood on them too?'

Butty held his fingers out in front of him. Nodded as if he'd expected nothing else. Slowly, he peeled them off and let them fall on his coat. A heap of blood-stained winter wear.

'For Christ's sake, Butty. What have you done?'

'It was an accident. I didn't mean it.'

Glancing back over her shoulder, Penny made sure her mother wasn't coming to see who their uninvited guest was. Staring at Butty, she shouted, 'It's okay, Mum. Go and see to

94

Dad. It's just Butty. We're going to the Trumpet Room for a chat. Okay?'

Her mother appeared suddenly behind Penny, surprisingly light-footed for such a curvaceously hefty woman. Butty jumped.

'Hello, Butty,' her mother said. 'Why not come into the house. It's much warmer. You look frozen. You poor boy. Come.' She advanced and scooped him up in a cuddle, her arms encircling him, trapping him. Penny could only watch with horror as Butty's white face popped up like a disembodied head over her mother's shoulder. 'I'm so, so sorry about Jack. What a dreadful thing to happen. If you need anything, you just come straight here, you promise?'

Released, the boy nodded mutely.

'I'm going to see James,' she said to Penny and then turned to Butty. 'My husband, James. Now I'll leave you with my daughter. She'll look after you. And remember, anything we can do, we're here to help. My love to your family. And a big special kiss to you.' She kissed her fingers and touched his forehead, like a religious smote of the hand. 'And why on earth have you taken off your coat? You've just dropped it. There, behind you. What are you thinking, you silly child? You'll freeze to death. Get inside, get warm. Penny will look after you. Don't you worry.'

Glaring at Butty, Penny thought, *I hope for everyone's sake you haven't just transferred blood onto my mother.*

'It's all right, Mum. I've got this. Go to Dad. We're going to the Trumpet Room. See you later. Come on, Butty. Follow me.'

Restraining herself from dragging him by his ear, she hoped, she prayed that he hadn't done something *really* bad.

Worried, frightened, Penny went through the arduous but necessary complex unlocking routine at the Trumpet Room door. Once in, she pushed Butty into the centre of the room and said, 'What have you done? And do *not* sit down. Do *not* touch. *Anything*. Good, you brought your coat. Got your gloves? Yes, good. Put them in a pile on the floor. Is there blood anywhere else? On you, I mean. Look, Butty, look. Jesus wept, *look*. Check yourself. All over.'

He didn't move. 'I've killed someone, Penny. I killed Cindy. But it was an accident.'

'Who's Cindy?'

'Jack's girlfriend. She was Jack's girlfriend, but she isn't anymore.'

Penny rubbed her temples with both of her hands, massaging away the tension. 'Tell me exactly what happened and don't miss anything out. Nothing at all.'

He spoke clearly and well, keeping it brief but in chronological order, briefly banging on about what seemed to Penny to be inconsequential teenage disputes. Eventually he got to the really *bad* part of his story. She went and got some latex gloves from the box in the en-suite bathroom. The more she heard, the more scared and concerned she became.

'And then I thought, nobody will believe me, that it was an accident, so I made it look like a murder. You know, like a sexual attack. By a nutter.' He stopped talking, waiting for her to nod her understanding.

'If you're waiting for a round of applause, think again. What the bloody hell did you *do*? I mean *exactly*. And keep absolutely still. Don't move off that spot. I do not want you tramping blood through this room. When you've finished telling me everything you did, you will have a bath and I'll lend you a pair of my old jogging bottoms and some boots. Take your trainers off. Now.'

'Okay.' He smiled, apparently hopeful that she'd relent and smile back. It wasn't going to happen. Blowing his cheeks out, he clasped his hands in front of him and said, 'I undressed her a bit, and then I cut her a bit. Just her arms and stomach.'

Something about his tone of voice, or lack of it, made Penny study him closely. *I cut her a bit. Just her arms and stomach.*

'I don't think you're telling me the whole truth here. You're lying.'

He carried on as if she hadn't spoken. 'I rolled her down the hill from the tree and hid her in some bushes, and covered her with her coat, in the lay-by. I left her bag but took her mobile in case she'd texted Tommy about the fight, like I told you just now, and I've got her pink penknife that I cut her with. Here. In my pocket. I wasn't sure if a murderer would leave it there or take it with him. I took it with me.' He patted his pocket as proof of possession.

Penny stared at him. 'You brought it here. And yourself? Why did *you* come here? What are you expecting me to do?'

His face did an almost comic double-take, as if he couldn't quite understand her reluctance to get involved.

Penny said, slowly, trying to keep calm, 'What do you want me to *do*? You should have left her after she hit her head. It sounds like it *was* an accident, so why bugger about with her body?'

'But I pushed her. If I hadn't pushed her, she wouldn't have fallen over and hit her head and died, would she?'

'There was no intent. You didn't push her in order to kill her. She fell. Accident. Now, though, now that you've messed up the scene, messed *her* up, *now* it looks like murder and that *is* your fault.'

'Yeah, but she was already dead and now nobody will suspect me, will they? I'm only a boy. It couldn't have been me, could it? Not a sex murder.'

'But it *was* you. You did that to her. You complicated the whole thing. Why? What made you do such a thing?'

'Because I panicked, all right? What do you ex*pect* from me? How would *I* know what to do with a dead body? Will you help me?'

'Help you what?'

He lifted his shoulders in a quick and desperate don't-know gesture. 'Get rid of the body?'

Why does he think I can get rid of the body?

Keith's body was her own business. She'd got rid of him, and yet was always surrounded by him. It had been perfect. But this… this she couldn't be involved with. It was inviting trouble to her own doorstep, and she didn't want *any* police interest focused in her direction.

Penny laughed. 'Why would I want to help you get rid of a dead body? What makes you think I'd even *know* how to dispose of a body. Even if I did help you, how would that make your situation any better?'

'Because then Cindy would just be missing. A missing girl. There're millions of girls every day who disappear, run away, die. And it would have nothing to do with me then.'

'That's quite a cold-hearted way of looking at things, Butty. And Cindy isn't missing, is she? You, and now I, both know where she is. What about her parents? How do you think they'll feel if they never know what happened to their daughter? Constantly waiting for the phone to ring. Frightened to leave the house in case she comes back. Forever searching for her. What about her parents, Butty?'

'Yeah, well, how will they feel if they find her messed-up body in the lay-by and think a man's been interfering with her before killing her? Which is worse? Missing daughter but her parents would always have hope, or dead daughter and they'll be forever broken. I know which one I'd pick.' He paused, clearly going over what he'd just said in his head. Nodding, he was more emphatic now. 'I'd definitely pick hope. Who wouldn't?'

What a strange and complicated way of thinking, Penny thought. *A harsh and cruel way of thinking.* 'Imagine it was your brother, Butty. Imagine what you've just described and instead of it happening to Cindy, imagine it was Jack. Would you still feel the same?'

His answer came swift and strong. 'Of course I'd wish him missing. *Of course* I would. Better than dead. Dead is forever. Missing might not be.'

'But we both know that Cindy *isn't* missing, don't we?'

'Yes,' he shouted back at her. 'So why not make it better and get rid of the body and make it less painful, less traumatic for her fucking family? What is wrong with that idea? Then at least they'll have hope. I don't have hope. But they will.'

'It's not right, though. I can't help you.'

He stamped his foot and balled his fists. 'I don't know how to get rid of her body. I shouldn't have cut her, okay? I panicked. I'm sorry. It's all my fault. Is that what you want to hear? I'm sorry. I really am.'

'I don't know how to get rid of a body,' she lied. 'And why would I get involved in your shit, that *you* created? That you made so much worse than it need be? Why should I help you?'

'Who else will?'

'You're asking me to get rid of a young girl's *dead body*. Do you realise how serious that is?'

'I'm not stupid. I know it's a lot to ask. Too much. But I don't know what else to do. And I think you could do it. If you wanted. I think you could do anything if you really wanted to, if you really put your mind to it. And you'd be saving me. Isn't that what you wanted to do when you asked me back here for hot chocolate. You wanted to help me get over Jack's death. You wanted me to accept it. Get on with my life. I can't get on with my life now, because I sort of killed Cindy. By mistake. Then made it worse. I know all that. But I know you could help me. Make it better.' He sank to the floor, simply bending his knees and ended up, sitting cross-legged, looking up at her.

'What's happened to you, Butty? What's changed your

grief into such total hatred and callousness? You defaced a *body*, for Christ's sake. That's not normal behaviour.'

'What *is* normal? Are you normal, Penny? I don't think you are. You've got some weird vibe going on.'

Penny was shocked at his ability to read her, to diagnose her as a 'bit off'. He was right. She kept silent. He didn't.

'Now I have a dead girl to get rid of, and I've still got a dead brother which I can't, and will never, accept. Gone.' He blinked at her quickly and changed position, squatting on his haunches. Dropping his head to the floor he then raised his eyes to hers. 'Please help me, Penny. I don't know who else to ask. Please.'

'Where's the necklace?' she said, knowing that with the question asked out loud, there came with it an informal acknowledgement, a kind of unspoken agreement between them, that she'd help him. How could she leave him to extricate himself from a situation from which he couldn't escape? It was too cruel. She couldn't leave him. On his own. Alone and terrified.

And she literally *could* help. She had the means.

Penny watched with a sudden and growing sense of dread, as Butty's eyeballs went as round as marbles. He jumped up, tearing his clothes off, not caring that she was there, and pulled out every pocket. Feverishly examining them. Again and again and again. Turning each and every one inside out. He started crying and sniffing and wiped his nose with his arm as he stood there wearing only socks and a baggy pair of red pants.

'I must have left it. I left the necklace there. With Cindy. What am I going to do? The necklace is with the dead body.'

He's left the necklace in the copse. How much worse can this get?

Thinking quickly, she said, 'Did Jack tell anyone else he was giving Cindy the necklace?'

'If he did, how would I know?'

'And tonight, she grabbed it from you, right? Trying to get it, she touched it, with her hands?'

He nodded.

Shit. Penny didn't know a lot about forensics, but she knew that it was possible that Cindy's DNA might be on the bloody necklace. Butty's DNA might be on the bloody necklace. Skin cells from her fingers, hair from her furry coat. Skin and hair from *him.* Penny had to find it. To keep Butty out of it.

'Where did Jack buy it? Did he pay for it with cash?'

'What's that got to do with anything?' Butty was nearly crying with frustration.

'I'm just trying to work out if the necklace is that important. If it ties you to Jack and if you're the only one who knew about it, it ties you to Cindy. If I can't find it and the police find it instead, you might be implicated. Understand?'

He nodded miserably and said, 'You need to find it then. Please find it.'

She and Butty had only known each other for days, but her initial realisation that their relationship might end in an explosion, had been fulfilled much quicker than she would have guessed.

And the devastation it had caused was so much worse than she'd ever anticipated.

EIGHTEEN

Penny

I *cannot believe I am doing this.*
Penny drove one of her father's old beaten-up jeeps down country lanes, turning off the headlights when she felt it necessary. She'd smeared the numberplate with mud, making it illegal, and, knowing that beaten-up, dented vehicles like her father's in this part of the countryside were commonplace, she wasn't unduly worried that she'd be recognised or picked up and identified by any CCTV. Such as it was.

Her father had used the jeep to tend the garden and to occasionally fell a tree when he was feeling particularly boisterous. Now, he liked to go for drives, when well enough, and sometimes get out and sit in his wheelchair and admire the countryside. Consequently, Penny had a wheelchair ramp which could be attached to the rear of the vehicle and ran from the base of the jeep to the ground.

Good for an improvised body ramp, she thought sourly.

Penny kept to the backroads. Gritting her teeth, seriously pissed off with Butty for putting her in this outrageous position, she eventually neared the lay-by. Next to her, Baggage sat on the passenger seat, nose forward, ears pricked.

Her heart bounced like a ball in her chest, beat that little bit faster, her gardening-gloved hands tightened on the steering wheel, and she shivered: because of the cold or because of fear, she didn't know. It didn't even matter, she decided, as she pulled the jeep off the road.

Making sure there were no fellow motorists out, nor serial killers on a similar mission, she manoeuvred the truck so that its zipped cover at the rear was angled towards the undergrowth. She hoped that any cars that might pass by would carry on passing by, not picking her up in their headlights, but only seeing the jeep side-on if they did.

If anyone approached her, she had Baggage to point to: just out walking the dog on the common, no, no, I'm fine, thanks. Yes, dreadful weather, isn't it. Yes, okay and thanks, bye.

Presuming that Cindy's body would be easily found – a difficult thing to miss in a relatively small space, however overgrown – Penny guessed that this would take ten minutes, tops.

Panic threatened. Just because she'd killed and, yes, disposed of Keith's dead body, did not mean this was an easy task. This was *entirely* different. With Keith's demise, she'd had the moral high ground. Here, she had nothing. Nothing heroic, noble nor fair: just the getting rid of a girl's corpse.

Keep it neutral. Keep it impersonal. Keep it cold.

She couldn't engage on any real emotional level with what she was doing. It was too awful. Already, guilt made her physical movement awkward, as if it were stopping her natural ability to function. It risked paralysing her. Sitting for a second, she dragged up a breath from the bottom of her lungs and opened the jeep's door. Penny soothed Baggage who wanted to follow. 'Later, I promise,' she said. 'We'll have a walk later, Baggy. Scout's honour.'

Moving quickly now, uninvited panic set up house

determinedly in her gut, gate-crashing her innards. With fumbling hands she plunged her torch into the gorse and brambles and switched it on. Immediately, the light picked up a shapeless form; covered bizarrely with fur. Her coat. Cindy's fur coat. It was a horrible reminder that this *thing* in the bushes, wasn't a thing at all. It was in fact a young girl. A girl who would never breathe again.

Who Penny was dispensing with. Like rubbish.

Don't think like this. Stop it.

Penny wished it was Keith. At least there'd been a serious point in his dismissal from the world. This poor girl was simply a tragic victim of an horrific accidental death, which left Penny as the very deliberate but seriously reluctant body-dumper.

But it was for Butty, she reminded herself. She had to save Butty. No one else would.

Standing and looking and taking in the position of the girl, the thicket, the exit from the bushes, the entry point into the rear end of the jeep, Penny eventually dragged the large tarpaulin from the back of the vehicle. This all had to be done quickly. She wouldn't get a second chance if someone saw her.

All efficiency now, understanding the mechanics of the job in hand, Penny was swift and sure of movement, her actions seamless. Cindy had come to rest, lying on her front, thankfully face down, her head furthest away. Making a quick noose with rope, Penny secured it around the girl's ankles. Tightly.

Pulling the body slightly nearer with the heavy cord, she managed to tuck, coax, fold and wedge a tarpaulin beneath the girl. Once all was set, she'd only to fix the wheelchair ramp and lower it to the ground. Before leaving the house, Penny had already greased and primed it, making it slippery. Making sure that Cindy was properly weighted and centred on the tarpaulin, Penny jumped back into the vehicle and pulled on the ropes which she'd drawn through the large eyelets of the tarpaulin, prior to coming here. It was all about preparation.

And manoeuvring.

The body was still heavy. *Cindy* was still heavy, but after Penny tugged on the looped ropes, once she had the momentum on her side, the tarpaulin slid up the greased ramp and vanished into the back of the jeep. Penny let out a breath. Gasped out a breath.

Gasped out guilt.

Balling her fists with frustration she said out loud, 'And now for the bloody necklace.'

Going around to the passenger side she opened the door. 'Come on, Baggage. Walkies. Come on, boy.' Grabbing his leash, woman and dog climbed the two separate inclines with the tree at the top, beckoning them both. Hopefully, this was where the necklace would be. According to Butty, it couldn't be anywhere else. She wasn't convinced.

Torch held in now-steadier hands, she endeavoured to keep the light pointed down at the ground, loath to be picked up by passers-by, be they on foot or in car. Baggage barked with excitement, and she tried to 'shh' him. Unleashing him, confident that he would stay close, she reached the tree and went around it. To the covered side. Preferring to be hidden, at least partially, for the meantime. If luck was on her side, the necklace would glitter out its presence.

Ten minutes later, she found it. Held it dangling in her gloved hands: brightly yellow, it screamed out its innocence and its cheapness. She smiled, remembering how Butty described Jack's excitement and childish pride about his present for Cindy. Curling her fingers around it, she slipped it in her pocket. The goodness and naivete of the necklace made her feel less wicked. She'd found something that had been precious to Butty's brother and that was about all the good she could get out of this evening's events.

Turning, ready to return to the truck, calling out quietly to Baggage, she nearly tripped. Glancing down, shining the torch at her feet, she saw it. A round white stone. With blood on it. Still red and shining. It made her stop and consider the various possibilities. As Butty had seesawed with his should-I, shouldn't-I bring Cindy's penknife with me, so now, Penny thought, should-I, shouldn't-I take the offending stone away?

Deciding to go with 'take it, take it far away from this awful place,' she picked it up and slid down the two hills with Baggage in tow. The night was still quiet, the roads still empty, her heart still heavy. She appreciated how lucky she'd been not to be seen by anyone. Avoiding the impulse to screech away from the lay-by like a maniac, she instead pulled away sedately and drove home.

As she left the scene, it started raining hard. The drops trampolined from her windscreen, and she realised that once again, if you believed in a God, he was indeed smiling down on her. Rain meant lack of tyre-treads, no evidence of greased ramps, no boot prints, no paw prints. *Thank you, God-that-I-don't-believe-in. Thank you.*

It was only after Penny had transported Cindy's body across the lawn in her wheelbarrow and into the Trumpet Room, that she made the mistake of looking at the girl's face.

Butty had lied.

He'd cut her *cheeks*. He'd said he'd only cut her arms and stomach, but he'd lied.

He'd done so much more than that. He'd *ruined* Cindy's face. At least half a dozen slashes ribboned her cheeks. Penny's insides went cold. What had he done? Who was Butty? Who and what was he really?

She didn't want to know, but what she did know was that their friendship, or whatever it was, had to end. Penny thought that Butty really might be mad. Certainly unhinged. At worst, Butty could be *bad*. Very, very bad.

And she *still* had to dispose of poor little Cindy.

For a mad, bad, sad boy.

A dead child and a lunatic child.

She'd much preferred her own personal crusade: that of finding men and ending men.

To make herself feel better, feel clean, feel *herself*, she promised, right there and then, that she'd go man-whispering again.

As soon as she could.

NINETEEN

Butty

I'd run home in the dark, through the forest which surrounded both sides of our road. Wearing stupid clothes that Penny had insisted on: baggy tracksuit bottoms, wellington boots – too big – and an old jumper of hers. I was to return them all tomorrow and pick up my washed clean bloodied coat and stuff.

Stripping out of Penny's wardrobe, quiet as a mouse in my bedroom, I re-dressed as me.

Penny had saved me.

And for that I owed her.

Big time.

There was a knock on my door and without me calling out to 'come in,' Dad bowled in anyway. 'What're you doing in here, Jack? And why are you dressed up like your little brother? Look…' He crouched down, so that his face was close to mine. His breath still stank of whisky, but he wasn't obviously drunk anymore.

But he was still obviously mad.

He took my hands in his, squeezed them and sucked in his breath through his teeth, remarking on the icy temperature of my fingers. He tried rubbing my hands within his, blew his stinky breath on them to warm them, but I pulled away: uncomfortable and awkward and embarrassed.

'I know you dressing like Butty makes you feel better, Jack, and being here in his room, makes you feel closer to him, like he hasn't really gone. But he has gone. You need to accept that. Right now, you need to go back to your own bedroom, and start wearing your clothes again. You don't have to pretend anymore, okay, little man? I've got your back. Me and your mother, we'll look after you and we'll all get through this.'

I didn't think Mum would be up for Dad thinking I was Jack. *I* definitely wasn't up for it.

But I'd play along.

Because it was easier all round. It would keep Dad off my back, and hopefully he'd come out of his trance or whatever it was. His pretence, his wish, his big fat lie. That's what I was now, a lie-of-a-boy. Fake me. *Hello, everyone, my name is Butty/Jack. I answer to both and/or either, because I* am *both.*

More worryingly, I thought this game might make me neither boy. Neither me nor you. I'd ceased to be anyone specifically.

Except to Mum.

And to Penny.

At least they were normal. Well, Mum was. I'd have to mollycoddle Dad along, push him gently down the tracks and hopefully he wouldn't end up in the loony bin at the end of the line.

The Outside world, without you, had become definitely and suddenly smaller. It decreased and contracted until it swallowed me up whole. I'd mistakenly thought that having beaten up Tommy, I was king of the world, an emperor in my own realm. Now it didn't feel like that at all.

All the badness of the Outside world had come in. My

Inside existence and Outside life had merged. I'd been shrink-wrapped.

I was all upside-down and Inside-Out.

It was a lonely place to be.

My anger at Dad had weirdly gone and had been replaced with concern. I wasn't sure what he'd do if I insisted I was me. Going for what felt the safer option, I said, 'I'm just returning some stuff to Butty's room. I'll go and get dressed in my own clothes now. I only wanted to feel closer to him for a bit, you know, because I miss him.'

By playing Dad's game, by allowing him his fantasy, I realised I might as well have been self-harming. I was helping Dad delete me.

I'd always wanted to be you, Jack. Turns out, Dad had always wanted the same thing so I could hardly blame him.

But I didn't like the game.

It felt bad.

My whole life had gone horribly wrong, and I didn't know what to do.

Dad patted me on the head, ruffled my hair and said, 'Good boy, Jack. Off you go, then. Me and your mother have to discuss Butty's funeral now. Helen's up now, so you can join us if you like. We both want you included; you do know that don't you?'

I didn't want to be included. I couldn't think of anything less I'd rather do. Shoot me now.

'No, thanks, Dad. I'll grab something to eat and go to bed, if that's okay?' *Don't poke the bear. Smile and play along. Everything's just fine and dandy here. Honest.*

'There's some chicken in the oven for you. Your favourite. Eat that, get into your jimjams, go to bed and sleep.'

Thankfully he let me go.

Dressing up as you was a betrayal. That's how it felt. And stupid. Like I really thought I *was* you. *Knowing* I wasn't but *looking* like I believed I was you. Willy would think I'd gone round the bend. Sneaking out of the house, I ran to him, hoping for a bit of normality.

You'd been killed. I'd killed Cindy. Dad had killed me.

I wondered who'd be next in this new Inside-Out world.

TWENTY

Butty
————

It was only half-past ten in the evening, but I knew that Willy's parents could be a bit strict. They might accept a visit from me, but they might not. Good old Butty/Jack, the boy with the dead brother: now was that Jack or Butty? Even I was getting confused, dressed as I was in your khaki army jacket and red shirt and jeans and trainers and your big winter coat.

I decided to run around the side of the house and throw stones at Willy's window.

Because I wasn't you, I was pretty crap at actually hitting the window with my missiles, but eventually one pebble hit the framework of the little casement window, and Willy's worried little face popped up in between the open crack of his curtains. Opening the window, he hissed down at me, 'Butty, what are you doing here this late?'

God, he sounded like a little worried old man. Worried about the lateness of the hour, worried about the suspected anger of his parents should they catch him having nocturnal visitors, and worried, I suppose, about what I might want.

I don't think he'd forgiven me for beating up Tommy. He

was frightened by violence. I was too. Well, I *had* been. Not so much now.

Laughing at his old ladyish ways, I held up a bottle of vodka. Waved it at him in the night air: it was still drizzling and I was wet but didn't care. Mrs Evans had sold the alcohol to me, tucking it into a plastic bag, thinking, because that is what I'd told her, that it was for my parents who were too upset to come to the shop themselves.

Willy did this sort of opening-fish-mouth thing, his lips forming a perfect O. An O of horror and fear, instead of excitement and the risk of doing something daring and naughty. Although what I thought of as 'naughty' had widened its parameters. A lot.

I waved my hands at him, gesturing him down, not wanting to shout and definitely not wanting to see his parents. But my hand signals did not have the desired effect so finally I had to speak, 'Come on, Willy. Get dressed and come downstairs.' I waved the bottle again and put the neck up to my mouth, staggered about a bit, mimed drunkenness and threw my arms around in a beckoning wave for him to come down. *Semaphore boy is here.*

He looked appalled. As if I were asking him to join me in a midnight murder bash. Sometimes he was so wet it seriously pissed me off. Willy needed to toughen up and I was the man for the job.

It seemed I was the man for most jobs these days. Except the rather important one of actually being me. Dad couldn't grasp that one and didn't think I was the right boy for that job at the moment.

I needed a drink, anyway. Felt I bloody deserved one after you. Then Cindy. *Then* Dad. After everything. Impatient now, I had to stop myself from shouting at Willy. 'Right, I'm coming in,' I said, knowing that would completely freak him out. And it did the trick.

He waved his hands frantically, trying to stop me from even *thinking* about coming into the house. 'I'll be down, wait there. Give me a sec.'

Jumping up and down to keep warm, I wound up waiting near the road. I was in a terrible hurry. I didn't know why, but it felt like everything needed to be done now, no waiting about, now, now, now.

I was still running, running, running.

Grief was an odd fucker.

It kept on chasing, chasing, chasing.

At last, Willy shuffled around the corner of the house, glancing over his shoulder nervously. 'Mum and Dad will kill me if they find me out here.'

'Well, don't let them find you, then. They'll think you're all tucked up in bed, safe and sound. Come on, let's go. Follow me.'

I swear I could hear the reluctance in his footsteps as they plodded along behind me. Imagining his shoulders slumped in defeat, I had to physically stop myself from shouting at him to get his bloody shit together. Stop behaving like a stupid girl.

'Butty, wait. Where are we going? And why are you dressed up like that? Like Jack?'

'We're here. Almost. Just a bit further. And I'm dressed like this because I felt like it. Because I can.'

And then we were there. By the big kissing tree in the forest: the one that was too babyish for you, Jack. But it was all right for me and Willy. I spread out the plastic bag on the ground, at the base of the tree, and daintily perched one buttock on it, offering up the other side to Willy's cheek.

'It's wet. I don't want to.'

'Fuck's sake, Willy. It's just a drink. For Jack. We're going to raise a glass to him. It's his funeral on Saturday, but I want a private, more personal ceremony for him. And you're invited so sit down and drink up.'

I unscrewed the top and took a swig. Shuddered. I should have brought some orange juice and plastic cups, but I hadn't thought. Too busy escaping Dad. I held up the bottle to Willy, who'd remained standing. 'I don't drink.'

'You do now, Willy. For Jack. And for me. Do it for me. We've been friends forever – it's the least you could do. I'm not asking much.' The laying on of guilt. It was a cheap move, but I was all out of sophisticated ideas.

Grudgingly, Willy lowered himself, oh-so-gently, onto the tiny piece of plastic. Like he was a fairy princess being told to bathe in shit. It made me angry: his pathetic-ness, his weakness. After everything I'd been through, all I was asking him to do was have a drink. It wouldn't *kill* him, for Christ's sake. He took the bottle and surreptitiously, or so he thought, wiped the bottle neck with his sleeve before taking a very tentative sip.

'I haven't got herpes, Willy. What's wrong with you?'

He ignored me and I watched as the bottle tipped up to his mouth and tipped back down again. I wasn't even convinced any alcohol had actually passed his lips. 'And again. Have another sip. Go on.' I was being mean. Like Tommy. I was bullying my best friend but I couldn't seem to stop myself. He was like watching a bad out-take of what I might have become if it hadn't been for you. You shielding me. Willy was so scared of life, had never had a 'Jack' to protect him. All he'd had was me, and right now, I wasn't sure he even had that anymore. Wasn't sure he deserved it.

Because he just didn't try. He'd given up on life already. How bloody dare he? What was his excuse? He didn't have the right to feel as battered by life as he so obviously did. Who'd died that he loved? No one, that's who.

So I made him drink.

Even as I did it, I felt so bad. I mean, really, really bad. Cruel.

But I carried on. No longer wanting a drink myself. Just wanting to make Willy drink. Make him drunk. Make him sick. Make him understand that life wasn't to be wasted. You had to *do* shit to survive in this stupid Inside-Outside world.

In the end I had to hold the bottle up to his lips. Forced him to swallow.

I lay back on the ground and looked up at the sky. Inky black, almost blue, and clear. Pointing up with my finger held out, I told him what was there. 'There, Willy. See? It's so clear you can see the constellations really well. That there, is Taurus. That's Orion, also known as The Hunter. And see there? The Big Dipper – follow it down from the two stars on the side of the bowl, and there's the North Star. Great, isn't it?'

He didn't reply. I said, 'The Big Dipper, is also known as Ursa Major, which means The Great Bear – how cool is that? That's where I'd like to be. Far, far away. Miles and miles away from both the Outside and the Inside world here. In fact, I sometimes feel like I *am* Ursa Major – in disguise.' Laughing, I turned and checked on Willy.

He was drunk enough. Pissed enough that I thought he might actually understand about how shit life really was and that really, in his little world, he didn't have much to complain about.

He was sick. Very sick. All over himself.

I sat back and watched him vomit everywhere and finally stagger to a semi-vertical position. Throwing the mostly full bottle away – what a waste of money – I escorted him back to his doorstep. It was raining harder again now, and I was cold and annoyed and wasn't enjoying the smell of Willy's sick nor the sound of his very familiar sobbing, whingeing, crying thing that he resorted to so often.

Willy's mother opened the door: all tight-lipped and buttoned-up like an old-fashioned librarian.

'Good evening, Mrs Brown. Willy's had a bit too much to

drink, I'm afraid. And he's been sick. I brought him home. Think he needs to go to bed.'

There was some inaudible muttering from Willy's mother. She grabbed her son and pulled him into the house. I could hear more vomiting on the always spotless parquet flooring. Mrs Brown's lips tightened.

'Thank you for bringing him home, Butty. And I'm so so sorry about Jack. How are you all coping?'

Mum's taken to drugs and lies in bed most of the time; Dad thinks I'm Jack reincarnated; and I, by mistake, murdered Cindy. Other than that, I'm coping just fine, thanks.

'Fine, thank you, Mrs Brown. And sorry about Willy. I told him not to, but he said he wanted to try vodka. I don't think it agreed with him. Sorry.'

Again with the tightening of the lips, like she was trying to zip her face up, but she nodded at me and thanked me for looking after her son.

'Not at all. Any time.'

'We'll all be there on Saturday, Butty. For the funeral. Chin up.'

I went home and ate your favourite dish. I wasn't overly keen on chicken myself, but now that I'm you, it doesn't really matter whether I like it or not. You do, and that's what counts.

Lying in your bed with your pyjamas on, I thought about Mrs Brown's parting comment to me.

Chin up.

More like what a fuck up.

TWENTY-ONE

Penny

Penny wasn't too sure what to do. If it wasn't about murder and body dumping, she might have asked her father his advice, but that wasn't an option, and she had no one else to ask. It wasn't the sort of thing you could bring up at your local evening piss-up. Not that she went to any these days.

She sat next to her father, looking out of the window onto the garden. It all ended up here. This house or its garden. This was ground zero. The beginning and end of all that had happened over the past two years. Including Butty.

Tugging at her hair, she was warm and cosy in body: cold and frightened in mind.

'What bugs you, Pen?'

'God, Dad, you nearly gave me a coronary. I thought you were asleep.'

'I was. Now I'm not. And stop tugging at your hair – it won't make it grow any faster.' He leant forward on his chair and coughed. A little cough, not an out-of-control torrent of choking, but it would become that. Any minute now. Penny tightened and scrunched her toes in dreaded anticipation and preparation for the onslaught of a cough-before-dying. It was like listening to her father *literally* drawing his last breath. Probably because he *was* literally dying. And there was always the risk that it would in fact *be* his last breath.

Averting her gaze from his face, wanting to stick her fingers in her ears, she had no choice but to listen to every single gasp of wet, choking, suffocating cough as it enveloped and rattled his body, making his eyes stream, and his face redden. It sounded like a very inexperienced wind section in an orchestra warming up, with perversely off-key instruments.

In between coughs, he spat phlegm into a cup, only to continue to cough. It felt never-ending. His breath, wheezy and desperate, sounded, as always, like it might be his last. Penny automatically got the oxygen mask and held it over his mouth and nose. Eventually he calmed and his breathing resumed some kind of temporary but calmer normality.

'Could murder a ciggie,' he said, through his mask.

'Ha-dee-ha-ha.'

'Tell me what's wrong.'

'What is it with you and Mum? There's nothing wrong. Honest.'

'I don't mean what was wrong *then*, whatever happened that you refuse to speak of, not that, but what's wrong *now*. Now this minute. You look frightened.'

She shrugged, surprised that she was so transparent. 'Nothing's wrong. Suppose I'm just not looking forward to Jack's funeral tomorrow. It'll be awful, Dad. A young boy. I can't bear it. And if I can't bear it, imagine how his bloody family are coping.'

'Maybe they're *not* coping. Why should they cope? It's not the bloody law. I know I couldn't cope if anything happened to you. I think I might die.'

Penny kissed him on his cheek. 'Nothing's going to happen to me, Dad. I'm more worried about you.'

He removed his mask to speak, 'This isn't a who's-worried-about-who-more competition.'

'No, it isn't. Put your mask back on. It's about life. And life's shite.'

'Yup. Life can definitely be shite. That's the fun of life. When you can see the sky and the sun, *despite* the shite. When life isn't shite, when life is totally without shite, *that's* when it's time to celebrate.' He smiled.

'Confucius say,' Penny said.

'Indeed, my wise grasshopper. Now tell me your shite.'

'I am wholly without shite, thanks. Shite-less.'

'Bullshit. I know fear. It's the way you looked two years ago and I recognise it again now. It's not the same thing is it, not that I know what that is?'

'No, not the same. Different. I'll sort it out, Dad. Please don't worry.' She stood up. 'Do you need anything? Hungry?'

'I need you to stop lying to your old man and let me help.'

'Wish you could, but you can't, so there.' She kissed him hard on his forehead. 'Ring your bell if my services are required.'

'Will do and thank you. Would you tell your mother to come and talk to me. Promise I won't cough and freak her out too much.'

Penny nodded and having told her mother to go up, she wandered into the garden. It was bitterly cold and still raining. She wondered how Cindy's parents would be today: one ghastly night after their daughter had failed to return from her karate class. Would they be shouting, wailing, screaming, weeping? None or all of the above? Penny couldn't think of anything worse than the not-knowing, the forever-hoping, but perhaps, trying to be optimistic, Butty had been right. Hoping is better than the finality of death. When hope abandons you forever.

She didn't like her involvement in it. Felt that guilt had

become her permanent lodger and she desperately wanted to evict it, like some irritating guest who had outstayed their welcome.

Penny walked past the Trumpet Room and couldn't help but shudder. As she remembered. Remembered the details of last night. The little details that she'd had to finish in order to thoroughly dispose of Cindy.

Forever.

God help me.

TWENTY-TWO

Butty

T oday is the day. The day I've been trying to pretend was never going to happen. Your funeral. Once you disappear in your coffin, behind the curtains, and your body burns, I can't even pretend that you'll come back. You'll be gone forever, even though, of course, you've been gone forever since the car hit you.

Dad still thinks I'm you. Stupid old fart, you'd say. But you'd be pleased if you could see Mum. She seems more on the ball today. Yesterday too. The funeral's made her focus. She's not so stoned off her face but looks to be operating on autopilot. Greeting and meeting and pretending that she's fine, thank you very much. Too proud to cry in public. *Yet.* Her grip was tight on my shoulders, keeping me close. Keeping me safe.

Keeping me away from Dad, the looney tunes who calls me Jack.

It was a really good turn-out, that's what Dad kept on saying proudly, like your funeral was some sort of sporting event. He's really losing it, Jack. Any marbles he might once had, have now well and truly rolled far, far away, never to be retrieved from under the sofa, or even from behind the fridge. They're gone, mate. Gone, gone, gone.

Mum looked nice. She wore that red dress that she only ever wore for very special occasions. She'd been adamant that she didn't want people to wear black. Too sombre. Too sad. Too *final*. Black gave her no wriggle room, so she'd opted for serious in-your-face bright red and to give her credit she looked great. Not radiant, mind you. She looked ravaged, like a completely ruined person with a plastic, painted on face to cover up the cracks. But still they showed through. Nobody had to even look closely to see them. I avoided looking altogether.

I wore a suit. A blue one with a red tie. A bit of colour coordination a good thing, according to Mum. Solidarity and all that. Mum, Dad and me, stood outside the chapel and shook hands and bobbed heads with everyone. And I swear, Jack, there were millions of people. Standing room only inside, and the grieving hoards spilled outside as well. Inside and Outside – mourners. You'd have been well pleased. I was proud that such a lot of people came. It showed how loved you were. How very perfect you were.

Now that I'm you, according to Dad, I'll have to brush up on my perfection.

There was a bit of an awkward time when there was a delay for a little while, and people had run out of platitudes and stood with downcast eyes. The air was dry and cold and every time they exhaled, it looked like they were all smoking. A mass tobacco gathering, like a cigarette convention. I really wanted a fag but didn't think it would look proper, so I kept my hands in my pockets.

Finally, the music started and us, The Family, led the procession in. It felt very grand and very non-grand all at the same time. Too much but not enough. And the chapel, it had that weird, holy smell to it: a dusty, musky, deathly atmosphere that both cleansed and suffocated.

Dad did a reading. Mum had written it, making sure he said the right name. He'd followed his script and hadn't veered from it. He'd looked completely blank as if he weren't connecting with any of it. I didn't think he was.

Throughout the entire thing, Mum gripped my hand and her shoulders shuddered as she was inevitably and tragically unable to contain her tears. I squeezed her hand tightly, not wanting to let go. Of her or you.

I'd seen Penny and her mother earlier and had politely said 'Hello, thank you for coming,' and not much else. As if Penny was just some random person and not my saviour. I didn't look for Cindy's parents – I couldn't bear it.

Of course Willy and his parents were here. Willy had glared at me and I'd blank-faced him back. Now was hardly the time to debate the merits or not of drinking to excess.

I stopped listening to the Vicar. Didn't hear the music as it played. I sat there and pretended I was somewhere else. *Any*where else would do. Your funeral seemed never-ending, and I started to recognise the feeling of wanting to escape, to run away from it all.

But I couldn't. So I sat there, holding Mum's hand and ignoring Dad's presence on the other side of me. It was like I'd gone temporarily deaf and blind. I was just a thing, sitting on a pew, waiting for it all to end. I didn't cry. People grieve in different ways – like thinking the wrong son has died – and I think I'm one of them. Or maybe I'm just different full-stop.

Finally it ended as you took your last curtain call and went into the flames.

It was over.

TWENTY-THREE

Butty

P eople milled about outside the chapel, admiring the blankets of flowers. I edged away from Dad who had his hand draped around my shoulder: proud father and surviving perfect son. Mum was helping various men and women and children into arriving taxis, or their respective cars – all efficiency now – her tears on temporary hold. Ushering them all off to the village hall where drinks and eats would be provided. In my new role, I hoped there'd be chicken.

I sidled away from bonkers Dad towards the back of Penny who seemed deep in conversation with her mother. A man cut across my path. A stupidly *hugely* tall man, like a giant, stopped in front of me and putting his hands on his knee and bending his head down to my hemisphere, said, 'Hello. You're Charlie, right? I'm DI Simon Cosgrove. Call me Simon.' He smiled and I politely smiled back. Trying to ignore the sudden trip-trip-tripping of my heart. I suddenly felt very young, *too* young, terrified that he'd somehow know about Cindy, but I carried on standing there, pretending. What I did best.

'I'm very sorry for your loss. Really, I am. My condolences to you and your family.'

'Thanks.'

'I know this is a bad time, but would you mind me asking you a few questions? Or we can do it later if you prefer?'

'Now's fine, thank you.'

He looked around. 'Think we need what we call an appropriate adult with you. This isn't an interview, just a chat. But better with a grown-up, I think.'

'I'm not a child.'

'I didn't say you were. Where're your parents?'

Thankfully Dad had drifted off somewhere into his fantastical world and was not in sight. 'Mum's busy. It's her son's funeral today. My brother's funeral.'

'I understand that, I really do and I apologise. Let's leave it until later, then, shall we? I could come to your house. Maybe six o'clock? Does that suit? With both your parents?'

'It suits now. *There's* an appropriate adult.' I pointed at Penny's back. I could tell she was listening and saw her shoulders stiffen. 'If this isn't an interview, then any old adult will do, right?' From quivering, rapid-heart-beating-baby to Superman in one giant leap.

'Who is she?'

'Penny Crisp. A neighbour. I've known her all my life. I want her with me.'

Penny turned around. *Whipped* around and faced us. 'Can I help?' Her tone was stony like flint walls.

The policeman introduced himself, wrote her name down in his little policeman's book, and said to me, 'I was just wondering if you've recalled anything more about the car that hit your brother that night.'

'No. I already told Mum. It didn't have any lights on, that's all I remember when it drove away. But it all happened so quickly. One minute my brother was there, the car was there, then both were gone.' I lifted my shoulders up and down to confirm my story and there was a little silence.

'We're having trouble finding the car, I'm afraid.'

'It doesn't matter, does it? If you find it or not, it won't bring Jack back, so what's the point?'

'Don't you want the person punished for driving away like that? For not even stopping?'

'Like I said, it won't change anything, will it? I don't care.'

And I didn't. But weirdly, I started to cry, and Penny stood a little closer, patted me awkwardly on the shoulder. She didn't say anything barmy or inappropriate. Probably because she was pretending to be an appropriate adult, I suppose.

'And what about Cindy? Do you know Cindy, Jack's girlfriend?'

Boom. Back with the heavily beating heart. 'Course I know Cindy. She goes to my school.'

'Have you seen her recently?'

'No. Well a couple of days ago outside school. With Tommy, at the bus stop. But not since then, no.' I was tempted to add stuff, stupid irrelevant stuff. I was tempted to ramble. I bit down on my lower lip to stop myself saying something seriously stupid.

And then thought of a good, sensible question. 'Why are you asking about Cindy at my brother's funeral? She's probably here with her family.'

'No, she's not, Charlie. She's missing.'

Penny spoke for the first time, trying to sound concerned and shocked and doing a very good job at it. 'Missing? What do you mean, missing?'

'Do you know the young woman, Miss Crisp?'

'No, I don't know any of the children around here. Just Charlie and Jack. We live in the same road,' she added: unnecessarily, I thought.

'How long's she been missing?' I said, relaxing into it now that it was actually happening. My questioning in the disappearance of a young girl. Who I'd sort of killed.

'Since last night. She hasn't been seen since she left her karate class at seven yesterday evening. Where were you then, Charlie?'

'Wandering about town, went to the cinema, crap film, left halfway through and then ran home. I've been running a lot since my brother died. It helps. Don't know why, but it does.'

'Did you like her?'

Lie or not lie? 'She was okay, I suppose. I don't know her that well, even though she went out with Jack. She's older than me. Nothing in common, really. Well, apart from Jack.' I laughed and decided it sounded like a nervous titter.

'Weren't you angry that she was going out with Tommy? So soon after Jack died. Surely that must have angered you?'

Penny jumped in. 'What are you accusing him of, exactly?'

DI Simon Cosgrove stood up, all ten million feet of him. 'Nothing, Miss Crisp. But Charlie, I *know* you were angry – certainly with Tommy. Because you beat him up. Furious apparently that he was dating Cindy.'

I stopped my jaw from leaving its socket. 'Who told you that? Tommy? I'm surprised he admitted it. He was embarrassed I beat him up. Little old me: my first fight and I won. So, yes, I was angry at him, because he's a bully and he's always bullying all the kids, including me, at school. Course I was angry. But not at her. At *him*. Because he's a real shit and he deserved it.'

'But not angry at her?'

'No, course not. Why would I be? It's not like she and Jack were going to get married, is it? Just angry at stupid Tommy for taking advantage of her, that's all. I can't *believe* he told you.'

'He didn't. Your friend…' He consulted his notebook. 'Your friend, Willy, told us. Said you went "mental" and nearly killed Tommy.'

I laughed and this time I think anyone listening would have

heard the nervousness turn into hysteria-on-the-verge. Sounded like an address where Dad should be living.

'Don't listen to Willy. He doesn't like fighting. I've always looked after him. He probably exaggerated. A *lot*.'

'So you don't know anything about Cindy or where she may have gone? You haven't seen her?'

'No, honest. I'd say if I did. I don't know her well. At all.'

And that was also true. Sort of. Well, a bit true. True enough anyway.

Penny said, 'This is sounding more and more like an interview to me. It's Jack's funeral for God's sake. Have some bloody respect.'

The policeman straightened up fully. 'No disrespect intended, Miss. Just a little chat and now it's sorted. Thank you for your time and sorry again, Charlie, about your brother. I can't imagine that I'll need to speak to you again. I'll go and say goodbye to your parents. Tell them we've had a chat.' He turned to Penny. 'Tell them we've had an *unofficial* chat, not that I've conducted an interview, because I haven't. Wouldn't dream of it. It wouldn't be right and proper without his parents and at his brother's funeral, would it?'

He held his hand up in farewell and walked away. I thought, *Mum doesn't need to speak to that plank.* Not here. Not now. And God knew what Dad would say. He wasn't safe out in public at the moment.

I jumped as Penny's voice spat into my ear. 'Do not *ever* do that to me again, Butty. Do not involve me at all with Cindy. Leave me out of it.' She seemed to have a change of heart and punched me on the arm in a matey way, and kissed me roughly on the cheek. 'All funerals are shite, Butty. You did well. Me and my mother are going now, we won't be coming to the party afterwards. I'll explain to your mother. See you around.'

She huffed off.

Gee, thanks for the support, Penny-body-dumping-Crisp. We'd done something together, something bad and now she was just pretending that I didn't exist.

Fuck *her*.

If two people could form a queue, Mrs Crisp was next in line. She descended on me with outstretched arms like a crazed bat.

'Hello, Mrs Crisp.'

'Call me Sarah. It's my name after all.' She held my chin in her hand, tilting my face upwards. 'Well done for getting through that, Butty. Funerals are always dreadful things.' Then she swept me up in her arms and squished me up and into her big bosoms. I thought for a minute she'd swallowed me whole.

'Don't mind my daughter. She can be a little harsh with her words, but she doesn't mean it. I want you to know, both she and I will be here for you if you ever feel like popping in for a chat with us. Anytime. Okay?'

She kissed me loudly in the middle of my forehead: the sound of her lips smacking together resounding in my ears, making them tingle with the echo.

'Thank you very much, Mrs– Sarah. Thanks.' *You're wrong. Your daughter's just dumped me. She can't do that. She just can't. We're bonded.*

See you around, Penny had said, not meaning it. It was a brush-off. I'm not stupid. But she would be seeing me around. And I'd make her be friends with me again. Whether she liked it or not.

TWENTY-FOUR

Penny

I t had been a long funeral morning. There was never anything good about a funeral. Penny had been impressed with how Butty had managed to get through it. She could only imagine the trauma he'd suffered. She closed her eyes and stopped her work and forced herself to think of walking with her mother, or father when he'd been able, and pictured one of them being hit by a car. There, and then suddenly and forever gone.

No wonder Butty was angry. She'd be bloody furious and would most definitely want the bastard who'd driven the car to be locked up. At the very least. *Vengeance is mine*, she thought, but apparently not for Butty. He genuinely hadn't appeared to care about revenge, about justice meted out to the driver who'd mown down his brother.

Strange boy.

But she was still furious that he'd included her in the unofficial chat with the copper. She didn't want to be involved at all in *any*thing Cindy-related. She was already far more involved than was healthy. Butty was becoming a serious liability. And the more she learnt about him, the more time she spent with him, the more she wanted to extricate herself from him.

Trouble was, however unhinged and deranged Butty might prove to be in the future, if not already, she still sort of liked him. He had a very endearing quality. Even her mother had said so and her mother wasn't one of those types who 'liked all children and old people.'

'It's a stupid notion, Penny – this idea that all children are angels, like all animals are fluffy little darlings. And don't even get me started on "I love all old people." What utter bollocks. Old people can be and very often are complete twats. Think the world owes them a living. And children...' She rolled her eyes. 'Some children are obnoxious shits, in much the same way that some animals are real pains in the arse, despite their cutesy fur and big round baby eyes. Don't let them deceive you, Penny. Keep your guard up. Not all dogs are special like our Baggy-Baggage.' She'd stopped and massaged Baggy's ears. 'I do, however, like Charlie. I mean, Butty, or whatever he likes to call himself. Gentle and brave. A nice boy.'

Her mother had laughed at her own ridiculous rantings. Penny smiled at the memory of the conversation. Both her parents were great, and she wished she *could* confide in them. They'd have something to say that would be worth listening to, but of course she never would tell them about her rape. She loved them too much.

Bringing her mind back to Butty, *that* had been news, him beating up Tommy to that extent, if Willy was to be believed. Butty had gone 'mental.' That was the term used. That went with the slashing of Cindy's face. Too much physical violence from a boy who purported to be non-violent. Butty had lied about cutting Cindy's face and she felt, she knew, that he was lying about something else to her. Something horribly important that she needed to know.

Perhaps he *had* murdered Cindy.

The longer she knew him, the longer he battled with his grief, the more he didn't handle his grief, the stranger and more unpredictable his behaviour. The more out of control he became.

She'd only wanted to save him.

Who'll save me from him?

No, that was ludicrous. He wasn't a homicidal maniac. That was her. Maybe she only imagined the badness in Butty when really it was herself that she projected onto him. But there was something about the boy that was deeply unsettling. Trying to shrug off thoughts of Butty, Penny carried on gardening.

There were still bits of Keith left for the roses, but there were no roses in the winter. She liked to spread the love, spread the Keith in the mulch, but there was little call for it now in this weather.

But there was always *some*thing, however small, that she could give a little horticultural Keith-mulch-nutrient to, irrespective of whether or not it had any actual worth as a gardening feed. This last summer, the Keith Effect had brought extraordinary and very satisfying benefits to the various roses in the various gardens which she tended. Keith had truly proved to be the gift that never stopped giving.

He wouldn't last forever though. Perhaps now was a good time for another. It had been ten months after all, and it might very well prove a distraction to the Cindy investigation. A young female child and a young man: both missing: Penny didn't even know how old Keith had been. Perhaps the police would think there was some mad kidnapper on the loose.

They wouldn't think that. I'm just looking for an excuse to do another man.

Cindy and Keith couldn't be more different as victims, and she *knew* their respective disappearances would never be linked.

Because they weren't linked. Not really. Except by me. I'm a link. The only link between the two.

Here was the flaw in her reasoning. Cindy was missing and there'd be one great huge, monumental hoo-hah about it. And rightly so.

Officially, Keith was also missing. Difference was, no one really cared. There'd been absolutely no coverage of his disappearance in the local rag. There'd been, as far as she'd been able to find out without drawing attention to herself, no active search for him. Getting his name from his driving licence in his wallet, she'd found his full name and address. Checked the papers daily. Nothing.

Sadly, and rather pathetically for Keith, his demise had gone down with all the disappointing fizz of a damp firework that failed to ignite. It seemed his disappearance from life had created no more of a splash than his life had. As unimportant in his absence as he'd apparently been in his actual presence in the world. Not a great testament to his character and if there had been a splash, it would have gone as unnoticed as a boot stamping in the murky water of a puddle. A ripple at best.

No one, it seemed, had loved him. Not enough to make a big noise about it, anyway. Or if they had, she hadn't heard anything about it. And she'd looked, she really had. But there'd been nothing.

In a nutshell, the only thing Keith had bequeathed to the world, was shit, and Penny had happily taken on the mantle of executor of his paltry estate, and duly doled out his parting gift, having thoroughly composted it, to the flowers and plants with which she was surrounded.

Seemed fair.

Tragic, really, Penny conceded, but then again, he *could* have been a rapist. Any man could, so she'd done the world a favour and felt no guilt.

Not after what the Aniseed Man had done to her.

Keith had made her feel better for a time. Freer. Less shackled and weighted down by dark memories of her rapist. But the feel-good factor had been wearing out, fading, recently. Cindy had most definitely and categorically *not* rekindled any of the Keith Sparkle. Penny found the girl's death nothing less than tragic. Deeply and utterly sad.

Perhaps it *was* time for another one.

And she had her roses to think about. The next one would keep for spring. Manure was a keeper and was a good and fitting analogy for would-be rapists. Shit begets shit. Life worked well like that. Not often, but when it did, it made it all the more worth it. To paraphrase her father, she could see the roses better *because* of all the shite around them.

She was having one of her customary bonfires at a gardening client's house today. In amongst the cuttings, the deadwood, the general fire-food, were Butty's clothes. She'd burnt the lot to be on the safe side. Burnt her own gardening gloves and clothes she'd worn on that night to make doubly sure. She didn't want anything coming back to her.

Cindy's pink penknife had been broken and smashed and obliterated and scattered: some down drains in the next town over, some in random bins, some in fields. A bit on the overkill side but you couldn't be too careful. The white stone on which Cindy's head had made contact, Penny had washed, bleached and deposited whilst on a walk with Baggy, miles away. The necklace and the girl's clothes had all been completely destroyed. It felt like a full-stop to Penny. Everything was accounted for.

But in her mind, Penny kept on coming back to *him*. Butty was a continual worry. Penny thought he wouldn't only keep coming back to her, but would actively seek her out, thinking they were now inextricably linked by some form of unspoken blood-pact. The sacred union of death and disposal.

He needed handling carefully. And she had to remember

that. He was a child. And that's what frightened her the most. That a child could be so damaged. She supposed that that was the reason she'd warmed to him: pure and innocent youth so already damaged by grief. It saddened her on a very profound level.

Hence her predicament.

Refusing to think of him any further, she finished up her gardening job and returned home to the bungalow. Started to get ready for the evening ahead.

For a man.

Any man.

For a would-be/could-be rapist.

TWENTY-FIVE

Penny

S aturday night and Penny was ready to party.

She gave a quick thought to how Butty's 'party' was: the 'wake' or whatever you called them. She preferred the word 'party' after a funeral: a word and an event to celebrate the ending of a loved one, instead of a time to wail and lament your own loss which, frankly, made it more about yourself than them.

Checking herself in the mirror, she realised with a shock that physically, her reflection looked a lot better than it had the last time she'd stood here, ten months ago, pre-man-kidnapping. Her eyes showed signs of life, her hair had definitely improved; sleeker, quite a bit longer and thicker. Her cheeks were flushed with colour. That of course might just be the thrill of the chase to come, but she didn't think so. It looked almost as if she was dressed in calmness.

…Dressed in what *looked like* calmness, but of course she wasn't calm. Her life and thoughts were anything but calm. Perhaps it was more a look of acceptance. That felt right. Acceptance at the inevitability of what she had to do. It was all she *could* do. She had no choice, as far as she was concerned. Bring on Keith #2.

She buttoned up her coat – just the one button in the middle – making sure, as before, that she had speedy access to her toolbelt beneath.

Hearing the crinkle of the plastic on the floor as she approached her front door, she set her shoulders back and stepped out into the night. The ice-cold wind bit her face, bringing an immediate, stinging red to her cheeks, like a physical assault.

She was surprised to find that unlike the first time when she'd felt anxious and nervous and frightened, this time she felt only rage. She wasn't sure if that was a good thing. Trying to tamp down on her fury, tooled up as per the first taking, she walked briskly, fully prepared to man-whisper a would-be rapist to death.

Instead of loitering at the top of the main road, she instead stopped behind a tree halfway up her own road, and pretended a phone call on her mobile. It was dark and there were few people around. But still she was careful not to be seen. Standing and whispering to no one on the other end of a non-placed call, she waited, biting down on her impatience. Practised her whispering.

Two men turned into her road, laughing loudly. She couldn't tell if they were simply loud idiots or drunk. Either way, two was one too many.

A very old man came into view. Perhaps a neighbour. And anyway, he was too old. That would be wrong. Aniseed Man hadn't been old: therefore, it would be wrong and unfair to target this elderly man. She watched him as he walked the entire length of the road, before turning left down a street at the end. Not a neighbour then.

Getting more and more angry, Penny was tempted to be more upfront and bolder and simply go into a pub and drag out any man that fit the general description she had in her head. It wasn't even much of a mental picture: not old, not young, similar height to her and aniseed smelling. Not exactly brimming with detail and she'd never be able to describe any physical features to the police. An E-fit sketch. A faceless, hairless outline would be all she could muster. It annoyed her that she knew nothing about his hair, and saddened and aggrieved her that he'd defiled her own. But she'd work with what she had. It was *all* she had.

A man with a suit walked unsteadily into view. The wait for him to draw near seemed interminable. Only feet away, she could see that he had thin hair, was roughly the same height as her, and he was most definitely drunk. Older than Keith. Perhaps forty. Ish. But his build seemed right: what she'd seen of it in silhouette anyway – next to her bed.

He met the criteria, such as it was.

Stepping out in front of him, she went through the ridiculous ritual of mock-stumbling into him, faking drunkenness and said, 'Fancy a drink with me? I live just there.'

Realising she hadn't even bothered with a cover-story, hadn't prettied it up in the slightest, hadn't even tried, she wondered if her approach had been too brutal, too harsh. Her offer had barely been polite. More demanding than seductive. *He might be a delicate creature, a sensitive soul and I might put him off,* she thought with derision. *She* was the delicate creature here: not him.

Yeah, right.

She was definitely vengeful though.

He'd startled as she'd spoken, lost in some drunken world of his own making, and he squinted one eye at her. The mole on his upper lip could be seen now that they were up close and personal. It was repellent. Truly disfiguring; she briefly wondered why he'd never had it removed.

He didn't answer her. Carried on standing there, leaning against the wall to keep himself upright.

Penny found it increasingly difficult to maintain her composure, her anger threatening to leak out all over him. She reined it in with effort and softened her tone, placing her arm on his. 'I said, do you fancy a quick nightcap with me? Just a quick one. I could do with some cheering up. Feeling a little blue tonight. Would you mind?'

Sounds like I'm begging him.

Eventually finding his vocal cords, he cleared his throat to lubricate his clearly dry mouth and burst into tears.

It surprised her. 'I asked you for a drink. What's to cry about?'

It looked painful as he prepared to speak, trying to organise his lips into a formulation of words. 'Feeling blue, too.' He'd struggled to get those three words out and she nodded, knowing that she need only lead him to her house. Already, he was hers. Too drunk to be a threat. His legs had difficulty in coordinating themselves into a walk, so she propped him up and steered him into her house. Stumbling forward, he didn't even look behind him as she shut the front door, and then the heavy curtain.

When the baseball bat made contact, he went down, without even bending in the middle. It didn't take long to truss him up a la Keith, and deposit him in the wheelbarrow.

She checked on his breathing and decided she'd become a dab hand at knocking out men with a swift smack to the head. Got it down to a fine art already, and this only her second go.

She rootled through the pockets of his coat, which she'd already taken off, and found his wallet. Took out one of many credit and debit cards and said, 'Evening, Albert Winter, nice to meet you. I'm Penny, but you can call me whatever you want. Because I don't care.'

Taking up her place on the chair next to his head, she

quickly shaved off his hair. Took no pleasure in it this time because it clearly wasn't anything in which he took pride. It was thin, wispy and slightly greasy. Her very active non-enjoyment of the clipping process annoyed her. It was better if it was like-for-like. Aniseed Man took her hair, for all intents and purposes, but there seemed little if any point once she'd taken the Mole Man's hair. In fact, Albert Winter, looked better bald. She'd *improved* him.

Quickly, Penny carried out the aniseed check. Negative. Went through the waste-of-time waving the aniseed lollipop, still in its wrapper, under his nose.

'Recognise it? Bring back fond memories, does it? No? Well, thanks for looking, anyway.'

Studying him, she forced herself to feel better. His ugly, very big mole on his upper lip, made any hairstyle, even baldness, a by-the-way thing. All anyone would see looking at him, was a great big fuck-off mole. His blemish, well, it was so much more than a blemish, more of a belisha-beacon of an eyesore, overshadowed any other part of him. The one and only thing that people would immediately notice about him. Perhaps the only thing they'd remember about him. He was wearing a suit, badly cut, and his shoes were old and scuffed. He wasn't, physically at least, an obvious 'catch'.

He started making a snoring sound which further irritated her. 'Right, are you ready, Mole Man? I am. Ready, willing and able. I'm not bothering with the make-up, the slap – what's the point? You're already vulnerable and anyway, that's not the purpose of this evening's entertainment. I've done vulnerable with Keith. Tonight, we're doing "Consent". Are you aware of the concept?'

His silence was good enough for her as an affirmative. Standing up, her hands held out from her sides, her palms facing upwards in a can-you-believe-it gesture, she said, 'I know, right? Apparently, and this might come as a shock to you, it certainly did to me, *apparently*, silence means "Yes". Did you know that? I can safely say it came as news to me as well.'

Making her way into the kitchen, she turned towards the Mole. 'I have to tell you, Moley, brace yourself… There are more delights to come this evening. We're going to have a meal together. If we were on a date, eating can be a precursor to sex. It often precedes and paves the way to physical intimacy; it's a way to get to know each other, to find out each other's favourite colour, their lucky number, where they're thinking of going on holiday. Exciting stuff like that. So, that's the general plan – open, as always to changes from me, if and when I see fit.

'I hope you like Chinese. I ordered in before I left the house. I'll go and get it. Stay.' She turned her back on him, holding her palm out behind her, as if he were a dog, learning a new trick.

TWENTY-SIX

Penny

'I'm assuming, due to the casualness of this date, that you won't mind eating straight out of the containers? Bit heathen I know, but you'll forgive me for not giving a rat's arse. I do, however, hope you like sweet and sour. I thought it an appropriate choice. Rape being... and I'm only guessing here, but I'm pretty sure I'm right in saying, that the actual act of rape is sweet for the rapist. For the man. And a pretty sour experience for the rapee. That would be me. Those are our respective roles tonight, Moley. You're the rapist, in case you're finding it hard to keep up, and I'm the victim of it. Now, one sweet and sour pork ball or two?'

Penny, chopsticks in hand, deftly picked up an orangey, goo-covered pork ball and popped it in her mouth. 'Good, Moley. They're good. They always are from this particular Chinese. I'd recommend them. Open up. Say aaaargh.'

She needn't have bothered asking. His lips weren't shut as if he were deep in contented slumber. They gaped open as if the very thing he most wanted in the whole world was a sweet and sour pork ball. A bit too eager, Penny thought. She poked him in the cheek with one chopstick. 'Do you want something to eat? Yes or no?'

To her surprise, he answered. She thought it progress of sorts. Might make for a more chatty evening. More interesting if he were actually vocal.

'No,' he'd said.

She craned forward, cupping her hand to her earflap as if hard of hearing, and pulled it forward. 'Could you repeat that?'

'No.'

'That sounds like an unequivocal answer, an answer that cannot be misconstrued, doesn't it? *No.* You wouldn't assume there'd be any doubt in comprehending the meaning of the word, right?'

Silence.

'But I'll tell you that I'm a bit on the confused side, Moley. Is that a "No" that really means "Yes"? How am I possibly to know? I agree that you'd be forgiven for thinking that "No" means "No", but again, *apparently*, it can also mean "Yes". In the context of rape, I mean. What's the difference do you suppose? I mean, how can any confusion arise over the meaning? Do you suppose it could be intonation, vehemence used, volume of the word, perhaps? Does one have to shout "No" for it to actually mean "No"? It's a real puzzle, isn't it?'

Penny took another ball in her chopsticks and chewed on it thoughtfully. Had a little chow mein. Before speaking again, she had a couple of spring rolls, wiping her fingers on the Mole Man's shirt.

'Seems to me,' she said. 'You're damned if you do, and damned if you don't. Silence means "Yes", and "No" means "Yes". So how do you say "No" and have it heard and clearly understood when you really mean it? Any ideas?'

His conversation, such as it was, had dried up. But his stupid face appeared to be changing. Coming to life. She put down the food to be on the safe side and picked up her pepper spray. Just in case. 'Is someone waking up?' she said.

Moley's eyes opened with effort; fluttered once or twice before actually focusing and staying open. He looked straight up at the ceiling and then moving his head slowly, he finally turned his gaze on her.

'Hungry, now?' she said.

'No.'

'Please, not this again. We've been through this. Here you go *again* with "No". Don't confuse me.'

Approaching his face with a speared pork ball, she dangled it in front of his eyes. 'Looks good and you want to know why? Because it is. Now come on, this won't hurt a bit and I know you want to anyway. You're just pretending you're not hungry. You're probably secretly bloody *gagging* for a pork ball right this minute, aren't you?'

She wedged the ball into his mouth. 'And now swallow. I like men that swallow.'

He shook his head slowly and was obviously confused; unsure as to where he was or what was happening. *Good*, Penny thought. *Welcome to my world.* Trying his best to avoid ingesting the food, he blearily turned his face away, understanding on some level that his hands were tied and behind his back.

Penny patted him on the shoulder. 'Difficult, isn't it? When you've got nothing to fight with. When you physically can't – either because you lack the strength or because, as in your case, you're physically restrained – fight back. I'm stronger than you are tonight and can do anything I want to. How does that make you feel? Go on, I'm really interested in your answer. Surprise me.'

Albert the Mole Man turned his head as far as he was able and vomited over the side of the barrow and onto the plastic sheeting.

'Jesus Christ. What do you want, a bib? And you don't

need me telling you why that's happened, do you? That'll be all the alcohol you drank tonight at the pub. And yet, you couldn't resist one more nightcap with me, could you? And when you accept, in all innocence, a drink from a stranger, I believe that some people, some *men*, think that means you are giving them carte blanche to do with you as they want. It's a sort of tacit agreement. Sex often comes, so I'm reliably informed, with the excuse, "but you accepted a drink from me. You owe me." Now, that just *can't* be fair, can it? That's not consent, is it, Moley?

'That's a horrible and unfair misinterpretation by the rapist. "She came willingly and happily into my flat, officer. I didn't force her. She had a drink. She even kissed me. And *then* she said *No*. Come on, that's being a tease, isn't it, getting me all excited like that? She led me on, guvnor. It wasn't my fault. And most importantly, Your Honour, she never said *No*. She wanted it. It was clear that she did."'

'Why?' said the Mole.

'Well, I suppose, the only thing I can think of, is that he liked my hair. He told me so. That's how I led him on. By having beautiful hair. He wouldn't stop stroking it, like I was a mannequin in a shop. Running his hands through it. He wouldn't stop. That's why I cut it off.'

Penny re-focused her gaze on the man in her wheelbarrow. 'Good one, Moley. Really, very good. I can't believe it. Maybe it *was* my hair. Surely not? Do you think perhaps it was, Albert Winter? Was it really my beautiful hair that made a man come into my house and rape me? Can that have been the real reason? My fucking *hair*? *Why have I never even considered that before*? Because it's a ludicrous notion, that's why. You don't rape someone simply because they have nice hair. Do you? *Do* you, Moley? Could a man have that shallow a reason for rape? Although, there's obviously absolutely no *good* reason for rape, is there? And when I say "no" good reason, I do actually mean *no*.'

Albert the Mole had stopped vomiting and appeared to have lost consciousness again. Pity. He'd come up with a not-bad theory and she felt pained, embarrassed even, that she'd never thought that her hair could have been the primary target. And that, unfortunately for her, she'd been literally attached to it. Rape by proxy. No. That couldn't be it. It was too stupid to waste good thinking on. There must be much, much more to rape than a man simply liking a specific trait of a woman. There *must* be, or what hope was there?

But it tickled away at her. The thought that she'd attracted a man with her hairstyle. Had she invited sex into the house and not even known that she'd sent out the bloody invitation. No man was that mad, surely? That superficial? If not nice hair, it could just as easily have been because she'd had nice legs, had worn tight jeans, had big tits, small tits. Had a pair of stupid blue bloody Crocs. Perhaps she'd worn her steel-toe capped gardening boots too provocatively. How could she stop men if a rapist was working from such a frail framework, who had such a whimsical criterion, how could she bloody stop them all when the rape could be based on such inconsequential and meaningless parameters?

If the reasoning behind rape was so flimsy, what chance did she have of ever finding out the why of it?

She didn't know, but she *did* know that she had to carry on trying to find out what made men rape. It was what got her up in the morning.

She stood, tired, over-full with Chinese, but vaguely intrigued by the hair thing. Felt she'd made progress in some way. Although it got her nowhere. It meant nothing in the grand scheme of things. But big hooray to Albert for asking 'Why?' in the middle of her out-loud musings. Glancing with distaste at him now, covered in sick and with mole still *in situ*, she wondered what he'd wanted answering. Why what? *Why am I here? Why are you doing this? Why did you get Chinese, and not a curry?*

Shrugging, not caring, admitting she didn't have an answer for him, she got up and counted his teeth carefully. Making herself clinical. Ignoring her dislike at this very physical *oral* part of the proceedings.

Thirty. Not a full set. He must have had two wisdom teeth out. Pity he hadn't thought to remove his mole at the same time. People were strange, she conceded.

She then picked out her most unliked cushion. Placed it over Albert Winter's face and pushed down hard. She held it there for a long time, to make absolutely sure. Longer than was necessary, she knew.

It was only the doorbell that stopped her continuing to suffocate a man who she knew was already dead.

She froze.

It rang again and then she heard the rattle of the letterbox.

TWENTY-SEVEN

Penny

'Come on, open up. I know you're in there. I'm not leaving until you let me in.'

Rather lamely, Penny was tempted to turn off the lights and pretend she wasn't in. But of course she couldn't. Bloody Butty knew she was in. It wasn't like she could hide in a corner quietly and hope he'd go away. Anyway, how did he know where she lived?

'Go away, Butty. I'll see you another time. I'm a bit busy right now.'

'I'm not going anywhere. Let me in.'

Penny let the silence drag out. Another metallic flap of the letterbox.

'Please, Penny. I'm not going anywhere. It's cold out here.'

She wanted to shriek out her rising hysteria. She had a dead body in a wheelbarrow in the middle of her sitting room, and a fourteen-year-old boy demanding to be let in. It was like some stupid farce. She teetered on the brink. For a moment, she stood immobile, frightened if she moved, she might fall.

She braced herself. 'I told you, I'm busy, okay? Let's meet up tomorrow.'

As she spoke, she mentally kick-started herself and began hurriedly cleaning up, wearing her disposable latex gloves, wheeling Moley behind the sofa out of the way, before bending and folding up the plastic sheeting into neat square packets. Instead of having to grapple with one large plastic tarpaulin, she'd used four, over-lapping. Wrinkling her nose at the smell of vomit she made sure she avoided getting it on her and steered clear of any blood spatter.

She got rid of the takeaway containers. Carried on ignoring Butty.

'I'm waiting,' came Butty's voice: plaintive now, wheedling.

Her teeth ached with the severity with which she clamped them shut: furious with the boy, with the chaos he had brought to her. Was *still* bringing to her doorstep. Ignoring him, she went about her cleaning up business. She moved to the thump of her racing heart, and having wheeled Albert the Mole through the kitchen and into the adjoining garage, she transferred him into the back of the jeep, again using her father's ramp. Returning to the sitting room, she got a duster out, feeling her palms damp within her gloves. Fear sweat.

She wiped everything clean.

Her mobile vibrated on the kitchen worktop. She couldn't ignore it. It might be one of her parents needing her. Picking it up, she read the text:

> Guess who? Let me in.

Butty had her mobile number. She wanted to scream. Instead she spoke quietly, but loud enough for him to hear. 'Fuck off, Butty. I mean it. I. Am. Busy. Go away.'

Her heart rate was so fast it worried her. She panicked although she knew that Butty couldn't get in, but he felt so close, too close. To her. To murder. To a stupid man with a bald head and a mole in the back of the jeep.

She heard a soft laugh from behind the curtained door. 'You got a man in there?'

Penny balled her hands into fists and looked at her face in the mirror. Checked it for signs of what she had done; any visible evidence of Albert Winter that might be lurking. Made sure her face and body were blood-free. Made sure all the Mole's clothes were in the car, that she hadn't left anything on show. Made sure she looked normal, whatever that meant, when she opened the door to the boy.

Throwing the gloves into the rubbish bin – to be got rid of later – she walked towards the front door and ripped the curtain aside. Swinging open the door with more force than was needed, barely able to contain her anger, curdled as it was with anxiety at Butty's presence, she looked down at him.

She was so bloody furious she could kill him, although not actually. Obviously, she told herself. He was only a child, not a contender for her 'to-get' list. 'Who do you think you are, knocking so late at my door, demanding that I let you in? Am I with a man? Who are you, my mother? None of your business. Anyway, how did you get this address? And my mobile number?'

She watched as the child slapped his arms across his torso, trying to keep warm.

'Aren't you going to let me in? You can lecture me inside.' He grinned at her.

She didn't grin back. Still furious, she walked back inside, not even bothering to speak. Collapsing onto her sofa, allowing herself some relief knowing everything in the room looked normal, she pointed at an armchair. 'Sit.'

Butty peeled off an RAF jacket that was slightly too big for him. Underneath he was wearing an army jacket, and layers of striped tops, most of which swamped him. His un-gloved hands, red and sore-looking from the cold, were only partially visible under his cuffs. His trainers were far more fashionable than she'd grown used to seeing Butty wear, although anything this boy did, she could hardly say she was used to.

Holding her hand up in the air, she said, 'Wait, let me guess. Who have you come as? Someone different. Someone not you. Give me a clue.'

His shoulders shrugged and he refused to catch her eye, suddenly looking self-conscious.

'I've come as Jack. That's who I am, according to Dad, anyway. Mum knows I'm still me, Butty, but Dad insists I wear Jack's clothes, insists I *am* him, so that's who I am tonight. The one and only Jack Hawthorne. Favourite son extraordinaire.' He bowed theatrically. 'At your service, ma'am.'

Penny found herself speechless. Embarrassed that she'd teased his clothes, she said, 'God, Butty, that's awful. He can't do that, pretend you're Jack. That's horribly wrong. What does your mother say about it?'

'Not a lot. It's been a busy day what with the funeral and everything.' He didn't bother hiding his sarcasm. 'But she's aware of it. She told me to ignore the silly old fool – her words – and I do, but it's also easier just doing what Dad wants. No harm done. Not really.'

'But there is. It's harmful to you. You're not Jack. You're you.'

'Yeah, I'm me and I'm here.'

'Sounds like your father's in serious denial. Be you, Butty. It's who you are.'

'I know I'm me. But people always noticed Jack. Not me. I'm like the boy-in-the-background by comparison. I understand if Dad can't handle Jack not being here; him being disappointed it's just me. If I wish Jack was still here, imagine being one of his parents.'

'That's your father's problem, not yours. It sounds like he needs help. You need to hang on to who you are. You're not in denial about Jack, are you?'

He snorted. 'Don't be silly. How could I be? I saw Jack die in front of me. How can I deny that? Doesn't mean I have to accept it though.' He shrugged. 'Maybe that's why I'm angry because I can't accept it. You know what I mean. I know you do. You understand me. I don't know why you do, but you do. I'm angry – just like you.' He flicked his finger between the two of them. 'That's why we're alike. We're the same.'

'I'm not angry, and we're not alike,' she lied. 'And I've got nothing to accept. You have. I can help you. I hope I can, anyway.' And she meant it, her anger at him being here diluted by the words he'd spoken.

'I know you can help me. You have, already.' He bobbed his head. 'Thanks.'

Penny didn't know what to say, so kept silent. She wondered if he had some sort of silly crush on her: not sexual, but needier, more obsessive than that. He was under the illusion she could give him something. It almost felt like he was becoming fixated on her, wanted more from her than she was able to give.

He grinned inanely at her, and she decided to drop it. Come back to it another time. Talk to her mother about it. About Butty. Instead, she asked, 'Why *are* you here? And how did you know I lived here? And my bloody number. How did you get that?'

'I returned your clothes to your mother this afternoon, the ones you gave me to wear home after you got rid of Cindy. I said I wanted to see you and she told my where you lived. She offered to ring you to let you know I was coming, but I lied and said I wanted to surprise you. She gave me your mobile number, so I could text you. Give you time to bake me a cake.' He clapped his hands and laughed. 'Ta-dah. So here I am.'

'But what do you want? And don't say that – "After you got rid of Cindy". She was a little girl, not some piece of rubbish.'

'I know that. Don't be stupid. Course I know that. I didn't

mean it like that. But I think, Penny, that we need to… I don't know, talk about it.'

The fourteen-year-old equivalent of 'I think we need to talk'. It was never a good line from an adult and nearly always presaged something you didn't want to hear.

'About what?'

'I want to know why you knew *how* to get rid of a dead body. You just did it. Like you knew exactly what to do and how to do it. That's not normal. Is it? I'm only fourteen, but I'd have to think really long and hard if I was asked to dispose of a body. I wouldn't even know where to start. But you did.' He waited a bit – for dramatic tension, Penny thought – before delivering what he thought his devastating punchline. 'You did it like you'd done it before. Like it was something familiar to you – the whole process. But getting rid of a corpse must be difficult. I've been thinking about it all day. Sitting there at the stupid wake, listening to people who were heartbroken about Jack but not being able to say it properly, me avoiding Dad the whole time and trying to help Mum, and all the time, I was thinking, *How did Penny know how to get rid of a dead body*?'

'I didn't *know*. That's the honest answer. I just made it up as I went along. Used a bit of common sense, that's all. And for your information, it was bloody difficult and not something I ever, ever want to do again. Just so you know, in case you're thinking of accidentally knocking off someone else.'

She knew it was wrong to be pretending to joke with Butty like this, even engaging in this conversation at all, felt truly wrong, but how else to handle him? He was a child. Penny was desperate to disconnect Butty from her and her part in disposing of Cindy. And even more worrying, he'd guessed that she'd got rid of bodies before.

'What happened to you?' he said.

Penny's throat constricted. 'What do you mean?'

'Your mother told me she was happy I'd turned up in your life. That I'd made you "better". Better than what?'

Penny squeaked out a panicked laugh. 'Ignore my mother. You know what parents are like. She didn't mean anything by it. I'm not better because I'm perfect as I am.'

'Don't joke. Please don't. I'm being serious. Your mother was quite clear about it. I didn't ask what she meant, because I'm too polite, but I'm asking you. Maybe I could pay you back and help you, like you helped me. Get you to smile again. Your mother talked about your smile and said she hoped I could make you smile again. So, what are you better *from*?'

Penny held up her hand. 'I've just told you. I'm the best I could ever be right now. Really, I don't need your help, but thanks anyway.'

She was grateful Butty didn't insist on pursuing that particular line of questioning. God, her bloody mother. She'd have to have a word.

Now Butty had gone back to being all-business. 'Tell me where you put her body,' he said.

'Certainly not. It's not something you need to know. Forget it. It's done. But don't forget *her*, Cindy. Do not forget what happened. A young girl died. It's not an amusing conversation piece on how and where I concealed her. It's a bloody tragedy and you need to remember that.'

He looked disappointed. Didn't bother to hide it. He opened his mouth to speak but Penny stopped him.

'You told me you cut Cindy. On her stomach and arms. You didn't tell me you'd cut her face. What made you do it, Butty? It wasn't necessary.'

None of the cutting had been necessary.

His face coloured and he stood up. 'I don't know why I did that. Really, I don't. Just to make it look like a nutter, I suppose. It did look like that, didn't it?'

Before Penny could ask him more about the face-cutting,

about how he'd felt when he'd done it, frightened of his answer, he bent to the floor and picked up a credit card which had been hidden behind the leg of the chair. She'd missed it. Time and space seemed to slow down as if she were falling into some cosmic vortex. She listened with dread as he read it out loud. 'Albert Winter. Who's he then? Was that why you were busy and wouldn't let me in? Is he your boyfriend?'

Penny jumped up and grabbed the card from him. 'None of your bloody business, all right. Just leave it. Leave me alone.'

He looked downcast, seemingly embarrassed. Mumbling a "Sorry," he spoke as if talking to his feet. 'I'll never mention your boyfriend again.'

'He's not my bloody boyfriend. Just… someone I know. Not that I have to explain to you.'

'Okay.' He met her gaze. 'I'll move on then.'

Penny was aware that Butty was evolving. Becoming more adult in a way. More confident. She couldn't work out why. He could be heart-breakingly endearing one minute, the next he was a bit too bloody scary to think about. She wasn't sure whether to love him or be terrified by him.

'Before I go,' he said, his face all serious and trying too hard to be adult. 'I just wanted to make sure that you got rid of everything else that might connect me to the crime, right? The penknife and the necklace, I mean. Cindy's mobile. You destroyed them, didn't you?'

A firm nod and a confident smile reassured him. 'All sorted. Stop panicking.'

Worried, more than worried that he'd seen the credit card, she listened to Butty's parting words as he walked towards the door. 'You should let me know where Cindy's body is, you know. I should know – it's my right. We're in this together. We're partners.'

'No, we are not. We are most definitely not partners.'

He smiled, making his face painfully youthful again, heart-breakingly sweet again. 'Course we're partners. We're partners in crime.'

For a moment, she wanted to kiss this broken boy, stained as he was with a disturbing darkness. But she stopped herself, fearful that her lips might bleed on contact with his skin. So damaged was he.

So damaged was she.

Then he was gone.

TWENTY-EIGHT

Butty

I thought my visit to my co-conspirator last night had been a bit of a non-event. Penny could be very tight-lipped when it suited her, and I didn't know how to get past her defences. It was like she was coated in a metallic shield from top to toe, refusing to give anything away about herself.

She was almost as good a pretender as I was, and that's saying something.

I wondered who Albert Winter was. Maybe I'd Google him. Maybe that was why Penny was angry and sad. Maybe *he* was bad. I knew Penny had lied about him. Had freaked out when I found the card. She'd tried to keep her face neutral, but I'd spotted the fear, the panic. The shock.

Maybe that's why me turning up in Penny's life had made her better, like Penny's mother had told me. Maybe I could re-pay Penny and save her from this Albert Winter. I'd have to look into it.

If I could discover why I'd made Penny better, then I could perhaps really cement our partnership and I'd have her for always.

And I *should* know where Cindy was buried. Penny should have told me, because whether she liked it or not, we *were* partners. She and I are definitely linked. And I liked that. I liked being attached to her. Perhaps I was a little in love with her. Not in *that* way, not in a Cindy-Jack-lovey-dovey way, but I wanted to be with her, because she understood me when others didn't. No one understood me, and what I was going through. Not sure anyone ever had.

Reaching into the sweetie jar, I took out a chocolate bar for later and wondered what to do with myself. I decided Willy probably still hadn't forgiven me, and I did feel bad about that. I really did.

But it was his fault. It was time he grew up. *I'd* had to. Definitely had to since you'd gone and left me on my own. With Mum.

I'd been leaving Dad well alone, letting him believe what he wanted, dressing in your clothes as he wanted, and I didn't actually mind that. In fact, I rather liked it. It made me feel more like you and less like me. Bonus.

Even if I wanted, I couldn't go to school now. It had closed for the Christmas holidays. It was also Sunday. Checking my mobile, I saw it was only eleven o'clock in the morning. I was bored, numb, lonely, and sad. And still angry. I felt like I didn't really know who I was anymore.

Thankfully, Mum put in an appearance. 'Where have you been, Butty? I thought I'd lost you. I've just checked upstairs and there you were – gone. Not there.'

'I came down the back stairs. And I'm sleeping in Jack's room – you do know that don't you, Mum? Dad is sort of making me.'

She nodded but didn't speak, her lips stiff and unyielding; pressed together so tightly they appeared as two straight white lines. Bloodless. I thought if she opened them, she'd be frightened at what may come out. Busying herself, she put the coffee percolator on and got herself a mug. Sitting at the table she gestured for me to sit opposite.

'Ignore your father. I've had a word. You're not Jack. You're my Butty. And you always will be. I love you to ribbons. Ignore Gordon. He's not quite himself at the moment. Please don't listen to him. You'll never be Jack and I would never want you to be.'

She reached across to touch my face, but I pulled back. Not fully believing her. Wanting to, but unable. I pretended a nod, gave out a little-boy whimper, did a crinkling of my forehead, played the role she wanted and needed me to, but deep down, I wanted to physically lash out. Not at Mum, but someone: I wasn't sure who.

Yet.

After Willy, I'd recognised in myself the ability to do harm. Serious harm. I hadn't physically attacked him, but the outcome was the same. I'd lost my best friend and that was my fault. Willy should count himself lucky though, because I could have done a lot worse than making him drink. And I wasn't sure what to do with that knowledge. Knowing I could really *hurt* someone.

But I knew it wasn't good.

Without you, I'd lost myself.

And I wasn't sure who I was instead.

Not you, not me.

A high-risk nobody.

I reckoned it couldn't be that hard to work out who I was on my own, without you, but I needed to come up with some sort of answer quickly. Get me back to normal. The only person who I thought could help, could understand, was Penny, but I wasn't even sure she wanted to be my friend anymore.

It was me, after all. The unfavourite.

Unexpectedly, that thought made me angry. I shouldn't be so bloody pathetic. I needed to grow up and I actually thought

I had evolved since you left, Jack. It didn't matter what my name was.

I am me. Here I am. I should be proud. I'll pretend for the moment.

I realised Mum was looking at me, her face creased with concern but still her eyes weren't really connected with this world. They were misted over with memories of you. Life without you. Life with a mad husband and me. The other son.

Trying hard to sound brighter than real life was, she said, 'They're holding a kind of vigil this evening, for Cindy. A gathering of family and friends and everyone who knows her. I think we should go, don't you? Just you and me. Your father won't be coming.'

'Back to his trains, is he?'

'Butty, for God's sake, forget about Gordon. He's not well. I'm talking about Cindy now. She's fourteen years old and she's missing. She was Jack's girlfriend. I know her parents. We need to show that we care. And we do.'

I thought that last add-on, sounded exactly that: an add-on. A make-believe thing that you say because it sounds like the right thing to say. *Doesn't mean you mean it though, does it?*

'We're going,' Mum said firmly. 'The police have been searching the area she was last seen in, in town, the neighbourhood, the forest, the countryside. Everywhere. You must know that, must have seen them in the area. We must help. Jack would want us to help. *I* want to help. Don't you?'

'Course. When are we going?'

'Everyone's meeting at six o'clock this evening, outside Cindy's house. And we shall be there. Both of us.'

Denial. Acceptance. Avoidance. I hadn't even got as far as the arrival desk to acceptance; was still loitering about outside the double doors, refusing to go in. Dad was firmly sitting in the departure lounge of complete denial, and Mum had wholeheartedly checked into avoidance – clasping a little carry-on of denial – Dad's excess baggage, just in case. Mum always over-packed. Three Hawthorne nuts in the airport from hell.

I stood up. 'I'll see you later then, Mum. Meet you here at five, yeah? I'm off upstairs. Lose myself in a book. Or something,' I lied.

Immediately she moved on, as if I'd already left the room. Busied herself frantically cleaning the kitchen, putting something on to cook, putting a load of dirty clothes in the washing machine and turning the radio on full blast. *Way to go, Mum. Avoid it all.*

Running quickly up the stairs, I carried on up to the attic: Dad's domain. The railway station with my father at the helm. I wanted to test out his madness. We could have a competition: who was the more insane out of the two of us?

He looked at me, for a minute bewildered before he remembered to smile, as I climbed up through the hatch, my feet still on the top rung of the ladder. 'Just visiting,' I said.

'Hello, you. Look what came yesterday in the post. It was left in the porch. I've been waiting ages for it. You'll love it.'

He picked it up, as if it were made of something so delicate that it was in danger of crumbling in his hands. It was a big green bus. And when I say *big*, I mean out of all proportion big. Stupidly big. Dad's trains were normal model size, and that, as Dad had informed me forever ago, was a series gauge 00. It meant nothing to me, but to Dad it was very important. All train details were important.

But this bus was gigantic by comparison. It was the size of a toddler and looked as heavy. 'Why's it so big? It's *too* big, Dad, it doesn't match. It makes the trains look dwarf-size.'

Confused, he held the bus to his chest, like he was protecting it. Cradling it so it couldn't hear my criticism. Bloody barking or what? His face scowled and he said, speaking slowly as if *I* were the toddler here. 'It's big because it has to be. It's a rail replacement service. For all the people who need to get from A to B when there's a delay or cancellation. It's used to replace and transport people from all over the whole fucking world, okay? Understand? That's why it needs to be big. It's a crucial job replacing people, ferrying them around so that they're all in the right place at the right time.'

'Yeah, course it is.'

'You must understand that. It's a pretty simple concept to grasp. There are so many people in this world, millions and millions of them, who are in the wrong place. And it's my job to get the right people back to where they should be. Get it? It's a very important task and it'll take me some time to get it just right. If done correctly, everyone ends up where they belong. It's all about correct dispersal and the redistribution of people. Making sure that a few wrong-uns don't get stuck in the wrong place when they should have moved on.'

He looked pointedly at me. Sending me some sort of secret message. He smiled, but it seemed wolfish. Fiendish. Like I was prey.

I thought I understood his completely bonkers reasoning and to be charitable, Dad's fantasy was better than his reality. I could relate – up to a point. Except I wasn't a nut.

The big bus was his metaphor. He'd moved me out on it, probably strapped to the roof rack knowing my luck, and Jack had been brought back into his rightful place on this earth. By a big green bus. Wow. I mean, I didn't even realise Dad had lost it quite so monumentally.

I wasn't sure if I was impressed by his lunacy, saddened by it, angry with it, or didn't give a flying fuck. After all, I had every right to be angry. I'd been shipped off on a bloody bus. God knows where I'd been abandoned and forgotten. There probably wouldn't be another bus for ages and then two would come along. I smiled at my own joke, but deep down, I couldn't help but feel just a teeny bit freaked out by Dad.

I wondered if he was suffering with grief-induced psychosis.

Was that really a thing? I didn't know, but whatever, Dad was loop-dee-loo crackers.

'Good luck with all your organising, Dad. Hope you get people where they should be.'

'Thanks. I knew you'd understand.'

Wanting to punch my stupid father in the face, I instead, reversed down the ladder and away. Away from his madness and back to my own sanity.

Everything is relative.

TWENTY-NINE

Butty

I didn't want to be here. Cindy's parents appeared completely blown away. Understandably. I just hadn't prepared myself for their faces. They didn't look human. They were like life-size dolls with blank features. They didn't even bother trying to smile and why should they? I also understood that. But they still creeped me out.

Mum stood there with her arm around the shoulder of Cindy's mother, Mrs Blackman. Beckoning me forward, Mum said, 'Come and say hello to Louise, Butty.'

I'd expected to feel guilt seeing Cindy's parents, but comparing Cindy's mother with mine, as they stood together, seeing the difference between the two women, I realised I'd given Mrs Blackman the gift of hope, while my mother had absolutely nothing.

Whatever she told herself, Louise Blackman must have known that Cindy wouldn't have gone far in the Outside world. Even Jack had admitted, in one of his rare unloved-up moments, that his girlfriend was hardly the brain of Britain. It stood to reason that her parents also knew this, must have known it when they were wrapped up tight and snug in bed together in their cosy Inside world, they must have known that their daughter would never amount to much. They would have felt helpless because Cindy was so obviously hopeless.

Then along I'd come and given them hope. By making Cindy go missing. You could see that perhaps for the first time, Mrs Blackman was now full to bursting with hope. My present to the Blackmans. I'd saved them the inevitable disappointment in their daughter that would surely have come the older Cindy had got. Now they had something very positive to attach to their daughter. Because of me. I'd done them a huge favour so I smiled properly at Mrs Blackman, accepting her unspoken praise.

As an official giver-of-hope, I felt a lot better so my smile was warm and genuine.

But even knowing I'd handed out the prize of eternal hope to her, I still had no idea what to say, so I went for the old chestnut, what everyone had said to me at your wake. 'I'm so sorry, Mrs Blackman.'

Mum laughed over-loudly and said, quietly scolding me, 'There's nothing to be sorry for. Cindy will turn up, Butty.' She huddled closer into Cindy's mother, suffocating her with her inane but well-meaning remarks. 'You just wait and see, Louise, I'm sure she'll turn up as if nothing ever happened, embarrassed at all the fuss she's caused.' She gave Cindy's mother a little squeeze and I thought Mum was playing it all wrong. Overly chirpy – Mum wouldn't or couldn't stop twittering on, too jolly, too upbeat, *too much*. I tuned out, not wanting to hear Mum tweeting and chattering like some kind of mad sparrow.

Of course Cindy may not come back – I personally *knew* she wouldn't – but Mum needed to be more subtle about it. Hope was a fragile thing, and my mother was in danger of ripping it into shreds. It was stupid. Mum carried on and inside

I cringed a little as she said, 'Probably off on some lark with her friends. It happens all the time.'

The pasty-faced Louise Blackman didn't look convinced. Not in the slightest. I wasn't even sure she'd heard. Her eyes scanned the gathered crowd who stood in respectful silence, their faces downturned, holding long thin candles in their hands. She even turned her head from left to right, taking in everyone that was there and even though she couldn't possibly see anyone's faces in the gloom, I realised what she was doing. She was looking for her daughter. Hoping that she'd suddenly see Cindy who'd run to her, arms outstretched.

See, I thought. *There it is. Hope.* Cindy's mother has hope instead of the absolute nothing that death brings.

I'd done the right thing. It wasn't my fault that Cindy was dead. It wasn't. I wish I could have told her mother that, but then I'd be taking her hope away, and that would be cruel. So I said nothing.

A hand touched my shoulder, and I looked up to see Mr Blackman. 'Hello, Charlie. How are you? I'm very sorry for your loss.' His voice was all on one level, his words going neither up nor down as he spoke.

I answered in the same robotic fashion. 'Thank you. I hope they find Cindy soon.'

'Thank you. Why don't you give these out...' He handed me a pile of photocopied A4 pages with a photograph of Cindy's face smiling out from under a caption 'Have you seen this girl?' And then a telephone number to ring if you had any information.

Looking down, I thought how weird it all was, that this was all that was left of Cindy. A crappy smiling blurred picture; her teeth showing grey instead of white because of the poor quality of the printing. Cindy wouldn't have liked that; I was pretty sure.

It was my excuse to escape and taking the pile of

photographs, and a box of coloured drawing pins I wandered off. For a minute, I couldn't think why on earth Cindy's father had given me the pins and then it dawned. I pinned one to a big tree and then merged into the crowd, proudly handing out the cries of paper hope.

Keeping my face suitably sombre, I hid my pride well. Safe and warm, under wraps.

THIRTY

Penny

Three days had passed: Butty-free. Penny wondered what he'd been doing. She was glad that he'd stopped bothering her, but also, in an odd way, she found that she missed him.

She had spent an unpleasant morning wading through pig shit. She was looking for a fiendishly missing fang. Her guts churned as she searched. Not her favourite pastime. And it wasn't one of Keith's. It was almost certainly from Albert.

She'd go and search again later. And this time she'd find it. It absolutely couldn't be anywhere else, so she forced herself to relax a little about it.

The police weren't likely to come searching the grounds of her house, so she had nothing to fear. She had the time to sift through the manure and she knew it would be there, enamel glistening brightly in the surrounding shit.

Just stop panicking.

She moved her brain onto Butty. Never far from her thoughts, she realised. A big part of her wanted to rid herself of him. But there was also the other part of her that felt inextricably beholden to him. She wondered how she'd got

169

herself into this predicament. Having a dependant. Wasn't sure whether she liked the responsibility or not. The whole looking-after-Butty thing felt like tending an earthquake. He was volatile and likely to erupt given any excuse – the face-cutting on Cindy being a case in point – a violent aberration she didn't like to dwell on.

At other times, Butty was just there, a baby tremor, only threatening to become a full-on shock. She preferred him in his dormant phase, when he was just himself – a young, grieving boy: lost and hating in his big bad world. He didn't know what to do and neither did she.

At a loss, knowing her father was as comfortable as he could be for the moment, knowing her mother was out shopping and was then going to the library, Penny made herself tea and sat at the kitchen table. Baggy laid his head on her legs, his gaze upturned so they were staring into each other's eyes. She gave up. Couldn't out-stare him. Smiling, she ruffled his ears and picked up the local gazette that her mother had left out on the table.

Her stomach did a backflip. The central story still focused on missing Cindy. That wasn't what had drawn her attention. Halfway down and taking up the front lower right quadrant of the page was a picture. It screamed out at her until it was all she could see.

A picture of Albert Winter, mole obscenely prominent, was plastered in glorious Technicolor: there on display. Unmistakably him. Identifiably him. 'Local man missing. Worried friends plea for information.'

She read the piece quickly, her throat clicking as she drily swallowed. Her breathing became more ragged as she read on: he was single and a well-known and respected doctor in town. She couldn't believe it. From an unmissable Keith to a very missed Albert.

At least she'd got that right, the fact that he'd looked so

ordinary, so unashamedly boring, so very single. Thank God he hadn't been married with children. That would have made his murder more personal – details of an innocent grieving wife was a level that she didn't want or need to know about. Luckily she'd been spared that.

Reading the article, it wasn't in fact 'pleas from friends as to his whereabouts', that had brought his missing status to the attention of the police. It turned out that it was one of the other doctors at the surgery who had reported him missing when he'd failed to turn up for work. Not a friend at all. That made it far more clinical and let Penny off the emotional hook.

She was glad she hadn't killed a much-loved and adored family man because she knew that any woman could quite easily be involved with a rapist and never have any idea that she shared her bed with a monster. Just another woman in the wrong place again. Happened all the time. Yet another female victim of a man. Hurting innocent women wasn't what Penny was about so she was very relieved but unsurprised that Moley was single.

He'd last been seen on Saturday night when he'd been drinking alone in a pub in town and drunk, had simply vanished into the night, never to be seen again.

Except by me.

Albert the Mole had been a doctor. That was a surprise. A man who cured and treated the sick and the dying. A good man – on the face of it. A doctor. She breathed in and calmed herself down, knowing, absolutely knowing, that that detail did not mean he wasn't a rapist. Any man could be. A doctor could rape, as could a barrister, a barista or a bus driver. Albert hadn't been *her* rapist admittedly, he hadn't smelt of aniseed, he hadn't been in her room, but theoretically, it could have been him.

That thought cheered her somewhat. But not enough to make her fear go away.

If Butty saw the article in the newspaper, he'd recognise the name. And he'd contact her. He'd think he had something to capture her with. Something to make her his. And he'd be right.

Her mind scampered around her head, unable to settle, unable to see through the initial shock of seeing Moley in the newspaper and totally unable to make sense of any of it. Fear kicked in. Fear for herself and her parents.

Sadness and premature guilt joined the kicking party. Supposing she was caught? Supposing Butty told the police. Supposing her parents found out that their daughter killed would-be rapists. How could she protect them?

On a more practical level, she made herself go through the mechanics of actually taking Albert from the street, the killing of him, the disposal of him. She sipped from her mug and felt a little better. Everything was covered. She'd left no evidence of her involvement. Nothing could be traced back to her.

Butty remained her only problem. He'd seen the credit card. Penny suspected that he also recognised in her, as she recognised in him, the propensity for violence that they shared. That same madness. Sitting and brewing and waiting to be released when either of them saw fit. Yes, Butty had only killed by accident.

So he says.

She wasn't sure she believed him though. And that's what bound them together. That terrible recognition of each other's frailties.

Or each other's strengths. Difficult to know the difference, sometimes. It depended on the context. To kill a rapist was good, no doubt about that. To kill an innocent man, well... was there such a thing? A good man? Pre-rape, she'd never had such a low opinion of men. The rape had changed everything. Irrevocably and forever. For good or for bad, it didn't really matter. She still had no doubt that she had to carry on, doing what she did, her belief in her taking revenge not wavering. And for that she was grateful.

But the boy was most definitely a risk for her. As she supposed, she was for him. She could, but would never, tell the police about Butty's involvement in Cindy's death. It wasn't ever anything she'd do, but the boy surprisingly had absolute faith in her loyalty to him.

Butty was like having trouble waiting in the wings. She knew she had to nip his curiosity and fascination with her in the bud before he did or said something stupid. Equally, she was confident that in some strange way, they shared an understanding and up to a point, other than his naivete and lack of knowledge of how the world worked, due in part to his young age, she was fairly confident that she could trust him.

She stood up and washed her mug.

Went back to the pigs.

Looked again for the elusive tooth.

THIRTY-ONE

Butty

I had been playing Avoidance with my mother. Like a card game, but not as fun. I had definitely *not* been playing Denial with my father. I thought that a game too far, with him the likely winner. At this point, I didn't want to lose to Dad. It felt like a risky and unnecessary move and one that might prove seriously harmful for yours truly.

What would you do, Jack? What would your advice be to me, right now?

Run for the hills, you'd probably say. *And don't look back.*

I could run away. That was definitely an option, but where would I run to? And what about Penny? I couldn't and didn't want to leave her. She was my friend, my only friend, and I couldn't desert her. It wouldn't be fair on either of us.

And anyway, it was easier to avoid my denying-Dad because he now refused to come out of the attic. It was his old familiar world, but now his only one. Upstairs was my father's Inside world; his Outside world had disappeared and all he was left with was his stupid trains, now made worse by his disturbed vision of how the world should have been. With Jack. Not me.

Mum didn't venture up there much – only when absolutely

necessary. Like feeding time. She left meals at the bottom of the ladder which were collected, eaten and the plates left, awaiting collection, scraped clean. Food eaten. Dad lived on.

He seemed to have stopped working entirely. His study was actually slightly dirty. I knew because I'd gone in there and run my fingers across his desk. Left a satisfying slice of clean through the dusty coating on the mahogany wood. I suspected Mum was worrying about his lack of work as I assumed that he wasn't making any money, accounting for other people's money. She didn't seem too bothered though, so I didn't over-worry that one myself. I had enough on my plate just getting through life intact.

I also decided to ignore the suspicion that I had that Dad was up there in the attic, plotting and scheming. Like some mad demon. I didn't know where his brain had taken him, where his fantasies about good people and bad people had taken him, and where that left me. Was he planning to take me? On his stupid bloody bus.

I didn't feel safe.

It was nearly Christmas.

But not in this house.

Mum was often out, coming and going, and frantically smiling and bravely carrying on with life. Avoided talking about *it*.

I ambled around the place, eating, watching television, gazing out of the window. Finally, so bored I could barely bear to stand, I sat at the kitchen table and picked up the local newspaper from town. *The Gazette.*

I was genuinely pleased that the search for Cindy was still front-page news and almost forgot myself – found myself hoping they'd find her. That was hope for you. A powerful thing.

My eyes skittered across the page, seeing another photograph about a missing local man. I almost skimmed past it, turning to something else, before I saw his name. It was a shock seeing it in print. Knowing that he had some connection with Penny, the letters of his name looked huge, as if they'd been typed in extra bold black. They leapt from the page like tiny shiny inky alerts: Albert Winter. The not-boyfriend of Penny. Studying the photograph of him, I knew immediately that there was no way that he was Penny's boyfriend. He was ugly. I wasn't stupid enough to assume that she'd only go for handsome men, but this man was totally not her thing.

I had been right. He must have been a bad man and he'd been in Penny's house. How else would his credit card have been lying right there on her carpet? I couldn't imagine that she'd pick-pocketed him or had stolen his wallet. It wasn't in her nature. That was something else I just knew. Because me and Penny were partners and partners knew each other well.

In fact, reading on, I discovered that he'd last been seen on the night that I'd visited her house. Why had he been there? Had she invited him? Were they friends? What had happened? What had she done to him? Why had I even just thought that?

I wondered if she'd tell the police that she'd seen him, but knew that she wouldn't. She was guilty of something, but I wasn't sure what. That's why she was so flustered when I found his card. It was like I'd caught her out. He shouldn't have been there or why would Penny be so put out when I turned up? As if I'd interrupted them. Why had she taken so long to open the door after I'd rung the doorbell? She must be hiding something. Nothing else made sense.

Something bad had happened in her house.

I texted Penny.

We need to talk about Albert.

THIRTY-TWO

Penny

P enny's mobile vibrated. She knew without looking who it
would be. She read his message. Texted back:

Come to parents' house. In an hour.

Now that she was again up to her ankles in pig excrement,
she was determined to find the tooth. Once found, she'd allow
herself to concentrate on the Butty/Albert problem. Give it
her full attention. Confident, she knew her story was well
prepared and believable.

It was back-breaking work, bending down and
painstakingly sifting through every piece of turd that she could.
She changed position, squatting and checking as she shuffled
forward in her wellington boots. Like an organised grid search.
All the others had been easy to find; this one felt like it had
gone missing deliberately, just to freak her out.

Her mind was numb. The search didn't require any
thought, so she was able to close down her mind and give total
focus to the job at hand. It meant that for the moment, she

could lose herself in what was probably a pointless task anyway. But it still had to be done. Just in case.

So intent was she in her organised sifting, that she didn't hear the approach of Butty who startled her, his voice sudden and loud in her ear. 'Hello, Penny. Thought I'd come early. Nothing better to do.'

She catapulted into a standing position, her naked hands brown and sludgy – all the better to find things with. 'Jesus Christ, do not creep up on me like that.' Holding her hand to her chest, she was uncaring that she spread crap all over her coat. It was old and was worn for precisely this work: mucking out the pigs. 'I told you to come in an hour. Not now this minute. I'm busy, as you can see.' She held her hands out to him as proof. 'Why don't you go back into the house, and I'll join you in a minute?'

'What are you doing?'

'Cleaning out the pigs.'

'With your hands?'

'This isn't twenty questions, Butty. Go and wait in the house. Please.'

'Where are the pigs then?'

'In the bloody barn. While I gather up all their shit, and then I compost it down, see, over there in that big container. Then I use it as manure for the gardens I do. It's especially good for the roses.' She felt like she was over-explaining and stopped herself from talking any more.

'Why don't you use a shovel? That would be easier, wouldn't it? Instead of your hands. Gross or what?'

'Go and wait in the house, go on, go.'

'I want to see the pigs.'

'Fuck's sake, Butty. This isn't a zoo, and this isn't visiting time at the local piggery.'

'Go on. Please.' He waited and then said, 'And then we can talk about Albert.'

Bloody touché, she thought. But knowing she couldn't carry on searching for the missing tooth in front of the boy, she agreed to show him the pigs. It would be just her luck that with the next sweep of her hand she'd bring it up and out and there it would be: a glistening white tooth, and she'd have to explain why it was there, in a pile of pig shit.

'Come on then.'

Walking briskly, she led him to the barn. Inside she pointed. 'There they are. We've just got three at the moment. They're pets. Dad used to rear them, but since he's been ill, he sold them all off and we kept these ones. Just because.'

Excited like a small child who'd never seen pigs before – which he obviously had – he approached them, stepping quietly and gently nearer and nearer the animals, before leaning his arms on the top of the metal gate. He rested his boot on the lower horizontal rung. She took in the delight on his face as he stood and watched them. His smile was simple and genuine.

'What are their names?'

Stopping her sentimental musings, Penny wiped her hands on her top and pointed at each of them in turn, and said, 'That's Porky, that's Bacon and that one's Chop.'

Butty looked at her, laughing. It sounded like a laugh full of real amusement. 'Wow. You really put some time and effort into naming them, didn't you? Very original.' He snorted with fun. Teasing her.

Shrugging, Penny said, 'I like their names. They suit them, don't you think? Anyway, now you've seen them, let's go and get a drink inside. Don't know about you, but I'm filthy and freezing. Come on.'

Walking back past the outside pig enclosure, Butty stopped and peered down at something in the mound of manure. 'What's that?'

Penny instantly felt sick. 'What's what?'

Keep calm. Breathe.

He pointed at something and bent his knees, his bottom resting on the back of his ankles, to get a better look. Joining him, her knees popped as she again semi-knelt on the ground. Her eyes flew around, wanting to identify and grab whatever it was that Butty was about to pick up and rip it out of his hands before he had a chance to work out what he was seeing. Prayed it wasn't the tooth.

She was sure she'd accounted for all of Cindy's. The problem being that she couldn't be sure, to the exact number, how many teeth Cindy had. Because when she'd taken the girl into the Trumpet Room, Penny had been panicking and hurrying and wanted it all over. She'd actually forgotten to count them – that simple, that stupid.

After the final disposal, when it was too late, Penny had thought about it and ruled out the girl having wisdom teeth – too young. But she might have had a cap or God knew what. If she'd had an extraction, that made it harder and impossible to know if she was looking for a tooth that didn't exist. It bothered her. Her lack of professionalism in not knowing the number of teeth she was dealing with, rankled. It wasn't like her to be so slapdash. Then again, she blamed her inefficiency on being handed a random body of a child to get rid of, and not being in the right frame of mind to behave with her normal attention to detail.

And the undeniable fact that she genuinely grieved for the dead young girl. It had all been so wrong.

And now, here was Butty, sticking his hand into the manure, his index and thumb extended, ready to pick something up. *Don't be a tooth. Don't be a tooth.* Like pincers, his fingers pinched together and dipping them into the shit, he triumphantly held something aloft. They both looked at it: it was a small ring. A very small ring. Relief swamped her, although she wasn't sure who the ring could possibly belong to.

The boy brought the ring up close to his eyes and squinting, he rolled it slowly in his fingers, peering intently at the inside of the gold loop. Startling her, he jumped back; reacting like he'd been burnt, and almost fell over. Dropped the ring. Picked it up again, this time more gingerly. Wiped his fingers down his legs. His face was ashen. 'What the bloody hell is this doing here?'

Penny sensed immediately that she had to be very careful. He knew what it was. She didn't. 'How do you mean?'

'It's Cindy's toe-ring. Look inside the band.'

She took it from him and did as he told her. Nodded up at him, acknowledging that she'd seen. He said, 'That's her initials. Just like Jack said. I've seen her wearing it, in the summer when she had sandals on. There, can you see? C.B. Cindy Blackman. What's her toe-ring doing in this pile of pig shit?'

She was angry. Why hadn't he told her that Cindy wore a toe-ring? Thankfully, *he* wasn't angry. Not really. Not yet. He was more freaked out. Revolted. He took several paces backwards, wanting distance from the toe-ring. She thought it was the personal nature of the find that perhaps brought home to him the fact that it had been a real live dead girl that he'd asked her to make disappear.

Keeping her face unremarkable, giving nothing away, biting down on her rising panic, she said, 'I wondered where that had got to. Here, give it to me. I'll get rid of it. Stupid me. It must have fallen off. No worries. No harm done.'

'But what's it doing here, Penny? How did it come off? It's a toe-ring, for God's sake. Why was she barefoot and why was she here at all?'

Taking control, as the appropriate adult again, she adopted a suitable authoritative tone. 'Don't question me like I've done something wrong here, Butty. You asked me to dispose of Cindy's body. I did. I had to undress her. Completely. If her body was ever found – and it won't be – I promise, but *if*, then I didn't want her to be identified by her clothing. The toe-ring must have fallen off when I put her in the car. See, nothing sinister going on. Stop panicking.'

'But why was she here in the first place?'

'I've just explained. Do I have to spell it out for you? I had to undress her for reasons already given. Where exactly do you think would be the best place for me to do that? In the lay-by where I picked her up? In the back of the jeep in the field where I buried her? I don't think so. I undressed her in the privacy and safety of the Trumpet Room, knowing I wouldn't be disturbed. I gave her some dignity after the indignities that she'd already suffered.'

He dropped his eyes in shame.

'I then transferred her naked body from the Trumpet Room back into the jeep. Past the pigs. Okay? Satisfied?'

Penny was angry at having to explain herself to a child, for whom she'd had to get rid of a dead body. 'Where's the gratitude, Butty? God Almighty. A thank-you might not go amiss instead of a bloody grilling. Just who do you think you are? Remember who did who the favour here.'

He thought it through. Everything that she'd said. Fortunately, and finally, he nodded slowly. 'Okay. That makes sense. Sorry. But you really should tell me where you buried her, you know. Where's the field? Why the big secret? It's not like I'm going to tell anyone, is it? But I think I'd feel better knowing, that's all.'

'This is not a game. It's also not why you came here, is it? I thought you wanted to talk about Albert.'

He nodded again, his face sobering. 'Yeah, we definitely need to talk about him. You need to tell me exactly what happened, because it doesn't look good for you.'

She laughed. 'What cheap crappy films have you been

watching? No one talks like that in real life. Good God. "It doesn't look good for you." You crack me up, you really do.'

Striding back to the house she couldn't feel less like cracking up.

But this time, unlike the unexpected appearance of the bloody toe-ring, she was prepared.

The story of Albert the very bad Mole was to be told and Butty would believe everything she said. Already, she almost believed it herself.

THIRTY-THREE

Penny

'You've read the paper, I assume,' said Penny. 'That's why you're here. You recognised the name of the missing man.'

He nodded again; his hands clasped loosely together in his lap. They both took a sip of what now felt like their favourite shared tipple: hot chocolate.

'Tell me what happened. Why was he in your home?' he said.

Holding her index finger in the air, she waggled it back and forth. 'No. That is not how this conversation is going to go. First you have to tell me something, or I'm not saying diddley.'

He raised his eyebrows in surprise, not expecting Penny's response. He'd assumed he had the upper hand. 'What do you want me to tell you?'

'How did it make you feel when you cut Cindy's face? When you slashed it? After she was dead and there was really no need to touch her anymore. You'd already cut her stomach and arms, that would have had the desired look you were going for. I want you to tell me how it made you feel when you did that.'

Straight away, his arms crossed and he slung one leg over his knee, entwined one ankle around the other. Defensive. 'Speak, Butty. If you think we're partners, I need to know how you felt when you hurt Cindy. Tell me.'

'I didn't hurt her. She was already dead.' He made a show of scratching his nose. Thinking. 'If I tell you, you'll tell me why Albert was in your house? Because don't expect me to believe it was coincidental that his credit card was there on the floor on the night he went missing. Something happened.'

'Fair enough. You have yourself a deal.'

She was unhappy at the deal she'd had to strike, but she was willing to give up her truth, *some of it*, if it meant she found the real boy inside the angry casing. This wasn't a game: she had to know just how out of control his fury and hatred was. How far he would go. If he had to. She needed to know exactly who and what she was dealing with.

She needed to know how to cure him.

Needed to make sure he didn't turn into her.

He pitched his head back and stared at the ceiling, his hands cradling the back of his head. 'It made me feel... I don't really know how to describe it. Sort of excited. And I don't mean dirty excited. I mean, excited at how naughty it felt. How bad. How really wrong. I cut her more than once because I could. It's funny you asking me because I was literally interested in how it felt, when I was doing it. I was aware of thinking *This feels weird*. It was strangely... satisfying. Final. I mean, she was already dead, so you can't get any more final than that, can you? But to me, personally, it was like doing the worst, baddest thing in the whole wide world, and it made me feel good. Like I had some superpower or something. Do you understand?'

He held up his hand. 'Before you answer, I'd like to add that it also confused me. All that feeling from a little cutting of something that was already dead, I couldn't get my head around it, especially as I knew I wasn't physically hurting her. Wasn't causing her pain. Because she wasn't alive. And that made me feel sort of better about the whole thing.'

They sat in silence for a bit. Butty said, 'I'm sorry for what I did to her. I really am.'

Penny believed him, but had to ask, 'Were you experimenting? Would you do it again?'

The boy's eyes met hers. Gently his head shook from side to side. 'Genuinely? I couldn't honestly answer that. I don't think I'd do it again, but everything's changed since Jack died. I've changed. My parents have changed. Life has changed and I don't really know who I am or what I'm doing anymore. I don't think I'm really bad, I'm just not sure about *any*thing at the moment. You know?'

'Yeah, I do know. I understand.'

They sat in silence, digesting his words. Penny was sad and Butty was, what? Bad? Mad? She felt there was an awful similarity between them, and by encouraging the relationship between them, worried that she'd somehow, in a stupid and misguided way, created some sort of *folie á deux*. Would he have gone so off the rails had they not met? Had he picked up on her own madness, and was trying to emulate it?

She bloody hoped not.

Butty leant forward, propping his elbows on his knees and cupping his chin. The dog shifted its weight on the boy's feet, its body now lying across them. 'Your turn,' Butty said. 'What did you do to Albert Winter?'

She made an exaggerated sigh, as if loath to share the story but knowing she must. 'I didn't *do* anything to him. Well… not that he didn't deserve anyway. I was at home, upset after Jack's funeral, tired after working all afternoon in a client's garden, and I was just relaxing, watching television, when the doorbell rang.' *Untrue.*

Pausing, she drank again from her mug. 'Although it was late, I didn't realise how late, so, not really thinking about it, I opened the door. And he just barged in, pushed past me and fell into the room. Drunk. It was stupid of me.' She rolled her eyes, trying to keep the story light, but not too light. Striking a balance between plausible and painting herself in a sympathetic light. Feeling deceitful, she had to remind herself that she'd murdered Albert Winter so tricking a child wasn't the worst sin she'd committed that week.

Butty's eyes rounded in horror. 'What did you do? What did *he* do?'

'I wasn't sure what he wanted at first. I hoped, although I knew it wasn't likely, but I still hoped that perhaps he'd stumbled into my house, mistaking it for maybe his own, or a friend's. I know that sounds ridiculous. Sounds really stupid. If someone told me that story, I wouldn't believe them. I'd think they were lying. But that's how it was. I couldn't make any sense of it. It was like a sensory overload. I suddenly had a man lying on my carpet and I couldn't compute the information. It was like, what the hell?'

'What a bastard. Who did he think he was? He must have been slaughtered. How can you even get that drunk?'

'Like I'd know.' She smiled but realised Butty didn't get the joke. 'Anyway, I said that was what I *hoped* was happening. That he was drunk and confused and that once he realised his mistake, he'd bugger off politely. But it didn't work out like that.'

'What happened?'

Butty had forgotten his drink, his face avid for the story. Penny had prepared the telling in advance of him coming, had practised it, but now she wavered. Maybe a smidge of truth, only a morsel, might make it all sound more believable. Slotting in a little reality always made lying sound more palatable, so much easier to accept. And she thought she owed him: he'd been honest, so he deserved some honesty back from her.

Holding his gaze, she kept her tone even and calm. 'My dad, when he was at university, used to play baseball.' *True.*

'He gave me his bat as a present. For protection when I moved out into my bungalow. I love it. It makes me feel safe.' *True.*

'It's always propped up in the corner by my front door, in case the Bogey man comes a-calling. I've never actually hit anyone with it, obviously, but when this man came hurtling through the door and landed on the floor in front of me, I automatically picked it up, thinking I'd threaten him with it.' *Not true at all.*

Butty said, 'You should have whacked him over the head with it straight away. He could have been a real nutjob. You know, a pervert. Or worse. You know, like maybe he'd tie you up, rape you, torture you. Even kill you. How would you know?'

Her heart jumped in her chest when he said the word 'rape.' She ignored it, and carried on, with a forced breezy tone, squeezing out the words from her suddenly constricted vocal cords. It was like she'd forgotten how to string a sentence together. She wasn't enjoying lying to Butty, but she faked it.

'You're a strange boy. To leap to that scenario immediately: that he was a psychosexual torturing maniac.'

'Not such a leap. Not even a hop, skip and a jump. I just know that real life can be very crappy. Shit happens that you don't even see coming, haven't even ever imagined happening. It's why life is such a blast. Never fails to amuse.' He smiled sadly and then slapped his face gently with both of his hands. 'Right, Butty is back in the room. Bet you wondered where my scintillating witty views on the world had gone?' His pale cheeks pinked up after the slapping. 'Then what happened?'

'He got up. Saw me holding the bat and came towards me.

Staggering. He was so pissed he couldn't walk straight. I didn't want to get backed into a corner, so I held the bat up, swung it in the air a few times close to his face and asked him what he wanted. He said, "You." Obviously, it wasn't what I wanted to hear.'

'I bet. So he *was* a perv. Told you. Knew it.'

'It was him saying "You" that changed the situation. Made it worse. Made him more frightening. More of a real threat. I could feel he was dangerous: he seemed too big and too tall and heavy, standing there in my sitting room. He was a risk. To me. We circled each other for a bit, him wobbling all over the place, me gripping the baseball bat, keeping him at bay, waiting for him to attack.'

'And did he?'

'He lunged at me, and being a stupid drunken nasty twat, fell over. And *then* I hit him on the back of the head. Hard.' *True.*

'Good for you. The crowd cheers, the people roar, the winner is declared.' Butty laughed. And stopped quickly. 'Did you kill him?'

'What do you think?'

She watched closely as his face frowned, concentrating on her question. Interested in his answer, she quietly waited, drinking her now only-faintly-hot hot chocolate. He rested his forehead on his steepled fingers. As if a million pounds rested on him giving the right answer. Finally, he lifted his head and they stared into each other's eyes. Both fascinated with each other's responses.

'I think you might have. I think you definitely *could* kill someone. If you needed to.' He paused. 'If you wanted to.'

His voice was very quiet now – almost whispering.

Awe had crept into his voice and he was looking up at her with – and yes, there it was, definitely – respect on his face.

He's impressed. And he really shouldn't be.

Then he said it. 'What did it feel like when you hit him? When you killed him. How did it make *you* feel?'

The million-dollar question.

'Hitting Albert made me feel shocked.' *True.*

'But it was oddly gratifying. Knowing that I could incapacitate a man and be the only one left standing.' *True.*

'I felt powerful and that I'd righted a wrong: him coming into my life and me telling him, "No, you can't do that." So I felt righteous.' *Again true.*

'I didn't feel guilty, or bad, or frightened. I was taking back control, which is my right.' *Couldn't be more true.*

Butty looked shocked. 'You killed him?'

Penny laughed. 'No, I didn't kill him. What do you think I am? I stood over him, checked that he was still breathing and waited. I thought about calling the police, but I preferred handling it myself. Knew I could win. I could beat him and to me that was very important.' *Again, true.*

Butty threw his hands in the air in front of him, impatient. 'And…?'

'And, he finally came to. Threw up all over the bloody place. Then he sat up while I stood over him, with my bat. He looked up at me and he was all confused. I told him to get up, tapped him again with the baseball bat, not so hard, on the side of his head and said he had to get up and leave, or I'd kill him.'

She didn't know why she'd added that in. Unnecessary, but she had become so involved in the story, that she forgot that she was lying. She could picture the scene she was describing. And was very glad the reality had been worse for Albert Mole.

'He got up, holding his hands out in front of him, like he was warding off evil, and he backed away. But where could he go? There you were, knocking on the front door, which he heard. His face went all panicky. I put my finger to my mouth, meaning for him to be quiet because you were right there, and pushed him out into the back garden and told him to go.'

'And he just left?'

'He not only left, he thanked me. For not killing him, as would have been justifiable, I think, under the circs. Anyway, that's why I took so long answering the door to you. I was clearing up his vomit, tidying up the place as he'd knocked over a chair. And as it turned out, dropped his bloody credit card out of his pocket. What a moron. And that, Butty Hawthorne, is the story of the missing Albert Winter. He left my house, alive and well with a bit of a headache and he *is* actually missing. I have no idea where he is, and I don't care.'

'You didn't kill him?'

'No, I didn't kill him. And, more importantly, he didn't kill me.'

Butty waited for a bit, absorbing it all and then he stood up and walked over to her. Bending down, he kissed her on the cheek. 'Good. I'm glad Albert Winter is alive and missing. That's more hope given. Hope is good.'

'You're right, Butty. You should remember that yourself. Hope. There is always hope.'

'I hope we're partners now. Because I won't tell anyone your story. What's the point? I'm your partner and your friend.'

Penny hugged him. 'Yes. We're definitely partners. Forever.'

THIRTY-FOUR

Butty

I was happy. A big word for a boy like me, but after my talk
with Penny, her assurance that Cindy was indeed safely
buried in a field and would never be found, I felt calmer. More
importantly, after our conversation about my cutting and her
baseball-whacking, we seemed to have come to a kind of
understanding. She hadn't killed Albert Winter, he *was* missing,
and everything was okay.

And we were definitely partners now.

I walked into my house and found the kitchen was
unexpectedly crowded with people. People I'd never seen, lots I
had. All attention was focused on my mother who was holding
court, flipchart at the ready, black marker in one hand, a pencil
behind her ear and a ruler resting inches from her other hand:
one finger absent-mindedly tapping it. I wondered what she
was going to do with it.

Now she was focused in an unnatural way, her eyes
concentrated but blank. Only recognisably blank if you knew
our mother. And I did.

Normally – before your death – her eyes had been soft and
warm. They'd crinkled when she laughed. Now there was

nothing behind them. She was hiding behind two empty sockets, blinded by grief, but pretending so hard that she was okay that it hurt to look at her.

Cindy's mother, sat like a statue, grey-faced but apparently attentive, leaning forward to hear Mum's words, as if they could save her. Others sat taking notes, nodding wisely, looking respectfully mournful, and there was a lot of hugging and squeezing of arms. There were some tears, a lot of tissues, a few red chaffed noses and too many phony simpering expressions: insincere smiles, pretending loads, heavily weighted, but meaning nothing.

'Butty,' said Mum. 'I'm so glad you're here. We're sorting things out. Working out how to get Cindy back. Working with the police on where to search. Please join us. You can help too.'

Avoid, kiss or promise. I decided to follow in my mother's footsteps and join her for this particular event, on the road to avoidance. We'd walk hand in hand. Her chosen route seemed to be working for her, and I took up my customary position, accepting the path of least resistance. It was a familiar journey for me, so used was I to being one step behind you, Jack. It's what I did best, what I was used to. I settled in for the ride, following this time behind my mother, instead of you.

It was difficult watching Mum orchestrating the meeting and knowing at the same time that she was missing a son. You were missing forever though, not Cindy-missing where people hoped you'd at some point put in an appearance and everything would be all right. You weren't missing. You were dead. Gone. Finito.

There was no hope for you.

Cindy still might turn up. That's what this room full of neighbours and friends thought. What her mother yearned for.

I was the only one who knew that she wouldn't turn up. Not ever.

My mother's quiet inability to talk about you was so loud, I wished I had earplugs to drown out the bloody great noise that boomed silently from her. Felt like clapping my hands over my ears to drown out her anguish. It wasn't difficult to know why she was behaving like this: it was achingly heart-breaking, and I hated watching her self-destruct so politely.

Perhaps it was simply easier for her to concentrate her world on someone else's tragedy; made her own more distant.

Not being realistic about your absence was what Dad and I were doing as well. I thought my way was best, though. Anger got things done. Avoidance avoided and denial denied. Not much you could do with either. At least my rage gave me impetus.

Having to dig around a bit for my good manners, I smiled at the assembled mess of people, but thought it was a mess I could do without. I had enough of my own mess to wade through. I'd pass on this one.

Mrs Evans, of the local shop fame, tried to get my attention. She gave me a sort of conspiratorial look: after all, she'd seen you dead – clearly, in her mind, that made her special; a member of some exclusive club. Trying not to look as if she were enjoying the occasion too much, she clamped her lips together to stem the gossip which must already be building up behind her tongue, causing a word-jam.

It appeared that this was headquarters for the 'Find Cindy' campaign. New leaflets with a different Cindy photograph sat neatly on the table. I wondered if my mother was canvassing for votes in some weird election with God, and guessed the two sides, us – the Hawthornes – and them – the Blackmans – were fighting to change what had happened to their respective children. They had both lost, both had a dead child: only one of them knew it.

My mother importantly shuffled already-tidy piles and then glanced at other papers and scanned them as if they were top secret: the contents only for those who needed to know. That would be Mum. Self-elected commander-in-chief of operations.

Cindy's mother put her hand up, *yes, really*, as if she were a child at school, and said, 'My husband was thinking of offering a reward. It would encourage people to come forward, don't you think?'

Mum shook her head and managed to look like she was tutting without actually doing it. 'No, no, Louise. I don't think that's a good idea at all. The police wouldn't like it. It would only encourage dishonest information from greedy people, wanting money. The police would spend their whole time having to follow up every reported fake sighting of Cindy. It's not a good idea at all. It would only waste time and time is precious. No, no, Louise. Definitely not.'

My mother, trying to be kind, but coming over condescending and thoughtless. Mrs Blackman sat back in her chair – crushed and feeling foolish. Wanting to help her out, I said, 'It's not a bad idea, Mrs Blackman. But if people knew anything, they wouldn't need persuading to come forward. If they really knew anything, they'd say. Without promises of money. I think Mum's right.'

She'd just said it all wrong.

Cindy's mother glanced at me briefly, so deflated that I wasn't sure she'd heard me. It was clear that she thought I was only a child and therefore could offer little sensible advice, but she wasn't aware that as I stood there, if I chose to simply open my mouth, I could destroy her entire world. Just like that.

For a moment, I toyed with the idea, angry at her dismissal of me, but equally I knew what strange things grief could do to a person, so I gave her a break. Also, I wasn't cruel for the sake of it – I had no reason to further hurt Mrs Blackman. Thought I'd done quite enough on that front. As resident accidental-killer, I took a stool and manoeuvred it into the corner so that I could better watch the proceedings.

First, I noticed Tommy standing near the fridge. And behind him, Willy. Had they buddied-up? Was Willy that alone that he now sought care and protection from Tommy? I couldn't believe it. If so, it made a mockery of our friendship – was he that fragile that he was willing to be looked after by *any*one? That wasn't a person I wanted anything to do with. I nodded at Willy, making a point of overly bending my body around in order to see past Tommy, taking care that Willy saw that I knew he was hiding from me, and raised my hand to him. Smiled.

No response.

Silly boy.

Tommy sneered, comfortable and relaxed and safe in the knowledge that I wouldn't beat him up again in front of everyone; assured and secure amongst so many witnesses.

Sillier boy.

I could do whatever I wanted, but I'd lost interest in Tommy. I was above all that.

Taking in their united front against Butty-the-bonkers, I was strangely and forever detached from them. In an instant, I cut them loose. Suddenly both of them appeared as if they were the school children that they really were. Gone was the bully who I'd been frightened of for years and protected from by you, Jack. Gone was the vulnerable boy whom *I'd* protected for so long. In their place was an idiot and a saddo.

Crossing my legs, I felt a million years older than both of them. As if I existed on another, more adult planet. A one-boy planet, but a grown-up, mature and suddenly developed one, where the air I breathed was cleaner and so much more honest than either of them could ever imagine.

Silently and without moving, I deleted both of them from my orbit. I was my own star, shining bright. Penny swirled around inside my head, and together I thought we could take over the world. Neither of us had the time to waste with morons like Tommy and Willy. They were two giant black holes full of hot air: about as useful as intergalactic debris. Realising that they needed me more than I needed them, made me feel superior and untouchable. Beyond their grasp. They didn't know that I'd moved on, but I had. I didn't need anyone. I'd moved to a higher plane.

And then there was Penny. She was my saviour and my leader. I'd do anything for her. She'd taken over from you, Jack. Become everything that you had been to me, but better. We were equals. I was never equal with you. I hadn't even tried. I'd just followed you blindly and accepted.

Now my eyes were wide open.

I closed them and happily allowed myself to jettison into space, leaving the weaklings behind.

Mum's voice interrupted my astrological travelling. 'Now see here, Louise.'

Opening my eyes, I finally understood the presence of the ruler. It was for banging self-importantly on the flipchart. Mid-bang, she took it in both hands and bent it so that it arced, threatening to snap. She then tapped it against the side of her thigh: *Six of the best, anyone?* Back to the flipchart banging. 'These are the areas that have already been searched by the police. You can see how organised they've been on the map. They've used something like a grid system, and they've covered every inch. But this is where we come in. Us, this group, the people who know and love Cindy. I've spoken to the officer in charge of the case, and he's happy for us to go over these areas again – I've highlighted them in red. All on the understanding that I keep him updated and let him know where we shall be searching and how many of us there will be, et cetera et cetera. It's more than possible that we could find something that they overlooked or missed purely because they don't know and love

Cindy as we do. We'll also ambush the town, flood it with posters and leaflets. We can do this, people.'

Vote for me, vote for me, I am your leader.

There were reverential murmurings of appreciation at this plan. Except from Mrs Blackman, who remained completely silent. She'd disassociated herself from the stupid blathering of my mother, and I for one couldn't blame her.

She kept on checking her phone and then excused herself, mumbling that she had to check in with her husband who'd remained at home. Waiting for Cindy.

It was all very sad. And it was very strange sitting there in my corner of the universe, knowing where Cindy really was. In a field, naked and buried.

Without her toe-ring.

Eventually, after a lot more of nothing, they all drifted away, back to their happy Inside worlds, breathing sighs of relief that it wasn't them, their children were safe, saying quietly so that no one else could hear, 'There but for grace of God go I.' Thinking they'd got it made, so smug and grateful for their lives, thinking they'd escaped and nothing bad would ever happen to them – the Outside world wouldn't get them.

If only they knew.

Mum slumped in her chair, all out of pretending. I went over to her and let her hug me. I hugged her back.

'Thank God for you, Butty. Do you want to know a secret?'

I nodded, feigning enthusiasm.

'I've been thinking. Let's run away. We'll leave your father to his trains. He'll be fine. We can start life again. Together. How about it? Just you and me. Would you like that?'

And there it was: the ultimate avoidance. *Let's just run away and pretend none of it ever happened.* A new life, without you, without Dad – that bit didn't sound too bad – but also without Penny.

I couldn't leave her.

And I wouldn't.

Smiling, knowing that it would never happen, I kissed Mum on her cheek and held her hand. 'Yeah, course, Mum. Sounds great.'

Then I went to bed.

In your bed.

THIRTY-FIVE

Penny

T hey'd all eaten an early lunch; possibly better described as brunch, in her father's bedroom, on trays balanced on their knees. He was feeling better, was fully saturated with oxygen for the time being, and the three of them were enjoying a meal together where he could breathe without coughing. For now.

Penny sat on the end of his bed, whilst her mother relaxed back into the armchair, surrounded by cushions. They chatted easily and happily like any normal, loving family. Baggage's nose rested on her father's slippered feet: both seemed content with the arrangement. It added a homely feel to the occasion. It was where she belonged.

Not out in the night, killing men.

This was a place where she could be truly herself. Her home, where she didn't have to be a grown-up. A child, adored by her parents. Whether she was thirty years old or three years old, it didn't matter. She would always be their baby. Penny was accepted for who she was. As damaged as she was. It was ironic that it was here, in this family home, that she had been so wholly defiled. And what made it worse was that her parents had been so physically close, but unable to help. Her heart cracked a little every time she was with her mother and father. It was greedily snatched happiness in her world of hurt and hate. A beautiful relationship with them – spoilt.

By a man who smelt of aniseed.

No one would ever guess at Penny's other life: her bungalow and her men. She wondered why she couldn't be happy with this slice of domestic normality in which she was now firmly wrapped; why it wasn't enough for her. Why the constant need for revenge? It wouldn't leave her alone, this need to punish men.

It is my only way to salvation, she thought. She enjoyed her role as an avenging angel and she was good at it. But would it save her? Penny didn't know.

Her mother cut into her thoughts with all the subtlety of a meat cleaver. 'What's eating you, Penny? Is it shame?'

'Where did that come from, Mum? Why should I be feeling bloody shameful? What have *I* done?'

Her mother smiled knowingly, crossing her swollen ankles, one over the other, keeping her pepper-grinding body concertinaed. 'I thought I might surprise you into answering. Where's your smile? Your real, knock 'em dead smile? That's what I want for Christmas and it's what you'll give me, right? Not much for your old mother to ask for, is it?'

'Fuck's sake, Mum. I can still smile. I just don't feel like it, right now this second. Here, look – here you go.' She pulled her lips back in a parody of happiness, convincing neither herself nor her parents.

'You've bloody buried it, Penny, that's what you've done,' her father said. 'Hope you only used a trowel, and not a fucking great shovel. Bury a smile too deep and you may lose it forever.' He smiled to remind her how it was done.

Penny did smile then, but it wasn't a full-beam one. It was a watered down, diluted one: hardly worthy of her natural smile that she knew was a magnificent thing, although deep down she did wonder if it still existed. She worried that she'd had it raped right out of her.

She pushed out a laugh. 'Stop it both of you. Leave me alone. I'm not three years old. I'm all grown up so bugger off and tell me what's happening tomorrow night. Christmas Eve.'

Her mother rolled her eyes. 'What are you expecting? It's the same old thing we do every year, thank God. We all love it so why change it? But as you appear to have forgotten, I'll remind you of the night's festivities: dinner, drinks, one present each, more drinks, bed.'

Putting her tray on the floor, her mother bent forward. 'But I tell you what, why don't we add something a little different this year?'

Suspicious, Penny squinted her eyes. 'Like what?'

'We could ask the Hawthornes over for drinks tomorrow night. I know it's short notice, but it would be a nice gesture, don't you think? Think how empty that house must feel without Jack there. Their first Christmas without their son. It's the least we can do. What do you think?'

'Great idea,' her father said.

Worst idea ever, Penny thought. Not wanting to be disloyal to Butty, she wasn't sure if it were right to tell her mother of Gordon Hawthorne's belief that Butty was now Jack. It sounded unhinged even as she thought it. It had also been told to her in confidence. She bit down on her lip, unsure.

Seeing her expression, her mother said, 'Why is that not a good idea?'

'I'll have a word with Butty today. I'll text him. In a minute. I'll ask him. I think the situation is… delicate – that would cover it. Tricky. Not sure the father's coping all that well. But I'll ask the boy. See what he thinks.'

'Sarah, would you mind making me another drink? A small one this time, but hold the tonic anyway,' her father said.

'Small drinks aren't in my repertoire, but I'll give it a go. Gin and a splash?'

'Please.'

Her mother ground out of the room and her father said, 'I saw you the other night. With Butty. Couldn't see everything because of the bloody trees, but I saw enough. I saw you elbow deep in pig shit. And then he joined you. I could only see both of your arms, yours and his, I mean, mucking about in the muck. What the hell were you doing?'

She had to stop herself from gasping. Covered her shock with a reprimand. 'What the hell were you doing out of bed, Dad? You could fall, you idiot. You're meant to use the hoist, or at the very least, use my arm for support. You'll break a bloody hip.'

'I was fine. And I didn't fall, did I? I was feeling especially good for once and fancied looking out over the garden. You know how much I miss it. And all I saw was you in shit. *Are* you in some sort of deep shit that you want to tell me about? Metaphorical or literal; I'll accept either answer. I think it's got something to do with that child, Butty. Tell me. I might be ill, but stupid, I ain't.'

'I'd dropped my phone in the pigsty. Must have trampled it into the manure. Butty saw it. Got it out for me. End of thrilling story.'

'Is it, though?'

'What else were you expecting? Dead bodies piled high in the pig poo? Prostitutes in the whore frost? It was just my phone, Dad. Nothing exciting.'

Her father made a kind of unconvinced noise. Blew air threw his lips, making them flap. 'You're a big fat liar, Penny Crisp. I know my daughter, and I know, I absolutely *know* that you're worrying about something. I also know Butty visited this house the night that Cindy went missing. Your mother told me. Is he involved?'

'No. Absolutely not. Why would you think that? He's a child, for God's sake, not a monster. He was visiting me, that's it. Nothing more sinister than that.'

He didn't look convinced. 'You've been struggling with something new, something that happened relatively recently. The arrival of Butty into your life fits. Why won't you tell me what's going on? I won't shout at you. Promise.'

'Honest, Dad. There's nothing wrong at all. Why are you so convinced something's wrong with me? I'm telling you; everything is fine. And Butty isn't a baddie, I swear.'

Her mother reappeared with drinks for each of them, and both Penny and her father startled, as if caught out, talking about something forbidden. Her mother saw their expressions and handing them their drinks, she took her seat and said, 'You're talking about Butty, aren't you?'

'No,' Penny said.

'Yes,' her father said.

'He's a strange one,' her mother said as she sipped from her glass, the ice chinking against the crystal, the lemon bumping against the sides of the tumbler. 'An odd child. Half boy and half man. Too young to be a man, so I think that's why I find him slightly unsettling. He reminds me of something about to go off pop. It's more than the loss of his brother, I think. Or perhaps it's *because* of the loss of his brother. Either way, he's fixating on you, Penny, so keep an eye out. There's something not quite right going on there, in my humble estimation, and I should bloody know.'

She adjusted her topknot. 'But there is also something terribly endearing about him. Very lovable. Hence him tricking me into giving him your address and mobile number. He charmed me. He's broken but charming. Strange combination. Naturally I worry. It's my job. You're my daughter. And be aware, I absolutely recognise broken when I see it. You showed me what broken was two years ago, and I still haven't learnt how to repair you.'

Her father asked, 'What exactly does Butty want with you, Penny?'

'Apart from my sparkling wit, you mean? I think he needs me; probably anyone would do, but he's latched onto me. I'm trying to save him,' Penny said, surprised once the words were out that she'd been coerced so smoothly and effortlessly by her parents into telling the truth.

'You can't even save yourself, Penny,' her mother said. 'If you'd let me, I could still save you. It's what mothers do best – it's why I'm here. You and Butty, you're almost like two peas in a pod, you the bigger pea who should know better, and he the baby pea, trying to… I don't know, is he trying to impress you? It's almost as if he's obsessed with you. You need to take care if you're wanting to save him. Save yourself first would be my advice. Broken can't save broken. You just get broken squared.'

Penny drank quietly. She didn't know what to say and was surprised at her parent's astuteness. Her father must have picked up her anxiety over Butty and linked it to him purely based on the timeline.

And he'd made the connection with Cindy.

Unexpectedly, she felt like bursting into tears. Her world was slowly unravelling, strands of her existence becoming loose and tangled. She was like an ever-decreasing ball of thread.

Her mother recognised broken.

Broken can't save broken.

THIRTY-SIX

Butty

M aybe it was because it was Christmas Eve tomorrow, or maybe I felt like living a little dangerously: whatever the reason, I decided to visit the strange man who now lived in the attic. A teeny-tiny part of me couldn't help but feel a bit sorry for the old bastard. Up there, all alone, with his trains and his big new bus and his mind playing tricks on him. Bloody pathetic really.

He wasn't actually a homicidal maniac; I was pretty sure of that. He was just behaving like one. We're all allowed to pretend now and again. *Live and let live*, I thought charitably. For this was the season to be jolly – the time to be merry, charitable *and* jolly. Fa-la-la-la-lah. I could hardly contain myself.

Mum was out, as usual, doing something else, *any*thing else, *always* doing something else. She point-blank refused to do what she should be doing – grieving. It wasn't rocket science, it shouldn't be that hard, but she refused to even give it a bash.

I'd *chosen* not to actively mourn, so that made it different – I'd given it proper thought and acted accordingly. Having done her 'I've-taken-to-my-bed' routine, and having recovered from that, she'd then told herself that that was enough and convinced herself she was right to bravely ignore the grieving process entirely.

The five stages of grief: I was fascinated by it, and was aware, very aware, of exactly what I was doing. I acknowledged grief's presence and had decided to not give in to it because I didn't want to. Easy as.

I'd accept your death when I was good and ready.

Mum willed the loss of you away, ignored it, pretended she was fine. I didn't think that a healthy approach at all. She should be crying and wailing and not eating and gazing out of the window, looking sad and drawn and washed out. Her heart should be breaking.

And I would have helped her. I'd have been there for her, to support her through it. I was intelligent enough to know that her heart *had* been broken, was still broken, but it pissed me off that she couldn't even share that with me. The one thing I could have done for her, and she wouldn't let me.

I took it personally.

Like I'd said before, Jack, Mum was avoiding your passing. Did that make you angry? That you were no longer the centre of attention? Or maybe you still were. In fact, who was I kidding? I *knew* you were still the centre of everyone's attention *because* of your absence. Even though you weren't here, you somehow still were.

Didn't seem fair.

You were gone, Mum was never here, but *I* was here. With mad Dad upstairs.

That was why I now found myself attic-bound.

I couldn't carry on not confronting what was living above me. It wasn't normal. God knows what new fantasy my father was now breeding and cultivating. He was like some demented scientist, fiddling around with test tubes and a petri dish, adding thoughts and theories and hypotheses to it, trying to find some unanswerable answer to a nonsensical question.

Perhaps I was Jack again, although I didn't think it likely. I'd been cast in a different role by Dad now, and if I wasn't on that bus going from A to B, I'd want to know why I'd lost my seat.

'Dad, hello, you up there?'

No answer. I went to shout out again, now at the bottom of the ladder, but wasn't sure how to introduce myself. *Am I Jack, or am I Butty?* I didn't want to set him off before I'd even got into the room.

'Dad, it's me.' *Nothing if not ingenious*, I thought.

I heard banging and crashing about, and then silence. 'Is that you?' Dad said.

This game was harder than I'd have imagined. 'Yes, it's me.'

'Come on up, then. What are you waiting for? An invitation?'

Sticking my head through the hatch, I quickly scanned the room, wanting to know exactly where Dad was. Not being sure of his mental state, I couldn't be totally sure that he wouldn't jump me. Put me on the fucking bus by force and strap me in for my final journey to who-knew-where.

He was standing on the other side of the tracks which were laid out on a large table. *The wrong side of the tracks.* I'd made a Dad joke. I laughed inside at my own hilarity.

His appearance shocked me. I hadn't seen him for a couple of days, I'd lost count of exactly how many, but he looked like proper shit. He was dirty, had grown a beard and his hair stood up in clumpy tufts as if he'd been pulling his hands through it. A faint smell of sweat and general oldness came off him; his clothes were rumpled and I could see a stain of food down his shirt. His eyes proper weirded me out: they were black-ringed and had fallen back into his skull, like he was practising his skeleton look. Hadn't done a bad job, either.

'Hey, Dad. How you doing?'

'It's all coming together. Finally. I've managed to regain

some sort of order, set the world to rights. In the grand scheme of things, I do believe I've made substantial progress. Happy?'

Was I happy with what, in particular? I had to choose my words carefully. One wrong word and he'd go mental. That's how he looked. On the brink. Tottering, off balance – he could fall down on either side of the normal spectrum. I hopefully pushed him towards what is generally accepted as normal behaviour.

'I'm happy if you are, Dad. Clearly you know what you're doing, what needs to be done. Can you explain it to me again, then that way we can talk properly about it. In depth. With me knowing what your aim is here.'

'My aim? *My aim?* What do you think my bloody aim is? I've told you already. I am returning the world to how it was, how it should be, before everything changed. Good things shouldn't change without some warning. That's only fair. But I was presented with a situation that was grossly *un*fair.' He stopped talking suddenly, shook his head in a confused way, and scratched his head, as if he'd momentarily lost his train of thought.

God, there I go again. *Train of thought.* It must be catching, or I was turning into my father.

I wasn't sure how to move the conversation on, how to get more details, wasn't even sure if I should encourage any more of his ramblings, detailed or not. He was more agitated than he'd been the last time I'd seen him. More volatile. Madder.

'How's the bus thing going? You know, getting passengers from A to B? Have you got the right people going to the right places now?'

'Passengers.' He spat out the word with such derision that I took a small step back. '*Passengers?* They're not passengers, they're commuters. Although you actually make a good point. "Passengers" is the exact, right word. Passengers are those that are just along for the ride, not offering anything worthwhile, just piggybacking their way through life.'

Dad's eyes were almost spinning with passion. Spitting with intensity, he said, 'Commuters have a sense of purpose, a plan, they are needed in this world to keep the cogs of life well oiled. They are required to keep the universe spinning on its axis. They are the ones that keep the great machine going. They are the ones who keep the wheels of the train on, so that they don't fall off. Without them, the world would fall apart. *They* know where and when to get on and off without being told. They know their place.'

He nodded more emphatically. 'Yes, very good point. The passengers, they are the ones that have mixed everything up. They've buggered up the natural course of things. They just jump on and off when it suits them, never bothering or worrying about the effect they'll have on the decent people who are trying to just get on with it. All these unwanted, freewheeling passengers take up valuable space, they get in the way of the natural order. They're stopping the world from functioning properly. *I hate them.* It's all their fault. Damn freeloaders. Wanting everything for free and not expecting to pay their way – just assuming they have the God-given right to exist alongside the rest of us. We've all earned the right to be here. What have they done, except take what is not theirs to take? They need to be punished.'

I wasn't sure if I deserved praise for my accidental break-through in providing the vital word; I should have kept my big trap shut. However, I was positive that praise was *not* coming my way from Dad. He was difficult to read, and it was impossible to get on his wavelength, but I instinctively knew I was toast. I wasn't going to ask if I was a commuter or a passenger. I knew already.

I was a shitty passenger, getting in the way, and I stopped breathing, tried to make myself smaller, less there, hoping that

Dad would forget I was standing in his pretend world, taking up valuable space.

Of course, I knew that you, Jack, you'd definitely be a commuter. Right person, right place. Right person for the job. You deserved your place on Dad's stupid bus. I had a nasty feeling that our father would be picking you up on his fantasy ride, and where would that leave me?

I'd been relegated to unwanted baggage. I'd be turfed out as soon as was convenient for the fat controller of the whole wide world. As soon as he caught up with my reasoning and realised that I was responsible for life turning to complete shite. It was all my fault.

By just being here.

I could imagine you up there, laughing your socks off. It gave a whole new meaning to the phrase, Big Brother is watching you.

Dad tinkered about, moving his big bus around – randomly it seemed to me, without any logic or sense. But he was intent on his job, forgetting that I was there. Good. Perhaps now would be the best time for my own departure, on my own two feet. Retreating quietly, wishing my feet weightless and soundless, I backtracked to the open hatch. It seemed to take ages, but I carried on, so very slowly I wasn't sure I was making any progress at all.

My heel hit the opening to the attic and I exhaled in relief. Lowering one foot onto the top rung, I thought I was home free. Never would I come up here again. I'd leave Dad up here until the men in white coats came and collected him.

In their very own big bus.

Keeping him in sight, I carefully bent my first leg to allow my second leg to follow it down onto the ladder. Without moving his head, not bothering to look at me, Dad said, 'Hold it right there, Butty. You're not going anywhere.'

THIRTY-SEVEN

Butty

He called me Butty. Butty. I *am* Butty. I wasn't sure that was a good thing at this stage. Not at this particular moment with this particular father.

Dad smiled at me. A happy, normal father-to-son smile. Familiar and loving. No menace showed. No madness seeped out from his face. No I'm-an-out-of-control-lunatic vibe bled from his expression.

Paternal love was all that I could see. Even knowing that my father was living in some mental part of somewhere, his gentle smile made me stop. Automatically. Maybe I'd got it all wrong. I couldn't believe that I was doubting myself, after everything that I'd heard, but possibly it was loyalty that kept me there.

He was my father, I couldn't deny that.

He was mad. I couldn't deny that either.

But maybe he needed help. I could steer him in the right direction, instead of standing back and watching his chaotic descent into a world I didn't want to live in. I didn't suppose he was happy living there either.

And I was as sure as I could be that Mum wouldn't even

agree to be his neighbour in the part of town that he'd unwittingly strayed into.

However, I felt I owed him. I admitted to my own small madness; certainly small in comparison to his full-on craziness, so maybe I should be a tiny bit more willing to help him. There he was, stuck in denial, drowning in it, and I was happy to stand there and watch. Didn't seem fair or particularly loving. Dad had always been a bit of an idiot with his trains and his stupid jokes, but he'd never been nasty to us, hadn't hit us, had tried to be a fun father.

I stayed. Inched back up the ladder until I stood upright again, ready for anything. I wasn't blind to what he may do, wasn't sure of his intentions, but was prepared to give him a shot at explaining his lunacy to me. I could be the bigger person here.

Or was I being really stupid? Dicing with death. Risking my life at Dad's hands. I had *welcomed* risk with arms outstretched for Penny. She'd swept me up in her grasp, like a passing empty crisp packet swirling through the air and I'd let her catch me happily. And I hadn't let go since: couldn't stop bloody running back to her. Sprinting back, needing the woman who'd told me in the Trumpet Room, 'No one can hear you scream in here.'

There is no difference here, I thought. If I was prepared to see the batshit crazy woman and her Trumpet Room, the least I could do was give time to whack-job Dad and his trains. It seemed the polite thing to do.

Weirdly, I found myself standing to attention, as if awaiting orders. I was definitely waiting for something. Some cue from him as to what was expected of me. A show of gratitude from Dad that I was still here for him would have been nice, but Dad was past being nice. He was too busy being completely bonkers. Keeping my face neutral and as un-annoying as possible, I carried on standing there in the silence.

He ignored me for about ten minutes. I felt each and every second drag by, trapping me and keeping me there, unable to move without his permission. Eventually he glanced up and his face showed surprise. He'd forgotten I was there. That pissed me off. Here I'd been offering my services as dutiful son, and there he was, forgetting I was still in the room. If it hadn't been so sad, it might have been worthy of laughter. Instead, I only felt like weeping.

'You still here?'

'Yeah, Dad, still here.'

'Sit down. Take the weight off.' He pointed at the corner of the attic, flapping his hand at the knackered old armchair with holes in the seat. I went towards it, but before I'd reached the familiar cosy piece of furniture, Dad spoke again. 'Do me a favour, would you, Butty?' He glanced quickly at his watch, so quickly I didn't think he'd even registered the real time – it was an habitual movement and meant nothing. 'Would you mind terribly getting me my four o'clock treat. You know, my favourite. I'd be most grateful.'

To be honest, he was freaking me out more with his jolly back-to-normal Dad routine, because I knew it couldn't be real. Knowing that, I still played along. 'Fine, I'll be back in a jiffy.'

Sliding down the ladder, I carried on further, deeper into the house, into the kitchen and got him his special teatime treat. It had been the same for years and wasn't difficult to put together. I also picked up the Sunday roast carving knife, clean from the dishwasher – just in case – and put it, blade up, in my back pocket. Five minutes later I was in the attic again, goodies at the front of me, baddies at the back.

I sat down in the armchair and watched Dad as he ate and drank, sitting across the other side of the table from me. Before he'd finished his daily treat, he raised his head. 'Butty.'

I nodded. Couldn't think of anything more that was required.

'Butty, Butty, Butty. What am I going to do with you?'

Again, I relied on physical movement only, not knowing the words he wanted, and went for a nonchalant shoulder shrug. Not sure I pulled off nonchalance, though. I was too tense. Looking at the shoes on my feet as if they were fascinating, with your red laces on your black trainers, Jack, I waited and listened to Dad's next verbal offering.

'Always been a bit of a passenger, haven't you? You know what I mean. Lap-dogging around after your brother. Jack. Jack Hawthorne. A fine boy indeed.' He lifted his mug again and glared at me. Definitely a glare this time. I couldn't mistake it for anything sweet or loving this time.

It was full of hate.

And pity.

'Jack Hawthorne,' he said. 'And then there was you.'

He shook his head sadly, indicating what a monumental disappointment I'd been. Bracing my shoulders and inhaling, puffing out my chest, I felt outrage and a how-bloody-dare-you retort resting on my lips. But I bit down on the words, the angry reaction – knowing that I'd only make things worse. *If you're watching, Jack, enjoy. Because I will win this, whatever I have to do. Just you wait and watch, you arsehole. You made this happen. It's all your fault.*

Dad carried on, smiling all the while. 'Your mother adores you, you know. Never saw you as inferior or lesser or insignificant in comparison to Jack. Of course, I spotted the difference straight away, when you were very small. You lacked…'

He scratched his unshaven chin as if really giving it deep and profound consideration. Scratched and rubbed and bristled his chin with his huge clumsy hand.

Smacking his knee, and beaming with delight that he'd

finally found the right word, he said gleefully, 'You lacked *identity*, Butty. You had none. Certainly not your own. You borrowed your identity from Jack. Like an imposter. It was never yours, never truly belonged to you. Which made you a replica son. A poor, second-rate one at that. You simply didn't come up to par. You piggy-backed on your brother to get you through your sad, pathetic non-worthy life. But you never achieved that purity, that perfection that Jack had. He was born with it. Oodles of it. You never came close. Not ever. Not for me. For your mother…' He shrugged and rolled his eyes. 'She'd be happy with anything apparently – *you're* proof of that. But I never liked you. There. Now it's said. It's out in the open. I think it needed saying out loud, don't you? It's like we've cleared the air – I'm glad.'

He took a swig of his tea and added, in case I was in any doubt as to his beliefs, 'Basically, in a nutshell, Butty, if I can't have Jack, I don't want you. I hope that suits you because it suits me fine and I feel so much better for having got it off my chest.'

Staggered, I couldn't think of a witty response, not even a non-witty response. Furious, I stood up and my mouth started working; spewing out all the hurt. 'Who do you think you're talking to, Dad? I've been me all of my life. The real me. Never pretended to be anyone else. I've been me forever. You can't borrow someone else's personality, their character, their stupid fucking *identity* – I've always had mine, and it was way more than you ever noticed. Because you're blind. All you care about are your trains. Jack thought you were a weak freak. That's what he called you on the night he died. One of the last things he said. How's that make you feel, *Dad*?'

Not my finest speech, and his expression didn't change as he listened. Not a muscle twitched. My father, the cardboard cut-out. He managed to look bored by my mini speech. My hands ached with the need to smash his face in. I needed to *do* something, anything to stop him talking his crazy bollocks. Because I knew with a heart-breaking certainty, with an inevitable dread, his empty eyes staring blankly at me, that he wanted to kill me.

Question was, could I kill my father?

Or should I try and talk him out of it?

My feet decided for me.

Moving quickly, fists clenched, feeling the knife in my back pocket but not needing it now, knowing that I could kill him with my hands alone, I advanced towards him. He deserved it.

How dare he think that about me. How *dare* he?

But I hesitated. Stopped a few feet away from him. Realising that I must be adult about this, I forced myself to stay stopped. To calm down. After all, I had breaking, headline news to tell Dad before we fought to the death. His death would have to wait. The news was *that* important. I had to tell him something that would change his last moments on earth.

It was news that would stay with him and stain his last moments alive. I wanted him to hear my news and for it be his very last thought; rotting what was left of his decayed and stinking brain. A final piece of reality at its most cruel. I could give him that and I wanted to. Couldn't fucking wait.

But to my surprise, as I stood over him, knowing that he'd seen my anger; he wasn't blind – he sat there, not moving. Didn't bother standing up, didn't even try to defend himself. Maybe he was that sure of himself and that sure that I would never harm him.

He was wrong.

I stood there and remained silent. Gearing up for the great reveal. It would knock his stupid socks off.

He smiled, looking smug. Triumphant. But he did nothing.

Father versus unfavourite son.

'What are you planning, Dad? Are you going to will me dead with your laser eyes? How am I getting on your stupid bus? How are you reincarnating Jack? Will he be arriving by taxi and join the procession?'

Dad continued smiling and tapped his nose. 'That's for me to know and you to find out, Butty.'

On a one-on-one fight with him, man against boy, I suddenly had visions of losing the battle. A battle he suddenly wasn't participating in, having thrown down the challenge. He'd told me I was as good as dead. But still, he sat there. Doing nothing. Like he knew something I didn't.

His non-participation, his sudden not-playing-anymore, seriously creeped me out. I didn't know what to do.

I refused to lose this bizarre war of sudden no action. I had no option. I had to make him listen.

'Dad, there's something you should know.'

He held his hands up in mock surrender. 'Do you see me move? Am I attacking you? No. Stop being such a big girl, Butty. You're right, though. I am going to kill you. But not now, this precise second. Maybe in a minute. When I've finished my treat. You'll keep. I also know you'll stay here with me – because you're that stupid and think you can beat me. You can't. Do your worst. And Butty...' He leant forward. 'Good luck.'

He roared with merry laughter as if this was all a game. Wagging his finger at me, shaking his head at my idiocy, he wiped his hand across his wet mouth. 'There's nothing you can tell me that will change my decision, Butty. You're getting on the bus to nowhere and Jack will come back. Believe me, I will have the right son back in his rightful place. And that means getting rid of the plankton. That's you, you complete waste of space. I loathe you.' All this, said in a gentle but horribly upbeat voice, his teeth showing in a mad grin of yellowish white.

It was like those evenings when you and me were young, Jack, and we'd play board games with Mum and Dad. That's what Dad reminded me of now. It was like we were playing Snakes and Ladders, and I was one hop away from the snake's head: he sitting pretty on ninety-nine.

'Before you do whatever it is you've got planned,' I said. 'You really need to hear this. You'll thank me for it, I promise.'

'Think it'll change my mind?'

I think it might tip you over the edge.

'It might.'

Then I texted Penny for back-up.

THIRTY-EIGHT

Penny

It was December the twenty-third, half-past two in the afternoon, and it was cold and windy. Harsh weather for a harsh woman. Penny recognised the diseased blackness within herself: she'd successfully managed to separate herself from anything that could be deemed as even remotely normal.

With her family, as happy as they made her feel when she was with them, she felt as if it wasn't real, that she was only marking time until she could go back to man-whispering. All the love in the world, couldn't stop her desire to find and destroy men.

Her parents couldn't save her. With all the love they had for her, that she had for them, she'd crossed a line with her murdering, and she unhappily admitted to herself that she hadn't finished crossing that particular hard black line that she'd drawn. It was in danger of becoming blacker every time she crossed it by killing.

Another crossing was calling her.

She knew she wasn't finished.

Will I ever be finished with my men-finishing?

Penny was feeling particularly un-festive. She hadn't

bothered contacting Butty about drinks with his family at her parents' house tomorrow night. Absolutely no way was that happening. Butty was too much of an unknown quantity. As was, by Butty's own account, his father – pretending his remaining son was Jack. It was sick and disturbed.

Maybe she'd do something about it.

Before the rape, she'd always enjoyed Christmas, but as her life continued to spiral ever downwards, she had to dig deep now to get the Father Crimble rush. Despite the superficially happy lunch with her parents, her existence, so divided as it was between good and bad, was bereft, confused, and still so bloody hateful.

I wonder what Butty's doing.

Dithering in the shops, wanting to buy the perfect presents for her parents, she decided on impulse to buy Butty something. Something nice and normal and filled with fourteen-year-old innocent Christmas fun.

She finally settled on her original plan, and bought her mother three paperback thrillers, and a black-and-white photography book, and for her father she'd had, by luck, stumbled on the ideal present: a selection of the finest gins. He might be dying, but she knew he still enjoyed a drink. Pleased, the gift made her smile. As it would, her father.

Now, she struggled with what to buy the boy. Wondered if it actually mattered. He'd be happy with the gesture, but she wanted to get it right. It felt important.

Wanting to get home, she hurriedly chose and bought a book on astronomy. It was a vague memory that had stayed with her: Butty's interest in the planetary system. Relieved, job done, she headed out of the shop, her bags weighted down with her presents and loads of culinary treats for Christmas Eve with her parents.

Back out on the street, she hunched her shoulders, trying to protect herself from the gale that gusted, making her feel as though she were trapped inside a wind tunnel. So strong was the force of the wind, she feared that it might rip her face from her skull. Gritting her teeth, she pointed herself in the direction of the bungalow, and trudged onwards; each hand icily gripping the straps of her two shopping bags.

The pavements were full of annoying people doing annoyingly Christmassy things, getting in her way. People suddenly stopped walking, giving no warning, always picking the spot into which she was about to step, and obsessively checked their mobiles – frightened they might have missed something important in the last five minutes since they'd last checked. She detested them all.

Especially the men. Bastards, all of them.

She picked her way through the male humans, who were out in force today – no doubt buying Christmas presents for their wives, daughters, sisters, aunts and grannies. Pretending they cared for the women in the lives. Pretending they were all loving men, would never do harm to a woman. Appalled, all mock outraged at the very thought of committing rape. *Oh, no, not me. Never. I'm not that sort of man.*

They were all that sort of man.

Working herself into a frenzied rage, Penny passed the pubs and shops nearer to her bungalow. At this time, not even three o clock in the afternoon, men stumbled out of bars, full of festive beer. Any excuse would do, and uncaring of others, some of them sang out-of-tune carols, laughing and burping, making a meal out of festive farting as they shouted out the words.

Already, the light was fading, the skies gloomy and cloudy. Early darkness was coming. With her fury warming her, Penny stomped down her road, relieved to be away from people, the world – men. The contrast of the quiet street hit her like a slap in the face. She didn't feel safe with her hands full. Exposed and suddenly vulnerable, she was annoyed that her fear was still there, deep inside. It never gave her any warning: it would creep up with shocking surprise, taking her unawares, and she hurried her footsteps, suddenly in desperate need for the sanctuary of home.

When the man appeared at her side, she nearly had a heart attack. 'Jesus bloody Christ.' She jumped so hard, her voice had come out in a squeak. Stopping on the pavement, she took a step backwards. 'What do you want?'

He held his hand to his chest, showing embarrassment at having scared her. 'I'm so sorry. I didn't mean to frighten you. Do forgive me.' His head nodded in a formal way, apologising silently. It was as if they were mirroring each other, both with hands to their chest.

A real, live gentleman, Penny thought derisively, trying hard to control her heart as it beat, too too fast. Tried to regain her fury and not give in to fear. Not moving, not giving him an opportunity to overwhelm her – either physically nor emotionally, she cocked her head at a confident angle that jarred with her more than it should were it real, and glared at him.

Come on. Get on with it. What do you really want?

And exactly how drunk are you? Are you actually drunk? If so, are you drunk enough for me to take advantage?

'I was wondering if I could give you some assistance. Your shopping looks heavy. May I?'

He was the same height as her she saw, remembering the obscene physical fit she'd had with the Aniseed Man.

His hand snaked out towards her, and she took a further step away from him. Unsure. Very unsettled. Normally, she could judge and correctly assess a man's level of sobriety, but now, she dithered. Was he sober or politely pissed? He certainly wasn't slaughtered, and therefore, her sensible brain told her to leave it. Walk on, say 'goodbye' and scuttle off home.

Her very *unsensible* brain said, *Why the fuck should I run away – frightened and freaked out by what was, ostensibly, an offer of help?*

But was it more than that?

Course it bloody was.

She hoped with the whole of herself that he *was* drunk. And she *knew* he was trying to pick her up. That he wanted sex from her. She'd give him shedloads more than sex.

Now her heart rate had slowed, she was ready. Ready for a fight. Ready for another man to whisper to.

The man didn't know it, but he was unwittingly offering himself up to her on a bloody plate, like a cheap bit of tinsel left over from the Christmas party. But it was a huge risk – the longer she stood there, she realised that she had accurately diagnosed his lack of drunkenness, however much she didn't want to. On some level she wondered if she were deliberately sabotaging her current one hundred per cent perfect murder record.

He was definitely sober, she wasn't armed with her essential kit, the wheelbarrow wasn't in its place and there was no plastic sheeting down on the floor to catch his blood. The only thing that was where it should be, was her baseball bat. Concern for her safety and the jeopardy she was about to put herself in, nearly overwhelmed her. She wasn't prepared at all. He could easily overpower her, attack her, rape her. Was it worth the risk?

Grabbing her gung-ho spirit with her two cold hands, she decided it was. Fuck it. Why get all precious about things now. Who gave a rat's arse if there was danger involved? *Life* was dangerous.

He was already guilty. What sort of man offered to carry a woman's bags these days? Unless he had an ulterior motive. She wasn't some frail, vulnerable old woman, who would be unable to put up any physical defence. She was young, strong and wasn't an obvious target.

Internally she rapped her knuckles against her temple at her own stupidity and naivete. *Oh, yes. I* am *an obvious target. Silly me. I'm a woman.*

Okay then, bring it on.

He still stood there, with hand on his beating heart, and said, 'Do you have far to go? It would be my pleasure if you'd allow me to assist.'

Penny felt trapped within a Dickensian novel, listening to his speech: so affected, so innocent sounding, so beguiling. Most women wouldn't view this man as a threat, but she knew better.

'No, not far. A couple of doors down, in fact. You don't have to carry my bags really.' She laughed. 'A bit of an out-dated gesture, don't you think?'

'Not at all. I'm walking this way, so why not? No skin off my proverbial hooter.'

Keeping her distance, Penny held her hands out, the shopping bags dangling, her arms rigid. 'There you go, then. Knock yourself out.'

Taking the bags, he started whistling as they walked. The noise unnerved her. She couldn't really get a handle on him and was not happy at not being in full control. Should she abort the entire idea?

Her anger told her to carry on. She knew what could happen to her. She also knew what could happen to him. Her life had taken on a direction of its own, and she was aware that part of her was going along for the ride, taking unwise decisions. She was passive, allowing life to happen *to* her, instead of actively giving life a run for its money.

Tired, a sad and pathetic part of her was eager to bring resolution and an end to everything. To hasten the onset of crossing the finish line. Not knowing what lay beyond that. It was all going wrong, anyway. How she'd got involved with

Butty's life, she didn't know, but knew instinctively, that together they would bring each other down.

I buried a child for him.

'What's your name?' the kindly gent said in his assumed accent of the day, cutting through her thoughts, like a splinter piercing skin.

'Penny. You?'

'Donald.'

'Great.'

'Don't you have your very own knight in shining armour to help you in times like this?'

Oh, very subtle. 'No, no. No man waiting in the wings for me. I'm very single.'

His expression shone out an insincere look of condolence and commiseration. *Never mind, I'm here now*, he silently said.

What a fool, she thought. Here he was, trying far too obviously to find out if she were single. *She* was reeling *him* in, not the other way round. He was too arrogant to imagine for a moment that it was him who had been caught, that he was the bait, not she, and that it was she who had won catch of the day. Penny was one step ahead of him. Of all men.

Instead of attempting to take her on, he should have been more intent on extricating the hook from his mouth, which Penny relentlessly and effortlessly tugged. She'd got him and she knew it.

It was hard to put on a show of friendliness; a charade, although there were social rules to adhere to, to get the bastard inside her house. She was keen to get her last man, and whisper him to death. It was all the palaver beforehand that was proving irritating. They both knew what he really wanted. Why couldn't he be honest about it, instead of them both having to go through this ridiculous rigmarole? All these niceties they were going through, when there was nothing approaching nice about either of their intent.

She came to a halt outside her door, remembering that as she hadn't gone out especially to get a man, she'd drawn closed the front door curtain to keep the draught out. Normally, it was left open when she was entertaining; alert always to the danger of getting tangled in the heavy drape as she manoeuvred the man through the door first.

This was her first time accompanied by an unexpected guest. She'd have to enter first. And move fast. Getting the key from her bag, she put it in the door and turned it. Pushing it open, there was an unexpected thrill as she drew back the curtain quickly. It was as if the door-opening was a little tease, a prelude to what was coming, and then, with a practised snap of the wrist, she pulled back the heavy velvet material – ta-dah: enter stage right.

Penny knew that for her companion, it would be his final act, so best and only polite to herald his last entrance onto the stage with a flourish. Turning, she said, 'Do come in. And wipe your feet on the mat, please.'

If they were being formal, she'd be buggered if she wouldn't out-formal him.

Carrying the two bags at his side, he stepped over the threshold and dutifully did as he was told. He stood there waiting for her to tell him where to go.

'If you wouldn't mind, Donald, could you take them through to the kitchen, there…' She pointed and stood back, allowing him to pass.

He was in.

Let the man-whispering commence.

THIRTY-NINE

Penny

Donald moved faster than she'd anticipated. Didn't loiter, with or without intent, and bowled boldly through the house, towards the kitchen. 'Here? Shall I leave them on the worktop for you? Would that suit?'

Nothing would suit until she had the baseball bat firmly in hand. Grasping its familiar handle, while he was momentarily out of sight, she raised her voice slightly. 'Yes, anywhere's fine. Dump it on the floor if that's easier.'

'No, no. They're on the worktop. Shall I unpack for you?'

Outrage at his forced intimacy and familiarity made her move. 'No, leave them. They're fine there.'

They could see each other's top half through the arch from the sitting room into the kitchen; a wall hid her bottom half. She needed to get behind him. Resting the bat against the wall, but with her fingers, her *trembling* fingers still in contact with the tip, she wanted to get him out of the kitchen. Standing in front of the bat, effectively hiding it from him, she said, 'Why not come and sit down. Perhaps we could share a Christmas drink together. My way of thanking you.'

Again, with the dipping of his head, his thick hair – nice

hair – staying in place, as he accepted her offer. 'Most kind, thank you.'

'Not at all. My pleasure.'

Bloody hell, the upper crust has come for a bevvy.

Confidently, he stepped out of the kitchen and headed towards the sofa: the most obvious place to sit. As he passed, she tightened her grip on the bat standing behind her legs. Prayed he wouldn't turn around, deflect her blow, mount an attack as he feinted to the right, pretending he was going for the sofa when in fact he'd be preparing for his own attack. She allowed him to take two steps past her, one more and then she struck.

At the very moment that he turned. For a brief second, their eyes met. Only hers remained open after she made her swing, connecting with the right side of his temple. For what seemed an eternity, he remained standing, looking stunned, blood already running freely.

Finally, he fell.

She hit him again. Hard. Uncaring if she killed him outright. She didn't like the situation – a living, breathing, very sober man who'd inveigled his way into her house. Bluffing his way into her safe place.

Now she was safe.

She smiled with relief.

Standing back, resting her weight on one hip, leaning her head back for better perspective, she surveyed the damage to his face. One side obliterated. Her breathing returned to a steadier rhythm, her fingers ceased their stupid trembling, and for a while, she luxuriated in her victory. Perhaps her final triumph. She felt fatalistic about her life but was most assuredly happy that she'd bagged herself another rapist-in-waiting. That was what it was all about. What *she* was about. Silently, she apologised to her parents, unable to cast off the belief that she'd come to the end of the road.

Blood was pooling around his head like a deflated red balloon. Annoyed that it was ruining the carpet and that she'd have to replace it, she sauntered into the kitchen and poured herself a large gin and tonic. With ice and lemon.

Came back. Squatted next to Donald and sniffed. Disproportionately disappointed there was no smell of aniseed lingering around his mouth, but not too disappointed with his lack of breathing, she lugged the armchair over to his body. She might as well be comfortable for the next bit.

Sticking to the rules, she got the aniseed lollipop and waved it at the man. 'Recognise this?'

It was very distinctive with its black and white swirly patten, the cellophane now so old that it stuck permanently to the sticky sweet.

Unsurprisingly, she got no response at all.

She decided to mix it up a bit, do something different. The theft of him from the street had already veered hugely from her usual pattern, so why not go the whole hog and go to town on the bastard? *Because he's dead, that's why.* What would be the point in hurting somebody who was no longer alive?

What Butty had done to the already-dead Cindy filled her mind. She would not lower herself to the same gratuitous violence as he'd perpetrated on the young girl. It was a step too far and she didn't consider herself to be that unhinged.

She was furious, that was all that ailed her. Psychopathy wasn't something she thought she was secretly harbouring. Upending her glass, she loudly inhaled the last drops of her drink from the bottom of the glass, sucked the lemon and ferociously crushed the ice with her teeth. Slammed the glass down on the table.

Penny got the clippers and shaved his head. It really was beautiful hair and the knowledge that she was taking it from him, cheered her. Studying his face, it wasn't a bad one. Handsome, if she were being generous, and if you liked that sort of thing. Late thirties, possibly forty at a push. Slim-ish build. Matching height. It all fit: all those similarities of her very own rapist and herself. It brightened her mood considerably. This was as like-for-like as she could get it. As it should be.

But no aniseed. Shrugging, she knew she couldn't have everything, but it would have been nice.

Crossing her feet at the ankles, she rested them in his groin. Coughing, she cleared her throat and whispered, 'Donald, or may I call you Donny? From the little I know of you, I'm sure that abbreviation of your name would rankle. Tough shit. I can call you what I want. Although, you never called me by my name, did you, Aniseed Man? When you came tiptoeing into my house to rape me? You never introduced yourself at all. Because what's in a name? Nothing. Names of the women you rape don't matter at all. Why on earth would they?'

She stared up at the ceiling. God, she was angry. How dare someone rape her? It wasn't fair. No wonder she felt no guilt as she killed these would-be rapists. If she could only physically rape them, it would have been better. But the act of stealing sex from someone was so repulsive she couldn't begin to entertain the notion, even if it were a possibility.

She got up and poured herself another large gin and tonic. Because she could and she wanted one. To calm herself down. Downing half the drink whilst standing, she went back to Donny.

'There is something I particularly wanted to discuss with you. If you want to add anything as I go, please feel free to interrupt. I'm all ears.'

Grinding her heels into his groin, she didn't bend to face him, confident that he could hear, but knowing he couldn't really – she hadn't lost the fucking plot – and she whispered into the air around her.

'Rape is an interesting concept. The penetration by a man

of a woman, without her consent. I'm sure there's some legal blather that makes it sound more removed and clinical than that, but you get my drift, I'm sure.

'And there are all sorts of theories that abound as to the reasons, the motivations that drive the poor little diddy rapist. Not a great deal on the victims of rape; it's all about the men and why they choose to do it. An odd emphasis, don't you think? An odd omission of the woman and how she ended up on the receiving end.'

Getting up again, she found some cigarettes in her bag and sitting again, ashtray at the ready, she lit up and inhaled. Blew smoke in a practised way, as if through a funnel. Made a smoke-ring, because she felt like it.

'The really interesting point I want to make, Donny, is a rather controversial one. Decried by many, but I think it's worth talking through. To see if it has any credence at all. A man like yourself with your oh-so-educated voice, must be well versed in the many and varied arguments bandied about, concerning the trigger points for a rapist. The old, poor-me-I-was-abused-as-a-child routine. That's always popular as a defence. "My Mummy made me do it," essentially. Bit weak in my view. What say you, Donald?'

She waited politely, cocking her ear in his general direction, playing the interested woman, hanging on his every unspoken word. Penny could guess at his answer anyway, so gave his silence minimal acknowledgement. She'd heard it all before.

Stubbing out her cigarette in the ashtray, she emptied the contents onto Donald's face.

'We all know about the degradation of women, the control and domination of the rapist. But let's for the moment, further explore all of the phony liberal bullshit about the "why" of it all. It's the oldest question in the book – Why do men rape? And one answer, and as I say, not one received in these modern times with rounds of thunderous applause and mad, frenzied cheering, but suppose, for a theoretical moment, that men rape because they want sex. It's as simple as that. No more, no less.'

Lighting another cigarette, she exhaled her next whisper with an accompaniment of smoke. 'It's not some namby-pamby bollocks about the mental well- or ill-being of the rapist. It's not as complicated as that. It's about sex. Pure and simple. By definition, if you can't get it up, Donny, you can't rape. Perhaps it really is a biological impulse; sexual desire winning out over common courtesy. I'd be being kind if I said I thought it were only a gender difference. Men take and women give. That's more bollocks yet again.

'It's far more basic than that. Men have a tool, women have an obliging orifice. Put the two together and what do you have? You have rape, Donny. Well done for listening, you tool.'

She sat back, enjoying her ciggie, and thought her mother would approve of this theory. It was so obvious it was bordering on the bloody ludicrous, but it would appeal to her mother's view of the world, where everything was fairly straight forward and uncomplicated.

The point Penny had just made irritated her and for a moment, she couldn't think why.

And then she got it.

If the man was a tool, then she'd 'outed' herself as a hole.

Fuck's sake.

Hatred at everything made her kick out at Donald. She kicked his body. Once, twice, three times before she was aware that her mobile had gone off.

Panting with exertion, she picked it up and read the text.

> Come now. Dad gonna kill me. Mum out. In attic. Back door open. B.

FORTY

Butty

Me and Dad had reached an agreement. He sat there in silence, and I stood over him in silence. Both of us eyed each other up, waiting for the other to make their move. It was more like a non-agreement. Deadlock.

But I had the upper hand. I had news. It was time for the news at half-past four. Checking my mobile, I waited patiently until it was indeed half-past four on the dot. Lift off.

'Good evening, Dad. Here is today's news.'

He held his hand up, stopping me. Again, I politely reacted to his interruption without complaint. I was, if nothing else, a polite boy. Mum had made sure of that.

'Before you start talking shite, Butty, I want you to know that I never *really* thought you were Jack. How mad do you think I am? You're a poor excuse for him. I just so wanted you to *be* Jack, that I tried to convince myself that you were. Stupid, I know. I tried to reinvent him in you. I forced you to be him, and of course you failed abysmally. The clothes helped, but only so much. Not enough for it ever to have worked properly for me. Like I said, you could never replace your brother. Never in a million years.'

'Thanks for the update, Dad. Glad you told me. You've just made everything all better. Where's my goodnight kiss?'

'Fuck off, Butty. Don't smart mouth me. I repeat, if I can't have Jack, then I don't want you. Without him, you appear even weaker, even more pathetic by comparison – even in his absence. *Especially* in his absence.

'Here, in my world, which I control, I get to say who stays and who goes'. He pointed at me. 'And you're going.' He pointed at the bus. 'On you get. Now.'

Really? I mean, *come on*. What the hell was his brain thinking? Did he want me to shrink myself into a teeny tiny boy and obligingly hop on the doomed bus? He clearly hadn't thought this bit through, and I almost felt sorry for the sad, mad old fart.

I chose to ignore his mental commentary, his madder-than-mad impossible method of killing me and bent in close so that he could smell my breath, so that he could feel the very real warmth from my very alive body. 'You're not listening, Dad. Listen to me. Stop putting off hearing something that will change your sad, crappy, rubbish life. Fucking listen to me.'

I inhaled before making my speech, knowing that as soon as I started, I'd have his full attention. For some reason, I wasn't even scared. Perhaps it was because I was proud of my news, and I knew it would destroy my father. He needed punishing for letting me know his view of me. No real father should speak to his son like that. To say that I wasn't worth it, that he wished me dead. It wasn't fair. But it gave me the right to speak, to say my piece without fear of being too cruel.

We'd see who trumped who when it came to cruel. I was confident that I'd win.

Glancing at my mobile again, I wished Penny here. I wanted her to hear my news too. She'd understand. I knew she would. Standing on tiptoe, careful to keep my pocket-full-of-knife out of Dad's eyeline, I peeked out of the sky light.

Obviously, it was the wrong angle and I couldn't see if she was coming or not. All I saw was sky.

But I'd hear her. Should I wait for her, or should I start? Excited, unable to wait any longer, but disappointed that Penny would miss the first bit of what I had to say; but knowing that she'd be able to catch up – it wasn't complicated – I couldn't stop myself from saying my opening line to Dad.

'I killed Jack. He didn't fall off the kerb like I said, and oopsy-daisy, never mind, splat. No, no. He didn't fall at all: he was pushed. By me. I killed my brother by pushing him under the wheels of the car. So there. Put that in your pipe and smoke it.'

Dad didn't react at first. Nothing showed on his face on hearing my great revelation. His blank eyes stared at me, unblinking.

'Did you hear what I said? I killed your precious, perfect son. It was me. And you want to know what? I don't feel guilty about it, not a bit. He deserved it.'

Again, I waited. I needed some sort of response because otherwise it was like talking into a big hole. All I could hear was the echo of my confession. The words sat heavily in the air, not knowing where to land. Dad continued to stare at me; like he'd moved out of his body, for the time being. Huffing with annoyance, I said, very clearly and very slowly so that he'd understand completely.

'I *knew* the car was coming. I *saw* it, larger than life, swerving down the road with its lights off. Guessed immediately that the driver was drunk, didn't *know* it, but guessed it. Looks like I was right, seeing as he never came forward. I pushed the perfect brother, the boy every other boy wanted to be, the boy every girl wanted to have, the child every parent wanted, I pushed him. On purpose. Deliberately. He didn't fall, he was pushed. By me.' I bowed. Realised I was weeping. Sobbing.

Finally, Dad got his voice back. 'What on earth are you talking about, you stupid boy?'

But I didn't want to answer his question. Not yet. I wanted to tell it my way. It was my story, and I wasn't about to let Dad spoil the telling of it.

Wanting him to truly understand the enormity of what I had done, I needed Dad to visualise it. Taking the knife out of my pocket, I squatted down in front of him. There was no need for me to brandish the knife. I had his attention all right. No doubt about it.

'I got the timing just right. Push and watch. Look and hear. A squidgy sound. Like a tomato being smashed by a brick. Not what I'd been expecting. And it completely freaked me out. Not just the sound. But the fact that I'd done it. I'd killed Jack. I'd murdered him. My own brother.' I clicked my fingers. 'Just like that. And the spooky thing was, it was so easy. I hadn't even planned it. Hadn't given it a second's premeditated thought – I just shoved and he disappeared. One minute he was there, all pink and laughing and healthy and alive. And then he was none of those things. He wasn't anything. He wasn't my brother. He was dead.'

I had to wipe my nose with my sleeve. For a minute I thought I had a nosebleed, but it turned out it was snot mixed up with tears. Finally, tears. Now that they'd started, I was frightened they'd never stop falling. I'd cry myself to death and drown.

Dad remained incapable of speech it seemed. All he could do was look down at me, sitting at his feet. Like he expected me to tie his shoelaces up.

'Don't you want to know *why* I killed him? Why is key. I'll bloody tell you why, *Daddy*. Because the perfect golden boy was leaving me behind. For that stupid tart, Cindy. You know the one: the girl with the one pink brain cell. He was leaving me: *for her*.'

Dad frowned, as if he wasn't keeping up.

'The missing girl, Dad. Cindy. Jack was dumping me for her. Can you believe it? You must understand. You never liked her. You saw through her. Saw that she was an idiot. Not worthy of Jack. And that's who I was dumped for. Fucking bloody Cindy.'

'I never did like that girl.'

Of all the things to respond to, he'd chosen Cindy to concentrate on. Maybe he didn't want to hear about how Jack had died, but I hadn't finished.

'You and Mum and everyone, you all got it wrong. It wasn't me who needed Jack. It was the other way round. *He* needed *me.* Depended on me. Don't you get it? With my constant and open love on display for him and everyone else to see, I bolstered his status, made him look like all powerful. My adoration of him, created a perfect monster. He thought he was untouchable, universally loved, immortal. He thought he was safe in the Outside world. Perhaps he might have been. But it was his Inside world, *me,* that got him there. It was me who put him on a throne.'

Dad nodded, as if we were talking about the weather or what was for supper. It really pissed me off. This was news, and my audience was a stupid, mean old man who didn't know what to say. But I couldn't stop talking. It had to all come out. Like it or not, Dad had to carry on listening, whether *he* liked it or not. He had no choice. Neither did I. I was a leaking dam and nothing could stop me talking.

'Jack didn't see the danger of leaving me behind. And he should have. He overlooked the real live risk that was right there on his doorstep – had always been there, watching and loving him. Don't get me wrong: I abso-fucking-lutely a*dored* him. He couldn't do any wrong in my eyes. And I couldn't get over the shock. After I pushed him, I couldn't believe he was dead. I swear. I swear to God. That's why I couldn't accept his death: real slap-you-in-the-face shock *and* grief. Do you understand? The knowledge of what I'd done, nearly killed *me*.'

I swished the knife through the air, as a sort of punctuation to my story. Getting nothing back from Dad made it difficult to say everything that I needed to. But I stuck at it.

'Jack grew up. Up, up and away. That was his mistake. After all my life of servitude, of undying love for him, he went and left me for some cheap-shit whore. It's all his fault. He made me do it. I hate him. I'm glad he's gone. I'm better off without him. Look how I've grown since he's been away. I'm a man, an adult. I'm free. I'm Butty. I am me. I am finally free.'

For a moment, maybe lots of tiny moments, I was jubilant. Weeping and jubilant. I really *was* free. Freed from the shadows of my own making. Standing up, I shouted with all the force I had, 'I am free. At last, I am free.'

I couldn't stop crying though, like a baby, and said, 'You know that expression, Dad, "Behind every man is a good woman?" – that's right, isn't it? It's the same difference here: behind every brother is a little brother. Me. I cemented his greatness, I was his support, I started it – I was his own personal fan club.'

'You're talking in riddles. Stop it. It's all rubbish.' Dad put his hands over his ears like a child. Desperate for me to stop. But I wouldn't.

'Without me, loving him so hard from the very beginning, he wouldn't have been favoured. I made him look great: without me he'd have been great, but not exceptional – I made him who he was. I led the stupid fucking adoring congregation, by my unwavering show of reliance and love of him. My open display of it. People followed me, not him. I made him who he was.'

Dad looked into the air, ignoring me. Started to quietly whistle.

'It's me who's the great one, not him. And Jack was

dumping me, like I was just a passing piece of shit. Flushed me down the loo, and for why? A stupid girl in pink. After everything I did for him.'

My father put his fingers in his ears and sang, 'La, la, la, la, la.'

Taking no notice of him, I finished my speech. 'That's why I did it. Anger. Anger that he'd dropped me. The ungrateful shit. But I'm also sorry I killed him. I really am.'

Then I heard footsteps on the ladder.

I hoped to God it was Penny.

I didn't want it to be Mum coming into the attic. It wouldn't be fair.

I'm not a cruel boy.

I'm a very confused boy. I'm happy I killed Jack: Sad I killed Jack. Shocked I killed him, horrified I killed him. I missed him, I loved him, I hated him for abandoning me.

But I've found myself.

At last, I have acceptance.

Finally.

FORTY-ONE

Penny

P enny closed her eyes and stood, without moving, dead Donald at her feet, mobile in her hand and re-read Butty's text. *Dad's going to kill me.*

Was Butty being melodramatic? She didn't think so. He was normally a straightforward boy, said precisely what he meant. Knowing this, she had no choice but to take him at his word. Already, the boy had upset and disturbed her with tales of his father's inability to discern his dead son from his live one. Sounded like a man on the edge. Believing the truth of Butty's message wasn't difficult.

Angry and frightened, she realised she had to go to his aid. Had to assume he wasn't lying. People did odd and unforgivable things, trapped in the darkness of tragedy, loss and sadness. She should know. Butty's father was suffering the trauma of losing a child. He sounded like a prime candidate for doing something unforgivable.

Penny couldn't bear the thought of ignoring the child and him dying as a consequence. Wouldn't be able to live with herself if he was killed because she'd ignored his pleas for help.

But she had a dead man inside her home. This interruption meant she'd have to rush. And that made her nervous.

A quick rinse of the face, a thorough wash of her hands, a change of jeans and top was all that she could do. Her killing clothes went into the washing machine – with bleach; who cared at this point as to the damage it would cause her wardrobe? – to be totally sure that nothing remained of the man's fluids. She was as ready as she possibly could be.

She'd have to leave the bloodied carpet as was. If not for Butty, she could at least start to sort out that particular problem. Now, she'd have to leave it for later. More pressing, she had to go through the motions of getting rid of Donald's body in what felt a haphazard and slapdash way: she feared it might have bad consequences for her in the long term.

Butty's immediate need for her aside, she'd already accepted that her time was running out. Everything felt off centre, out of kilter, like an uncontrolled slide down a snowy, icy mountain. Along for the ride, but without any of the equipment she'd normally have.

She understood, that on some level, she'd given up. She'd had enough.

Rushing now, knowing that she'd have to leave her gentleman in the Trumpet Room for some time, pre his final send-off – she had no option but to get on with it. Weighing up the possibilities in her head, there was nothing else she could do. She had to save Butty. It had always been her intent to rescue him: she had no excuse – couldn't fail him now. She'd have to risk her own life: pray to God that no one would suddenly want access to her father's music room before she'd finished with Donald.

Don't be stupid. The police don't know I'm a man-whisperer. They're not looking for me. No one is.

Automatically, she flew around the bungalow, dashing from

sitting room to garage, from body to jeep, wheelbarrow bumping and rolling along carpet and concrete. The body removal, after only two dead men, was already familiar and the ritual of it all fell into place. The repetition of her actions calmed her, and it wasn't long before Donny was wedged securely in the wheelbarrow, in the back of the jeep, en route to her parents' house.

Driving carefully, not wanting to be stopped for speeding whilst giving a lift to a cadaver, she reached home and quickly drove up as far as she could on the drive, before wheeling the now covered-with-cloth-and-logs dead Donny into the Trumpet Room. De-barrowing him into the bath, she hesitated, not happy leaving him in what felt like such open view. Unattended. Usually, the next phase would come immediately, but this time, she didn't have the opportunity to carry out his final adieu to the world.

More's the bloody pity.

Butty needed her.

She hadn't bothered texting him back. Wasn't sure of the situation and couldn't know if his text had been made secretly. She didn't want to make things worse, set off a volatile man who wanted to kill his son. Toying with the idea of ringing the doorbell when she arrived, she decided instead to follow Butty's instructions. The mother was out, father and son were in the attic. Again, no choice. She'd have to let herself in and hope for a warm reception from Daddy Hawthorne whose mind was apparently murderous.

Goddamn it. Her relationship with Butty ricocheted from one disaster, one crisis, to another. Nothing was ever easy or normal or calm with him. She hoped he wasn't lying and that it wouldn't turn out that it was he, Butty, who was holding his father at knife point.

Pulling onto the Hawthorne's drive, parking as near to the

side to make her van as invisible as possible, she approached the house on foot. Not able to help herself, she gave in to a childish fear that someone was watching her, some unnamed monster lurked in the bushes, in the dark – waiting to pounce. Her head swivelled behind her, right, then left, until she stopped and gazed hard into the undergrowth. *There, nothing.* She was being stupid.

Unable to put it off any longer, she went around the house and pushed open the back door. As promised, it wasn't locked. Licking her lips, she moved through the house quietly, finding and going up the stairs, until she came to the ladder leading to the attic.

She heard Butty's voice, crying and shouting. Listening for a bit, wanting to get a firmer grip on things, wanting to know what she was walking into, the boy's words chilled her.

His voice sobbed, young and sad, but proud and defiant all at the same time. It floated down to her: 'I made him who he was. It's me who's the great one, not him. And Jack was dumping me, like I was just a passing piece of shit. Flushed me down the loo, and for why? A stupid girl in pink. After everything I did for him. That's why I did it. Anger. Anger that he'd dropped me. The ungrateful shit. But I'm also sorry I killed him. I really am.'

Her stomach clenched and her heart dropped. 'I killed him.' That's what he'd said, and she realised she wasn't overly surprised. Just terribly, terribly sad and tired. Tired of everything. How could she save him now?

Deep down she'd always been unconvinced at his hurried and brief account of his brother's death but had never allowed herself the time to really think about it properly. She realised she'd suspected the true cause of Jack's death but had never permitted herself to linger on the thought. Had point-blank refused to ever explicitly think about Jack's death: hadn't wanted to go down that particular mental pathway.

Did it also mean that Butty had deliberately killed Cindy as well?

Not wanting to know the answer, she also knew that she couldn't shy away from it any longer.

Out of the three of them, Penny wasn't sure who needed saving most.

FORTY-TWO

Penny

'Penny,' Butty shouted, opening his arms out as if to hug her. 'You're here. Thank God.'

She wasn't about to change a habit of a lifetime and go all sugary-sweet-social-workery-do-gooder on him. There was no point. Hit him with it, full on. 'I heard what you said, Butty. That you killed your brother.'

She awaited his response, which came easily and freely, with no shame nor visible guilt. Butty was looking distraught but oddly happy. Like he was finally breathing. Breathing through a torrent of hiccuping sobs.

'Good. Good, I'm glad you heard. I wanted to wait until you got here before I said it, but I couldn't wait to tell Dad. I needed to say it out loud, to get it out of me, and as Dad needed waking up, needed a shock to get him back into the real world, I told him.' Butty turned to look at his father who sat in a chair, holding a big toy bus.

Daddy Hawthorne's expression told Penny nothing, except that he wasn't one hundred per cent all there. Something was missing deep within him. He certainly wasn't someone who you'd immediately choose to go up to, and recount jolly japes and the current state of the comedy circuit. He seemed trapped in a dark place, where there was no laughter. Or any tears. A nothing place.

Tiptoeing through the family mess that waited for her, both of them staring at her as if she were the one person in the whole world who could solve all this, she was caught in uncertainty. Unsure who to address first. Unsure *what* to address first. The murder of Jack, or the according-to-Butty, imminent death of himself. Both Hawthornes' eyes were glassy and shiny; Butty's still wet with tears; his father's frighteningly icy, slippery, wet-looking.

She went for the most obvious statement. 'You killed Jack because he grew away from you. Had a girlfriend. Cindy. He was choosing her instead of you.' Penny waited. 'You killed him because you were jealous? Really?'

'No, no, no.' Butty stamped his foot in frustration. He was speaking fast, his words tripped over themselves in an effort to escape his mouth: they poured from him, like tea from a spout. 'I was so shocked, Penny. I think that's why I could never accept his death, because *I'd* caused it.' For a moment, he looked truly shocked at that knowledge. As if it had only truly sunk in, that very second. She saw that in his eyes, she was his one true sounding board, and that the meaning and truth of his words had bounced back and smacked him squarely where it hurt.

After a brief, shocked hesitation, he carried on with his own brand of tea pouring into whatever vessel would take it. 'I wasn't jealous. Course not – *jealous?* That's stupid. No. I pushed him in front of the car because he was going to leave me all on my own, by going off with Cindy. After everything I'd done for him. It wasn't fair.'

He started crying again, had never really stopped, and Penny didn't know quite what to do. Christ, where was the bloody mother? This shouldn't be Penny's job.

But it was. It had always been her job ever since they'd bumped into each other. It was perhaps the one good thing she could do, to understand and help the child, in order that she redeem herself for her own misdeeds – heinous wrongdoings, as they would be perceived by other people. Normal people. She personally thought her killings were totally understandable, but she also knew that there'd be few who agreed with her.

Butty admitting to the murder of his brother, was a whole new walk in the park. She didn't want to go on that walk; she was all rambled-out with blisters on her feet and a sore back from too much bloody emotional baggage: not all of it hers. Not wanting to have to deal with all the shit that they'd have to wade through on that journey together, she was tempted to move on, as if Butty hadn't spoken, and talk about tea and crumpets. Hot chocolate and marshmallows.

Uncaring of the father's existence, ignoring Mr Hawthorne's totally uninvolved status, she asked Butty, 'Does that mean you killed Cindy?'

His face went white with shock and, she belatedly realised, fury. '*No*. What are you thinking? How can you not believe me, after everything we've been through together? It happened just the way I said it did. What the fuck, Penny?'

He was going to say something about her getting rid of the body, she knew it, braced herself for it, worried that however disengaged the father looked, he might not be that mad to let that particular piece of knowledge about her go without comment.

But Butty said nothing about it, and the father made no murmur. She wasn't even sure he'd heard any of it. Almost tempted to go over and check that he was in fact still alive, she instead decided to leave him to his self-imposed isolation. She wasn't going to mother him as well, for Christ's sake. Butty was enough to be getting on with.

And what to do with his confession? Give him a stern talking-to? High-five him in a congratulatory way? Call the police? Call the men in white coats? Contact his mother? Give him a bloody medal for coming in last?

'I'm sorry, Butty. Really, I am.'

How bloody feeble a thing was that to say? Made worse because he looked disappointed in her. As if she'd failed in some way. Hadn't said the right thing. And he was right.

They both startled as the father noisily crossed his legs, making an effort to be noticed. Coming out of some fog of his own creation. Knowing that he had their attention, Mr Hawthorne said, 'I don't believe him. He's lying. He didn't kill Jack – he hasn't got it in him. He's crying out for attention, and I, for one, am not giving it to him. He's pathetic. Lying to make himself seem more important than he is. And that...' He stood up. '*That* wouldn't be difficult, would it?'

'What sort of a father are you?' Penny asked. 'He's hurting. He's damaged. And so are you. I believe him and I wish I didn't, but I do. You should too. He's telling the truth.'

'Yes, I am,' said Butty – his voice was flat, his demeanour flat, his spirit flat. Total bloody flatline. The telling hadn't given him what he'd craved. He stood there, holding his knife, and wept for what seemed like forever.

Mr Hawthorne, who Penny only knew in passing and had never said anything more than a polite 'hello' to when they met, as they each went about their daily business, straightened his back as if it ached. He spoke to the floor. 'I've got one dead son, the perfect one, now perfectly dead. The other stands and blubbers before you, Penny. Impressed by him, are you?'

'More impressed by him than you, yes. And I like him. Very much. We're alike, me and Butty. He's my friend.' Penny surprised herself with this open and honest statement and was relieved that Butty's face lit up when he heard it. He smiled gently at her, so desperately grateful that *she* felt like weeping.

Swallowing down the rush of emotion she felt for the child, she turned her full attention to the father who averted his gaze. 'Butty tells me you're going to kill him. Is that true?'

Butty jumped in, his voice coming alive again, full of childish anticipation at revealing the depths to which his father had sunk. 'Yeah, it is true, isn't it, Dad? You said if you can't have Jack, you don't want me.'

The boy turned to her, his cheeks and nose pink from all that crying. 'Do you know how he's going to kill me, Penny? You'll love it, I swear. He's going to put me on that itsy-bitsy bus that he's holding like a baby and send me off to nowhere. Funny, isn't it? That that's how I'm going to die. On a fucking midget bus on the road to hell. And apparently, Jack's coming back on it, as far as I can make out. Taking my seat on the way back.' He laughed. 'Typical.'

Mr Hawthorne went into a gorilla-type stance, his legs planted firmly apart, his arms swinging loose, and his neck stuck out aggressively as if warning Butty not to come closer. 'Do not laugh at me, Butty. You ingrate. You imbecile. You have no idea what I'm going to do with you. But you're right. I'm definitely going to kill you. Ready?'

He stayed like that, not moving, not advancing. And for the first time since her arrival, he looked Penny directly in the eye. 'And you, Miss Penny Crisp, I'm surprised at you. Coming here. So brazen. So bold. I'm surprised but delighted at your presence, even if you're here for the wrong reason.'

He flashed his teeth at her in an odd sort of grimacing smile.

Confused, Penny gathered her thoughts with both hands, ready for a verbal attack, not understanding the man.

I'm too late to save Butty.

Perhaps I can at least save him from his father.

She braced herself for whatever was coming.

FORTY-THREE

Butty

W hat's the wrong reason? What about what I said? My confession? Dad doesn't believe me, and he doesn't even know Penny, not properly anyway, so why does he care that she's here? What's he on about?

Penny's face had scrumpled up into confusion and Butty watched her lips move as she spoke to his father. 'Brazen? Bold? Because I came into your house without your permission? I came because your son asked me to come. He needed me and I can see why.'

Dad straightened up from his ape impression, nodded his head sarcastically and covered his mouth with his hand as if trying not to laugh. 'If that's the way you want to play it, Penny, you go right ahead.'

'You're mad. And I bloody refuse to get into a conversation with a man who's threatening to murder his son. Whatever Butty's done. He needs help. Have you nothing to *say* about Butty's confession? All you've done is ignore it. Not believe it. It needs to be talked about. What are we going to do?'

'We? *We?* Who do you think you are? It's up to me to decide what to do with his stupid admission of murder. He couldn't murder a flea, much less my golden boy who was bursting with life. Butty was the weaker of the two; absolutely no way could he have harmed Jack. Jack was stronger. Butty didn't do it. I'm not even entertaining the idea. It's not worthy of my time.'

'I take it you're over the notion that Butty is Jack, then? Well done you. Progress.' She gave a mock round of applause and laughed. There was something about the sound that made me sad. *She* was definitely very sad. I really hoped I wasn't the cause. Maybe what I'd said about killing you, Jack, had released her own demons. I was pretty sure she had them. I think most people do. It was like I'd killed a bit of her.

It wasn't that I'd expected to be awarded a champion's cup for killing you, nor that I'd become the obvious choice for 'boy most likely to succeed'. Course not. But I had expected huge upheaval of some kind. It was after all, a revelation that would normally stop conversation. Even after I'd told, Dad refused to hear me, to notice me, to acknowledge what I'd done. According to him, it seemed I wasn't even worthy enough to kill you.

The tingle of my breaking news was replaced by a numbness. Detached now, deflated and disappointed by the lack of surprise shown at my brother's murder, I waited to see what would happen. Dad was acting weirdly. That wasn't anything new, but he seemed fascinated by Penny. As far as I knew, they didn't really know each other, were neighbours who rarely met. But he kept on staring at her, all sort of intense. And he seemed pleased that she was here.

I shuffled further to my left, so that I could see Penny's expression as she walked towards Dad. Cutting him off at the pass. I think she was trying to get nearer to Dad-the-volcano, in case he erupted, in case he went for me – trying to kill me in some way. Shrink me to death. I wasn't that bothered. Penny was here and she'd save me.

'Does your wife know how you feel about Butty?' Penny asked, sticking up for me, representing me, like a true friend. My heart warmed and my disappointment was lessened by the knowledge that she did care. She really did care about me.

'Who cares what my stupid wife thinks, says or does. She loved both boys and for that she either deserves a medal or a booby prize for being so stupid. No class, that woman. Always quick to love anything.' He turned to me. 'Or any*one*.'

'I know Mum loves me. It's what Mummies are for. Both me and Jack thought you were weak and stupid and pathetic. I don't care that you don't love me. Love your trains, instead. If they're better than me, I think that makes you the loser.'

And then I stopped talking. Anything else I wanted to say stalled in my throat, my words doing an abrupt emergency brake. I'd been keeping my eye on Penny, not sure what she was going to do, and then I saw it.

She smiled. It was sudden and extraordinary: like one lone bright star – the Northern Star – shining in an inky clear sky. It shone with a brilliance that defied description. It was transcendental; a total transformation that you could build a religion on. With a smile like that, people would believe anything you said. Do anything you wanted. She'd have an instant following and I, for one, would be first in the queue.

It was like being sucked into a cult. Not screaming and shouting but laughing at Penny's radiance. I wanted to run towards the light and be embraced by it. Be loved by it.

It was a smile to die for.

The smile vanished as if the electricity had been cut off. Sudden, violent and shocking in its disappearance. From white to black, in the snap of the finger.

It left only hardness on her face as if the smile had never been – a figment of the imagination only. A moment of being truly entranced, to an abandoned feeling of abject desolation. The contrast of her non-smile was like death had come early and unexpectedly. Her expression went from sunshine to unreadable: as cold as ice. And as unforgiving.

It chilled me and I was her biggest fan. It visibly frightened my father. He stepped back, needing distance from Penny.

But she wasn't looking at Dad. I followed her gaze and my eyes came to rest on my father's four o'clock treat: the mug of tea and his unfinished lollipop, only half-sucked and sticky looking. Its wrapper lay scrunched in a loose ball on the arm of the chair.

Penny couldn't take her eyes off it. Was transfixed by it. 'Where did you get that? It is yours, isn't it, Mr Hawthorne?'

Dad was pleased, had his stupid showing-off face on, like he'd achieved something when really he'd done nothing at all. He beamed. 'I'm thrilled you remember, Penny. Course it's mine. I make them. In a special machine which automatically seals them in their wrappers. I make all kinds of sweets. Ask Butty. He's always got his fist in the sweetie jar.'

She swung round, her face tight, white and bright with… something I couldn't recognise.

'Why don't you ever smell of aniseed, Butty?'

'Because I hate aniseed. Only Dad eats the lollipops. I eat all the other homemade stuff, but not them. The whole family hates aniseed. Except Dad.'

As I said this, I somehow knew that I was digging a grave for my father, getting him into deep, deep shit with Penny. I was glad but intrigued. What was so important about a bloody aniseed lollipop?

Penny went straight up to Dad and punched him in the chest. He hadn't been expecting it and the force of it made him fall back into his chair. I held my knife closer to me. I didn't know what the fuck was going on, but Penny was suddenly very frightening.

Standing over Dad, she was victorious. She was like a glorious female space hero from another planet, ready to unleash her power on the weak and cowering man beneath her. Penny was taller, bigger, stronger and more terrifying than anyone I'd ever seen. She was beautiful.

Her words bounced off the beams of the attic as she screamed at Dad. 'It was you. *You*. A fucking neighbour. All this time, there you were, living in the same road. You did it. It was you. You raped me, you bastard. *You raped me.*'

She started hitting his face, slapping, punching it, until I pulled her away and held her. I wasn't protecting Dad. I was protecting Penny. Tears poured down her face and saliva hung from her mouth. A long drool of it. A drool fuelled by such intense hatred, I was seriously scared, but I was so in awe of this woman, it took my breath away. She needed saving from herself. I could do that. I owed her after all.

But I couldn't take in what she'd said to Dad. I'm not an idiot, I understood the meaning of her words, 'You raped me.' The words themselves as single and separate things, weren't difficult to understand. But in a sentence – about my *father*?

I couldn't get my head round it. Dad was a rapist.

He'd *raped* Penny. Boring, normal-before-your-death Dad, model train collector, homemade sweetie man, had done something very out of the ordinary. He'd been more than bad. He'd been wicked.

Dad had to be punished.

He had to die.

FORTY-FOUR

Penny

P enny pushed Butty away, untangled his arms that circled
her body, trying to restrain her. He dropped the knife.
She saw him bend to pick it up and said, 'Leave it.'

Walking two steps to the side, she took the knife in her
hands, handling it with tenderness, glad to have something to
use. She knew as she looked at Mr Hawthorne, that her face
was full of disdain. But triumph also jostled for a home.

'Gotcha, Mr Hawthorne,' she said.

And she *had* got him, but disappointment threatened to
spoil her moment. He was so horribly boring and non-rapist
looking. An ordinary man, visually: on the surface. In her
mind, over the two years or so, *since he'd raped her*, she'd created
a monster of a man in her mind; not horned with pitchfork in
hand, but a man who looked at the very least, *capable* of evil.

And here he was. Finally. A nondescript figure. Very
*in*capable looking. And he had the cheek to be pleased that she
recognised and remembered the fucking lollipop. As if he
weren't guilty of anything.

The smell of aniseed. He was the same size as her. Not big,
nor small framed. Remembering how she'd thought they'd

obscenely and horribly fit, she could see that he was a similar size to her. Not young, not old.

It was him.

The lollipop proved it.

She'd been right all along. It could be any man. It could be all men. They were all the same. It just happened to be him. The grown-up boy next door.

For some reason, the fact that this complete bastard had lived within spitting distance made her angrier still. She could have had him any time she'd wanted. If only she'd known.

She asked what his first name was. It was how her encounters with Keith, Moley and Donny had started. With a show of common courtesy. She liked the tradition of it and followed her script accordingly. He answered, unaware that this was more than just any old over-the-garden-fence chat with a visiting neighbour. This was his *last* chat. She wished him well with it.

'My first name's Gordon. You know that, Penny. You know me. It's *me*.' He spread his arms out, pretending disbelief that she didn't know his name. She wanted to kill him right there, right then. But she couldn't. Not yet.

First, she had to go through her by-now, well-practised routine. Have *the conversation*. Find out, why her?

Putting the blade lengthways on the floor, she stood on the knife. 'Get me a chair, Butty.'

Waiting patiently, she searched Gordon's face. Tried to identify the rapist marker. It should be as obvious as the bloody stigmata. All she could see was 'ordinary'. It pissed her off. His face also had a smug expression plastered on it; as if she were making a fuss over nothing. As if he couldn't understand her being here, her accusation seemed to have flown over his head, not bothering with hanging about in his brain where she'd hoped it would be heard and digested.

He most definitely did *not* look guilty or afraid. That was a mistake: one of many.

Mistake number one was obvious. He'd raped her.

Mistake number two: he didn't acknowledge that he'd done wrong. She could tell. That was predictable but horrifyingly puzzling. It was so wrong she couldn't quite take it all in.

Mistake number three: he didn't realise what was about to hit him.

A chair appeared, and she sat, feet on blade, trapping it. 'I don't want you here, Butty. You don't have to listen to this. You mustn't listen. I forbid it. Leave now.'

'No, I'm staying. I'll sit in the armchair, but I'm not going anywhere.'

She looked at the boy who smiled encouragingly at her. 'It's all right, Penny. I'm grown-up enough to hear it. And, who knows? You might need me. Think of me as Santa's little helper. Your little helper.' He bowed his head. 'At your disposal.'

'I don't need your help, but thanks for the thought. Go on. Off you trot.'

'Penny, everyone needs help some time. Even you. I'm staying.'

Tutting, she turned from him. Couldn't worry about him now. This was all about her. Her and Gordon. Butty's father. Of all the men in the world, why did it have to be him? She'd been right, again, when she'd recognised her life was drawing to an end. If she hadn't met Butty, it might have been different. But she had, and now she'd ruin the child further than he already was. She might damage him irreparably. Everything had turned to shit.

Except she *did* have Gordon.

Knowing he was the one, she was loath to hit him over the head into unconsciousness. Didn't have her baseball bat at her side anyway. She had a knife but didn't feel predisposed to use it. Caving in skulls was more her thing.

Gordon was sitting quietly, patiently, relaxed in his armchair and had again picked up his big bus and caressed it as it lay in his lap. Leaning forward, Penny took the knife in her hand, using it only as a don't-come-near-me thing to keep Gordy from escaping, to stop him attacking her. It worked as she flashed it in front of his face: he reared back in shock. She took the opportunity to remove his toy bus from his hands.

For a toy, a replica, it had some considerable heft to it. She played with it, tossing it from palm to palm, enjoying its weight. It was good. It would work. Surprisingly, if all went to plan, Gordy's head would hopefully explode on impact when she hit him. A crude way to die, but if it worked, she didn't give a fuck as to death's finesse. Or lack of.

'Give me my bus back, Penny Crisp. Right now, this minute.'

'Go fuck yourself, Gordon Hawthorne. I'm keeping it. I'm in the driving seat now, okay. So, shut up and listen. We need to talk, as they say.'

'What about?' His face was quizzical.

She found it unbelievable. He was behaving as if he had no idea as to why she might be more than a little angry with him. 'I've said it very clearly already, Gordon. You raped me and now I want to know why.'

He laughed. 'Don't be ridiculous. *Of course* I didn't rape you. Don't be silly. If I'd raped you, what on earth are you doing here?'

'I told you. I came here for your son. But ignore him. I know that won't be hard for you. I came for Butty, and I discovered you. Pretend it's just you and me in this room. Alone. Together.'

'See, alone. Together. Exactly. You remember. And wasn't it nice, our alone, together time? I knew, well, no, that's a bit of a lie, I *hoped* that you'd see sense and seek me out. And you have. I was right to wait for you to come to me. I was fairly confident you would, and let's not pretend you're here for Butty. You're here for me. You just couldn't wait to see me again. Come on, Penny. Be truthful for once. You've missed me.'

Her fingers tightened on the heavy, metal bus. She found it hard to take in his nonchalance, his complete inability to own up to his crime. She said it again. 'You raped me. I'm not here for a merry get-together, to talk about old times. I'm going to kill you. But first, I want to hear, why me? You missed that bit out. You made it all about you. I couldn't give two hoots about how you felt about it. All I want to know is *why me?*'

He shook his head like he was dealing with a particularly stupid child. 'Because you wanted me to come to your house. You told me so.'

'What are you talking about? When did we make this secret, completely fictional assignation? Was I even there?'

'You must remember. We passed each other in the road, you with your wheelbarrow, me on foot, and I said, "Hello." Do you not recall how you responded?'

'Remind me.'

'You stopped walking and looked me straight in the eye, and you smiled. Pretended to go all shy on me, and then you did it. You swept your hand through your long, beautiful hair, in that special way. And that's when I knew.'

'What special way?'

'Oh, come *on*. You were flirting with me. Outrageously so. Like you don't know. Flicking your hair, in that come-hither way. You practically invited me to come to your bedroom. You wouldn't stop running your hands through your hair. You wouldn't stop bouncing it in front of me, waving it across my face. I could even smell the shampoo on it. Lovely.'

He closed his eyes briefly, in memory. Penny felt like vomiting. He slowly opened his eyes and said, 'I'd have had to be blind not to see what you wanted. You might as well have screamed it out at me, "I want you." That's what you said with your hair. It was code, I'm not stupid. It was easier to play with your hair than to come right out with it, and tell me, to my face, that you wanted sex with me. So, don't start complaining that I came and gave you exactly what you asked for. It's a bit late to cry rape now, don't you think?'

Penny sat back. A wave of monumental disappointment washed over her; made her feel like she was drowning in a sea of complete pointlessness. Her hair. Was it really that simple?

'I knew you'd come back for me, Penny. When your hair was grown again. It could still do with a bit more length, but it's enough to make me happy. Initially, I admit felt a bit snubbed by you when you cut it. After we'd been together. But I accepted it. And I'm glad you decided to grow it back. It makes you as beautiful as ever.'

She barely heard him. Realised she'd nailed the reason with her first man-whispered rapist, Keith. They'd talked about whether rape was simply about taking advantage of an attractive woman: committing rape, because the woman was vulnerable and pretty. That was it. No more, no less.

The fact that his reason for rape was so unoriginal, so basic, so fucking ordinary and predictable, enraged her. She'd wanted the reason for her violation to be immense, complex, impossible to comprehend. Instead, she could have been talking to a teenage boy; Gordon's motivations were that juvenile and uninteresting.

I raped you because you had beautiful hair.

You gave me a secret, 'come to my bedroom' message when you touched your hair.

You flirted with me.

How could she argue with a man who had such a twisted view of women?

FORTY-FIVE

The Whisperer

Whatever Penny said, Gordon wasn't stupid. She was only saving face, not wanting to admit in front of Butty that she'd desired a real man like him. She'd virtually fucking told him, as good as, to come to her house. Her presence in his attic had brightened up his whole day. Made him forget stupid Butty and his meaningless lie of a 'confession'. Idiot child that he was.

He'd never dreamt that Penny would come to him. Hadn't thought that she'd be so openly willing to visit him again. In his very own home. He couldn't be more thrilled.

The only problem was her banging on and on that he'd raped her. She wouldn't let it go.

She was sitting on the chair, knife under her feet and holding his bus. That made him angry. How dare she touch it? 'Put my bus down and stop going on about me raping you. I didn't. If you hated it so much, if it *was* rape as you claim, why didn't you say, "No"? Why didn't you protest, even a little bit? You didn't attempt to push me off you. You didn't do either, because you were getting precisely what you'd asked for. Don't play the victim now, Penny Crisp. Both you and I know the truth. You wanted sex, and I gave you sex. Or to put it more crudely, I fucked you. There, satisfied? It's as simple as that. What are you complaining about?'

Her face flushed red with fury. She certainly had a temper, this one. There was something a bit frightening about her, and he shifted in his chair – uncomfortable.

He watched as she gripped his bus, threatening to crush it, bend it out of shape – *ruin* it. And then she spoke, very slowly, enunciating each and every word. 'Do excuse me for complaining, Gordon, but you don't seem to get it. You raped me. There was no invitation, no consent. I was terrified into submission: that's why I didn't physically fight you off. I was scared fucking witless. Which part of that are you not understanding?'

'I understand that you're lying; not only to me, but to yourself. You're angry. What's wrong with you? Time of the month, is it? If so, I suggest you go home and come back when you have your hormones under control.'

If he'd realised how delusional this woman was, he wouldn't have visited her that night. Bloody women. Always crying about something, an imagined slight, a wrong word here or there and they'd all have hysterics. No emotional control, that was their problem. He wasn't even sure he liked women very much. Except for the obvious reasons. A man needed sex and women were good for *that*, if nothing else. In fact, it was all they were good for. Smiling at her, he was more confident now that he'd reminded himself just who was at fault here.

It most certainly wasn't him. He'd done nothing wrong.

And now, he was having to deal with the weeping, hysterical shrieking of a woman. As per. All very normal and nothing he wasn't used to. He could handle her.

Except Penny wasn't weeping, nor hysterical. Instead, she was sitting very still. Again, he was unnerved by her. The longer he spent with her, the more convinced he became that she wasn't the full shilling. Turned out, she most undoubtedly had beautiful hair, but was undoubtedly a very unbeautiful person. Didn't know her place. She could really do with another damn good seeing-to. That'd knock her into shape. Show her who was boss.

Her voice, when it came, was spookily calm. Her tone so flat it literally made his skin crawl. 'I was going to ask you if you'd raped other women before, Gordon, but that's a stupid question, don't you agree? Silly little woman that I am. If you can't admit to raping me, then it stands to reason you wouldn't ever be able to confess to previous sexual crimes. Right?'

'Couldn't have said it better myself. See, you haven't a leg to stand on, *because I never raped you.* It's all up here...' He tapped the side of his head with his finger. 'In your imagination. How dare you come here, to my house and accuse me of rape. In front of my son. It's outrageous. I'd like you to leave now. You've outstayed your welcome. Next time, wait for *me* to visit *you*. Get out. You're not wanted here.'

To make a point, he picked up his unfinished lollipop and sucked it, licked it as lewdly as he could, with his tongue stretched out as far as it would go. That would show her what she was missing, silly cow.

FORTY-SIX

Penny

———————

Penny's stomach lurched in a very physical way; it leapt and cartwheeled, filled with utter disgust as she watched Gordon, so self-satisfied, so confident, eat his fucking lollipop in the most repulsive way imaginable.

The killing of Keith, Moley and Donny had been easy. At least she hadn't had to listen to their facile, unconvincing excuses. Gordon had thrown her by actually being as horrendous as she'd imagined. He was like a template for all men, all rapists. The realisation that her rapist was as misogynistic as she'd thought, almost paralysed her.

He'd shown how much he *despised* all women. It had never been about her personally. It wasn't anything she'd done. She could have been *any* woman. And he'd have used *any* excuse to see flirtation where there was none. If it hadn't been her hair, it would have been her beautiful lips, her perfect teeth, her well applied make-up. Anything. None of it would have made any difference. She'd been fucked by simply walking down the street at the wrong time and bumping into the wrong person. A man. In this case, Gordon.

On the plus side, it showed she'd been right all this time: all men were the same.

She wished she'd told him 'No', wished she'd at least tried to punch him, kick him, wished she'd screamed out loud at the top of her voice, but having listened to him, he'd given her some peace.

It wouldn't have made any difference at all.

He'd have raped her whatever she'd done.

She held the chunky toy in her hands tighter. Confident it would kill him with a few blows. Life was strange like that: you'd get up as normal and go about your daily routine, minding your own business and then, bam, you were hit by a bus. It happened all the time.

'One more thing, Gordon. Before we part ways, I want to know if your wife knows. Knows about me, I mean.'

'Course she knows. I told her all about it.'

'What did she say?'

'Said she didn't want to hear any more of it. Refused point-blank to talk about it at all. Every time I brought you up, wanting to let her know all about you, she covered her ears and started singing so she could drown out my words. But she wasn't jealous – that would have been ridiculous. Unlike most women, the green-eyed monster didn't come out to play. She knew there was no point, because she completely understood that you meant absolutely nothing to me. Couldn't have meant less. You were there to serve a purpose and you served it well. Congratulations. You were great.'

He beamed at her, making his smile as condescending as possible.

Penny stood up.

Gordon stood up and folded his arms. As if he were about to escort her to the front door.

'Aren't you going to at least say, "No", Gordy? Aren't you going to put up a fight?'

Slowly, too slowly, he uncrossed his arms.

Unfortunately for Penny, he literally didn't see it coming. She had wanted to see his face register fear that his life was about to end. But instead, there was a second only of utter incomprehension in his eyes. The bus hit him on the side of the face, knocking him sideways onto the floor. Kneeling over him, she continued to rain down blows with the big heavy metal bus. Down and down she crashed it, until its frame bent and buckled. Still she couldn't stop.

She was only aware that she was covered in blood when she felt Butty's arms around her. As he lifted her away from the train-wreck that had been his father, the very dead and smashed body of Gordon Hawthorne, all she could say was, 'Sorry, Butty. I'm so sorry.'

FORTY-SEVEN

Penny

'The wheels on the bus go round and round, round and round, round and round. The wheels on the bus–'

'Stop it. Please stop it, Butty. Put the bus down and be quiet. Sit down.'

Leading him to the armchair furthest away from the corpse, Penny pushed him gently into it. Kissing him on the cheek, she said again, 'I'm so sorry, Butty. Can you forgive me?'

He nodded, like a five-year-old; shocked, his face grey. Having pried the bus from her hands, he'd stood and spun the wheels with his fingers, although they were still spinning from the assault. All on their own.

At last, he spoke, his voice so quiet that she had to lean in to hear him. 'You don't have to apologise to me, Penny. I should apologise to you. My father raped you. I can't believe it. And worse, Mum knew. Can you believe it, Mum knew.'

Penny agreed that she'd have to grapple with Helen Hawthorne knowing about the rape all this time and doing nothing about it.

She'd try and understand Helen's behaviour and could only imagine what it must have been like living with a man like Gordon. Having to listen as he'd gloated about raping her. What must Helen have thought? Or perhaps it was a frequent subject, often visited, but instead of it being Penny's story, maybe Helen had had to listen to a whole glut of rape stories of countless raped women, told gleefully and proudly by Gordon. It was another form of abuse and Penny found that she felt sorry for Helen. They shared a common monster.

Sitting on the arm of the chair, she held Butty's hand. 'Don't blame your mother. It must have been difficult for her hearing your father boast about rape. But for the moment, don't worry about her. She loves you. What's most important now, is that you really shouldn't have had to see your father's murder. Or hear what he'd done. It wasn't meant to end like this. How could I have known, when we first made friends, that it was your father who'd raped me? I never knew.'

Nodding again, he pulled back his shoulders, took back his sweaty fingers from her grasp, and bracing himself for this new world and everything that it would mean, he said, 'I won't tell, Penny. Never. He deserved it. He was going to kill me, and I know he would have, but I'll never tell that you killed him. I swear.'

Squeezing his hand, kissing him again on his face, she said, 'I don't think we can get away with that lie, Butty. The police will know I killed him. Primarily because I'll tell them that I did, because I feared for my life – it was self-defence. How can I deny it? I'm covered in his blood, my fingerprints are all over the bus, they'll know it was me, there's no way I can pretend it wasn't me.' She laughed. 'It certainly wasn't you. And I won't tell, either. About what you did to Jack. That's between me and you. For ever and ever. Okay?'

'Why are you so eager to save me, Penny? You've always been like that.'

'Because we're alike, that's why. And we already share a

secret. The Cindy secret. What's one more secret between friends.'

'I don't want you to go to prison, Penny.'

'You know what? I don't care. Not one bit. I'm kind of glad it's over. And prison… how bad can it be?'

It was the truth: she'd finally got her rapist. Nothing else mattered. She almost welcomed the idea of prison. A safe place with no men: only women. She'd cope.

She thought of something. 'Butty, where did the knife come from?'

'I brought it up from the kitchen because I didn't trust what Dad may do.'

'Let's keep that to ourselves, shall we. Let's say that your father already had the knife with him in the attic. So that he could threaten you or me with it? Okay? Would you mind saying that?'

'No, sounds good to me. The bloody bastard. It was his knife and he was going to hurt me with it. Or you. Got it. Sorted.'

Penny smiled gratefully at him, knowing that she could trust him, and quickly moved across the attic towards Gordon. 'Whose fingerprints are on the knife?' she asked the boy.

'Just mine. It was clean. I got it straight from the dishwasher.'

'Good.' She picked the knife up in her fingertips and wiped the handle thoroughly. Picked up one of Gordon's hands and made them grasp the knife. 'There. Now only his prints. We're safe.'

Butty nodded. 'No problem. Understood. Mission accomplished.'

Smiling briefly at him, her mind skittered on. Her parents would have to know about the rape and that thought was the worst. It would destroy them. Neatly swerving the detail of that truth, she was also genuinely appalled that Butty had been witness to the killing of his father and heard that Gordon had raped her. But she couldn't change that. Couldn't change any of it. It was done. Whatever happened was now not up to her. It was almost a relief. She settled down to wait, sitting next to Butty, careful not to get blood on him.

It crossed her mind that there would be no one to look after Butty when she went to prison. His mother wasn't aware of how bad her remaining son was. That he'd murdered her other son. What kind of a boy kills his brother and leaves it at that? Perhaps he had dived straight into his disturbed world and killed Jack and before that, nothing.

But she feared what he might go on to do. If he'd started with murder, how would he finish?

Her friend, the baby psychopath. Nutty Butty. There was nothing further she could do for him. She feared who he'd kill next. She knew he'd kill *some*one but she couldn't stop it.

He'd only just started and there was bugger all she could do about it. Nothing at all. It was morally wrong to keep quiet about him, but her faith in the justice system, authority in general, coppers in particular, was tainted. Her own joint-smoking escapade as a girl – hardly comparable she knew – had taught her that fairness didn't come into it. She was in little doubt that *more* harm would be done, were Butty taken into an institution. The system would devour and consume him.

It would further damage him.

It would make him *worse*. He'd feed off the environment, other inmates. Other disturbed minors. He'd learn how to do it better. How to kill better.

She couldn't save everyone, so she chose to save the boy. To give him a chance and she'd pray hard that he took it.

Feared he wouldn't.

They both heard Helen's voice, all jolly and bright, shouting up from the bottom of the house. 'Butty? Are you up there? I'm home, and I have doughnuts. Come quickly or all I'll eat them all myself. Butty? Doughnuts, and then we'll do the Christmas lights on the tree. Hurry up, young man.'

They both heard her clap her hands. It was strange to be brought back to reality with the promise of doughnuts and Christmas lights.

Penny didn't think she'd be staying for either treat.

And then it hit her. The shock of what she'd left in the Trumpet Room almost made her physically sick.

How could I have forgotten?

Fucking Donald. He was still in the bath. Very dead in the bath.

Would she get bail? She bloody well hoped so, otherwise she'd be charged with that idiot's murder and that was *not* acceptable. She desperately needed time to get rid of him, and no one would be any the wiser.

About Donald, or Keith, or Moley.

God, please give me bloody bail. I don't believe in You, but if You're listening, give me bail. Please.

And I promise I'll never be bad again.

Not ever.

FORTY-EIGHT

Penny

_____

P enny got bail after her initial arrest, not considered a risk to either herself or anyone else. She awaited her trial date: all prim and proper and angelic.

After being released that evening, after she'd happily killed Gordon Hawthorne, she'd rushed to the Trumpet Room. It was early the next morning – Christmas Eve – and she had a very important task to do.

Getting her power-saw, she'd neatly, efficiently and deftly dismembered the now rigid body of Donald. It didn't need to be pretty, only practicable. Small pieces were what she needed – purely for necessity, not manners. Pigs would eat anything, and they didn't give a flying fuck whether their meals were chopped into bite size chunks or not. She wasn't running a bloody meat on a cocktail-stick buffet here. Smaller body parts made the consumption of the body quicker and easier for her pigs. That was all that mattered. They were getting quite a taste for it.

She'd even remembered to count Donald's teeth before dicing him up, and managed to find them all and pick them out as they were excreted from the other end of the pig, a day or so later.

As well as teeth, her porcine friends were averse to human hair. Couldn't digest either. The teeth were smashed into smithereens in a sack by a ballpeen hammer and then scattered hither and thither. The small sack and the hair were burnt. Easy enough.

It had occurred to her early on that it would have been simpler to extract the teeth before dismembering the rapists, but because she was so squeamish about teeth in other people's mouths, she'd thought it easier to wait patiently for them to put in an appearance in the pig shit.

Penny never did find the missing tooth from Albert the Mole, but thought she was pretty safe, nevertheless. She'd got away with it.

Pre-trial, Donald, had in time, after he'd composted down with the pig shit, become rose food – the flowers loved it, albeit the manure was a little on the acidic side. But she enjoyed the muck-spreading. It was all part of the ritual.

She'd got rid of the bloodied carpet in the bungalow. Her parents decided to rent it out and were adamant Penny move back home. If she hadn't been expecting a prison sentence, she would have completely relaxed and enjoyed the time spent with them. It was reassuringly normal and happy and loving.

She did still have nightmares that Cindy had gone the same piggish way as the man-whispered rapists, and the guilt never left her. But the girl had *not* become rose food. That hadn't been necessary. Thankfully, Butty believed that Cindy was buried in a nameless field, so Penny didn't have to worry about him suspecting her of anything other than killing his father.

She was constantly having to remind herself that all she'd done was bury an already dead girl — had simply returned her to the earth with as much respect as was possible. It was the only way to accept her role in the disposal of Cindy, without weeping with dismayed horror at her involvement.

Penny stuck her finger through the bars of her cell and touched the 'whore' frost. Smiling at the memory of her now dead father, she wept. She'd surprised herself with how many tears she'd shed once everything had been done and dusted. Since she'd been in this shithole which had been home to her for four years.

Her mother had been right. She'd repressed everything, even her to-die-for smile – not called that for nothing – for so long after the rape, that now she'd killed the baddie, the tears wouldn't stop coming. At odd times, her eyes would fill, and she'd be irritated but accepting of the now predictable deluge that would run down her face.

Her mother had visited her every week. They'd held each other, her mother berating her for keeping the rape a secret. They'd talked of trivial things, happier times, all times, especially about what a shite Christmas it had been for all concerned the year she'd killed Gordon Hawthorne. 'No bloody stockings that Christmas Eve, I can tell you,' Penny's mother had said. 'Me and your father got rollickingly rat-arsed drunk. If you hadn't been being interviewed by the police at the time, you'd have enjoyed it, Penny. A fucking laugh a minute it was, that night. We did miss you so very much, you silly girl.'

And then Dad had died. Penny been given compassionate leave and had gone to the funeral.

'How will I live without him, Penny? Without you? I loved him so much.'

'So did I, Mum. Too much. But we'll get through. Promise. I'll be home soon, and we can run away together. Move to a new city. Live in a smaller house. We'll survive with each other. You, me and Baggage.'

Her mother had wiped her eyes and held Penny's hand. 'Plenty of bloody baggage.'

Penny had served half her sentence and was now due for release. The judge, although sympathetic, hadn't been able to get over the excessive force used by Penny. Gordon had apparently been dead after the second blow. She, however, had given him an extra eleven whacks. Because she'd wanted to. To make absolutely sure. She hadn't admitted to that obviously, but had said instead, that she'd been caught up in the frenzy of it all, fearful for her own life and the possibility of having to defend Butty. Gordon had had a knife.

The prosecution had convinced the jury that the rape was a figment of her imagination, something that could not be proved beyond a reasonable doubt. Butty had done his best, as surprisingly had his mother, Helen. Both had given their testimony, saying they believed that Gordon had raped her.

'Dad admitted he'd raped Penny and then he went a bit mental. Jumped up from his chair, waving a knife. We didn't know who he was going for, me or Penny. She *had* to hit him. It was him or her. It wasn't her fault.'

Faithful Butty.

Helen had been slightly less solid. 'Yes, my husband told me he'd raped Penny. But he told me he'd raped many women. He was a cruel man and I'm not sorry he's dead.'

That had shocked the court; but the way she'd spoken, as vulnerable and as destroyed as she'd looked, her eldest son dead, she hadn't come over as a convincing witness. She made it sound possible that the rapes Gordon boasted about, could have been just that. Boasts. Therefore, potentially untrue. Ultimately, Penny's rape couldn't be *proved*. It was circumstantial and therefore, disregarded.

What *could* be proved, however, was the state of mind of Gordon Hawthorne. This was backed up again by Helen. His warped belief that Butty was Jack. People had noticed his odd behaviour at Jack's funeral. Hearing that Gordon had forced Butty to dress in Jack's clothes and to sleep in his dead brother's room had upset the jury. Their collective expressions had shown disgust and sadness for what Butty had gone through.

Gordon's tenuous grip on reality had swayed the twelve men and women that he might very well have intended to attack his son. Or Penny. After all, he'd had a knife hidden up there, which went a long way to proving how delusional and potentially dangerous he was. That had helped her cause, most definitely. And Gordon's prints on said knife. All in her favour. Enough not to get her life in prison.

What scuppered her was the manner and ferocity of her attack. It was considered seriously too bloody much, too unacceptable to go unpunished. Eight years' worth of punishment. She'd been shocked. The media had gasped at what they thought harsh punishment. Her parents had been distraught; Butty had sobbed.

She'd remained stoic.

After a second appeal, she shut up and got on with her sentence.

Fuck it. She was happy she'd killed the bastard. And three more could-be rapists. Probable-rapists. The police didn't know about any of men she'd man-whispered to death.

Smiling, she wondered, for the millionth time, what Butty was up to.

During her incarceration, he'd written weekly letters to her. She'd written back but had slowly stopped answering, gradually creating distance between them. She'd told her mother to keep away from Butty. Hadn't explained and her mother hadn't wanted to know.

After her beloved father had died, she and her mother decided to move away from the big house in the tiny hamlet and downsize to a smaller house. Perhaps the Isle of Wight. When she was released from prison, they'd start again.

It was imperative that they got some land. That was important. Penny needed pigs. She liked them and they always came in handy. They made her feel safe.

Any man, and I do mean, any *man, that tries to chat me up, pick me up, anyone male who comes into my space, don't even* think *about it. I have pigs on my side.*

She'd got her Aniseed Man. But Penny wasn't stupid enough to think that there weren't still loads of them running about, searching for a new female victim: waiting, watching, hunting.

No man will ever get me again. Not ever.

And she'd be free from Butty at last.

But she did worry about him.

Worried a lot.

Wondered who he had killed, or would kill next.

But she and her mother would be safe from him.

She prayed that Butty wouldn't come looking for her. It was a scenario that she could too easily imagine.

Don't do it, Butty. Stay away from me. Because I guarantee, find me and you'll be sorry.

FORTY-NINE

Butty

4 YEARS LATER

No one called me Butty anymore, because I was all grown up now. All eighteen years of me. I was an adult, and my name was Charlie Hawthorne. I lived happily and normally in the Outside world.

As a child, I hadn't been blessed with the Midas touch. Everything I touched had turned to shite.

Now, people saw me; a strong, and, I'd say, handsome young man, with plenty of muscle: and that hadn't happened overnight – it was something that I'd worked on. Getting definition of muscle had given *me* definition. Given me focus. I was happy.

I kept on having to remind myself of the fact that I was happy.

Sometimes the Inside world crept into my life, and I dealt with it accordingly.

Tonight, was one of those nights.

As Judith-call-me-Jude turned to me, all eager looking, I punched that stupid face so hard that my fist hurt from the contact. Wasn't entirely sure that I hadn't actually broken a knuckle.

That was stupid and unnecessary.

And painful.

Grabbing her ankles, I hefted the deadweight into the middle of the floor. Fleetingly, I considered carrying it to the bedroom, but that seemed like too much of a faff. The floor would do just as well as the bed. I wasn't fussy and didn't suppose Jude was either. Didn't really give a fuck what her thoughts were on the subject.

Taking the knife out of its sheath, I held it to her throat, rested it in that tiny hollow at the front of the neck that seemed so achingly desperate to be filled. It fit nicely. Patiently and politely, I waited for her to regain consciousness.

It would be rude to start with one of us incapacitated.

I stroked her hair, trying to connect with it. For both my father and for Penny it had been the catalyst that had set everything in motion. Hair.

It didn't do it for me. I was searching for that very special Penny smile. The one that dazzled.

And Jude, no surprise, didn't possess anything like that smile. Instead, she had a fairly run-of-the-mill upturn to her lips; nothing that set the world on fire. Don't get me wrong, it wasn't a *bad* smile. At least she had one – of sorts. Couldn't afford to be too bloody picky about the whole thing. Jude was as good as any. A second-rate, second-best Penny. Good enough to be getting on with.

As I lay there, waiting for the girl to wake up, I allowed my mind to wander back over how I'd got here. Currently, at this precise moment, I was back in the now *bad* Inside world, which I frequented on occasion – when the mood took me. Or when life dictated that I must.

Over the years, things had changed: the Outside had become easier, but the Inside had become full of darkness. I didn't like it there, but sometimes I had no option but to visit.

The thing that kept pulling me back there was a simple and

embarrassing cliché. I suffered from fear of abandonment. And frankly, who the fuck could blame me? First, the ultimate betrayal by Jack – my own brother. It was all his fault. He'd started it. Abandoning me for the very pink and forever stupid Cindy.

I'd never got over it. The death of Jack. Trauma stayed with you: like a jagged scar – never letting you move on.

I sometimes thought my biggest trauma had been being born at all.

So, trauma one: Jack. The second traumatic nail in my coffin had been Dad. For him, after Jack's death, and probably even before, I'd ceased to exist to him, and I was only there, hanging around, waiting for him to kill me. Because I wasn't and never would be as good as Jack. Dumped again. And he *would* have killed me. If Penny hadn't saved me. Of that I'm absolutely bloody certain.

The third strike of the trauma gong was Mum. Two years after Penny had gone to prison, my mother had moved out, taking me with her – like a parcel she couldn't just dump on someone's porch en route – into the arms of her new man. A total pillock called Peter. He was wet, soft and so completely boring I couldn't understand what Mum saw in him. After they moved in together, with me loitering in the background like a bad case of acne, I became invisible. It was 'Peter this, Peter that, I'm sorry, did you say something, Butty? Are you still here, Butty? Why haven't you left home yet, Butty?'

When I'd happily moved out at eighteen, nearly ten months ago, she'd hardly had time to say goodbye. I'm not convinced she even noticed I'd gone. I think I frightened her. After the court case, her whole attitude towards me changed. As if everything was my fault. I was effectively dumped by my own mother. Helen Hawthorne at her avoiding, dumping best.

And the final, fourth and worst trauma of them all.

Penny dropped me.

She had the grace to do it politely, to pretend that she wasn't in fact, getting rid of me, but I wasn't stupid. Gradually her prison letters had dried up, and I had no way of maintaining contact. Her mother, early on in Penny's prison sentence, quietly but firmly shooed me away. Perhaps under orders from her daughter – how would I know?

But it left me with evidence that I couldn't ignore.

I was always dumped, abandoned, left on my own.

And I was fucking sick and tired of it.

It wasn't fair. I decided to do something about it. To reassert myself. To make sure that no one *ever* rejected me again.

I became Charlie: arrogant, bullish, physically strong and totally independent: reliant on no one. The new me would not allow Penny to get away with dumping the old me. The one woman who I'd loved like no other, who I'd shared my life with, such as it had been, when I was fourteen. Now I was stronger. I'd *make* her take me back.

My assignations with women, the unconscious Jude being a case in point, were all platonic. I didn't rape them because I wasn't my father. I'd been appalled by his behaviour: what he'd done to Penny. It made me want to vomit.

He'd let himself into Penny's house, crept in like a burglar, and sneaked into her bedroom. What he'd done to her had been cowardly and whatever he said, there is no way on this earth that his actions could have been misconstrued as anything other than rape. He was a virtual stranger to Penny. Imagine waking up with an unidentified man next to your bed – my *Dad*. Terrifying. I'd felt for her. I really had.

And I'd hated Dad for violating her. For *having* her, even for that one night.

After all, she was mine.

My way was much better than my father's. I'd pick up girls in pubs or nightclubs. And I was pretty bloody good at it too.

When it came to girls, I was like catnip to kittens; they'd push and shove their way through the throngs to get my attention. They always said 'Yes' to the offered nightcap back at my flat and they came, like a young child invited to their first birthday party, all flushed with excitement and anticipation, willing, more than willing – *desperate* – to have sex with me.

I forced myself from my nostalgic ramblings and concentrated on the girl on my floor. Bored with waiting for her to come to, I patted her softly around the face. 'Hey, Jude.' Her eyes finally opened, and instantly rounded in shock at finding herself lying on the carpet with a sore and bloody face.

'Hello, there,' I said. 'Better? Sorry about that. I had to hit you. Because you deserved it. I hope it didn't hurt too much?'

Her big brown eyes (same colour as Penny's) filled with tears. I didn't like women who cried. It irritated me beyond belief. It was so... so bloody pathetic. Try living my life – see how you like that, you stupid girl. If you knew me, the real, kind me, then you'd want to stay with me; if you could live my life for a day, you'd see how great I really was, and you'd never want to leave me. You'd love me.

But not like Penny loved me.

That wasn't possible.

I had to make myself listen to Jude. She was speaking. Kept on repeating, 'Why me? Why are you doing this? I agreed to have a drink with you, back in your flat, I never said I wanted sex. Why are you *doing* this? Please don't.'

'Just because I hit you, does *not* mean I want sex with you. I'm not going to rape you. You're not my type.'

You're not Penny.

I'd heard it all before. The 'I only wanted a drink' excuse. What complete fucking rubbish. How dare they lie like that? It was clear for anyone to see that Jude, like the others, had only one thing on her mind when she'd consented to come home with me to my ground-floor flat. That's why I had to teach them a lesson. Teach them not to be so careless with their bodies and their lives – not to put themselves in such a vulnerable position with a strange man.

Penny hadn't been so stupid. She'd woken up to a stranger in her room. She hadn't gone *looking* for sex. Not like the reckless women I picked up.

Look at how they all dressed. Jude was no different to any of them. Cheap tarty clothes, with her tits straining against her top, her skirt way too short and hinting and teasing and flirting at what lay beneath. Might as well have held her knickers in the air and said, 'Come and get me, it's yours.'

'Why are you behaving in such a risky way, Jude? I could be anyone. I could be a madman. I could rape you – if I wanted. You're asking for it, really, you are.'

'But you're not going to?'

'No, no. You're not Penny. I'm saving myself for her. I'm simply proving a point to you. Do not put yourself in such a precarious position with men. It's dangerous and silly and you should know better.'

'I won't, I promise I won't. Honest. Thanks.' She sat up, still looking dazed. 'Can I go now?' She tried smiling at me, her boring, non-dazzling smile not lighting up the room, and I grinned at her.

'Too late, Jude. You should never have come back here with me. Stupid girl.'

Her screams were muffled under my hand; her very real physical pain took away some of the hate I was still filled with. I'd never been able to get rid of it. It was the one constant in my life; it fuelled my existence and the only way to dim the hate, the anger, was to inflict it on others.

On women.

Every time I killed a woman, I was killing them for Penny – knowing she'd approve and would understand that I was only attempting to save them. If not for me, these girls would go out and get themselves raped. I was teaching them a lesson that they were unlikely to forget, and it pleased me that as they died, the last thing they saw as I released them from the danger they'd put themselves in, was my caring face. Saving them from themselves and from men who raped.

Naturally, I had something very different planned for Penny.

Penny, who had taught me how to get rid of bodies.

After I'd killed Jude with a hammer, smashed her stupid non-Penny face in, I waited until the coast was clear, and having backed the car right up to the back door, I only had to turf her into the boot.

And then we'd gone on a long drive to an empty field, in the middle of nowhere. I'd got out my spade and dug quickly in the pitch black and I buried her deep. Just like Cindy, following exactly how Penny had buried her, I now covered with earth the latest Penny look-alike. No one would ever find her: no one had ever found Cindy.

The next day, I was ready. Finally, I was ready to find Penny. I'd always known her release date and knew she'd go straight to her mother's new place. It wouldn't be too hard to find. I didn't suppose that Penny or her mother had changed their names or done anything radical like that.

It took me a while, but then I remembered old Mrs Evans, the local shop owner where we used to live. If she didn't know where Sarah Crisp and her daughter had moved to, I'd be astonished.

Dressing up smartly, making myself look younger and less bulky than I was, I travelled back to the small hamlet that used to be home, and went and had a little chat with the old gossip. She'd known me since I'd been a child and had immediately fussed all over me when she saw me again. Made me a cup of tea, made me another, offered me chocolate like I was a little boy. I let her blather on. How was I? How lovely it was to see me again. My, what a handsome young man you've grown into. Bet you have yourself a girlfriend, a nice boy like you. How was my mother? Blah, blah, blah.

After hours of sweet-talking, I'd asked the question. 'I don't suppose you have Sarah Crisp's new address, do you? She gave it to me, and I wrote it very carefully down on a piece of paper and now I've gone and lost it. Along with her telephone number. How stupid can you get?'

I'd rolled my eyes at my own stupidity, and Mrs Evans had patted me reassuringly on my knee. 'I do have it, actually. I'm not meant to pass it on to anyone, but you're not just *any*one, are you? I know, despite the ugliness of everything that happened, how you got on with Penny and her mother. A shame all round, the whole thing, don't you think?' She leant forward, as if someone were listening although the shop was empty, and said, cupping her hand around her mouth, 'They've got themselves a place on the Isle of Wight. Here, wait there and I'll get the address for you. Are you going to surprise them? They'll be delighted to see you. Especially Penny. After all this time.'

I made all the right noises and left, grinning.

Can't wait to see you, Penny. You'll feel the same. I promise.

I had it all planned out. I'd go to their new house and pretend to bump into Penny, accidentally on purpose, perhaps on the street, as she walked home. I'd act all surprised and ask her to come for a drink with me. She'd never guess that I had any motive other than to reconnect. Penny wouldn't have a suspicious mind, not when it came to being picked up by an old friend like me.

Maybe I'd even offer to carry her bags for her: if she had any. I'd politely ask if I could walk her home. Whatever method I used, and it would be something innocent like that, she'd be taken off guard. I'd be so totally and completely non-threatening, she wouldn't recognise the new charming, handsome me. She'd be so happily surprised to see me, she wouldn't know how to say *no* to me.

It would be as easy as that. Penny would never guess what I had in mind.

I would reclaim her as my partner. She'd said we were partners, and I knew she wouldn't have forgotten. We were life-long partners – I knew she'd understand *that*. We were a match. We were the same. And together, we'd consummate our reunion by having sex. Me losing my virginity to her. How perfect. We would finally be as one. As it should have been all along.

I'd forgive her for dumping me because I knew she'd welcome me into her bed, her life, and we'd be together again. Forever.

What could possibly go wrong?

I'd got it totally sorted.

This was my best-laid plan.

Ever.

THE END

Acknowledgements

Thank you, as ever, to the whole of the Bloodhound Team. Always a delight and a pleasure working with you all.

A very special thanks to my editor, Clare Law, with whom I always enjoy working. She has a simply ridiculous breadth and depth of knowledge that enabled her to pick out the errors in the most random and obscure things that I wrote: namely a minor mistake on model railways and a very badly and erroneously described constellation. A big thank you to her for improving my book. In the world of editing, Clare *is* the Law.

To PD of the North, from JD of the South, thank you for your word which lies discreetly near the end of chapter 12, as if it's a proper, grown-up, official *real* adjective. Now it is forever immortalised.

And of course, most importantly, thank you to Francesca, for everything.

A note from the publisher

Thank you for reading this book. If you enjoyed it please do consider leaving a review on Amazon to help others find it too.

We hate typos. All of our books have been rigorously edited and proofread, but sometimes mistakes do slip through. If you have spotted a typo, please do let us know and we can get it amended within hours.

info@bloodhoundbooks.com

Printed in Great Britain
by Amazon

20134058R10171